By Anna Jacobs

The Cotton Lass
and Other Stories

ANNA JACOBS

Allison & Busby Limited
11 Wardour Mews
London W1F 8AN
allisonandbusby.com

First published in Great Britain by Allison & Busby in 2018.

A CIP catalogue record for this book is available from
the British Library.

First Edition

ISBN 978-0-7490-2304-1

Typeset in 11/16 pt Sabon by
Allison & Busby Ltd

The paper used for this Allison & Busby publication
has been produced from trees that have been legally sourced
from well-managed and credibly certified forests.

Printed and bound by
CPI Group (UK) Ltd, Croydon, CR0 4YY

Contents

About These Stories

I wrote these stories over about twenty-five years and many of them have been published in women's magazines or in anthologies, sometimes in Australia, sometimes in the UK. Some have been read on Australian radio. A few of them haven't been published before.

However, these are all, without exception, new and longer versions of the original tales, because with all publishers of short stories, you have to comply with their word count, which is usually around 1,500–2,000. I like to include more colour and details.

A few years ago I used some of my other short stories in a collection called *Short and Sweet*. Before I turned them loose on the world, I did the same thing, put a lot more work into them, making all of them longer – some of them much longer.

I also wrote a preamble to each story in which I shared with readers how I'd come to write them, what had inspired me in the first place. Readers emailed me to say they'd enjoyed that insight, so I've done it again.

I've been thinking about putting together a second collection of my shorts for a while, which just about uses up my supply. I've written far more novels than I have short stories.

Once again, I've given myself the pleasure of rewriting them and adding the details I had to cut out the first time to meet the publishers' requirements. These form a more varied selection because they contain a couple of stories originally written under my Shannah Jay name. There are romances, modern tales, historical stories, suspense, fantasy and even a mock (and I hope humorous) fairy tale for adults.

I'd forgotten the exact details of the tales until I searched through my files and it was very interesting to revisit them. And polishing my work is my favourite job of all connected with writing, so I worked on this as my Christmas treat in 2017. Talk about a busman's holiday!

Therefore these stories are new in the sense that they've all been polished until they're as bright and shiny as I can make them, and some have more than doubled in size.

I do hope you enjoy them.

Anna

The Cotton Lass

Introduction

Starting in 2009, I wrote a series of novels set against the Lancashire Cotton Famine, when the civil war in America cut off the supply of cotton and the people of Lancashire starved for lack of work. No welfare state in those days, just charity. The novels were:

Freedom's Land
Beyond the Sunset
Destiny's Path

Because I'm from Lancashire myself, the history of that period, which was never so much as mentioned when we studied history at school, stayed with me. I'd read memoirs of people who'd gone through those terrible times, and of those who'd helped them. History is always more vivid to me if I can 'hear the voice' of someone who was there.

When a women's magazine asked me to do a serial I suggested the same background and they were happy about that, because they too hadn't heard of the Cotton Famine and they thought their readers would enjoy something different. They knew they could rely on me to provide a happy ending to my tale, because I always do. I have the choice and I can't bear to leave my characters unhappy; they're so real to me.

But as usual I had to be very careful to stick to the magazine's required word count for each episode because it had to fit in with their page extent. And of course there was so much more I could show, both about the characters' feelings and the details of their lives, not to mention the historical background.

So here you have the expanded story, offering you all that I'd have liked to include the first time round. I loved going through the tale and meeting Sarah and Ellis again.

The Cotton Lass

1

1863, Lancashire

Sarah Boswick had been hungry for so long she couldn't remember her last full meal. She stood quietly in the queue, not feeling lively enough to chat, not expecting more from the soup kitchen at the church than a bowl of thin soup and a chunk of stale bread. It would be her only food that day.

None of the mill workers had realised that the war between the states in America would affect Lancashire so badly, cutting off supplies of cotton and therefore putting people out of work. Sarah's husband had been delighted to think of all the slaves being freed. He'd been such an idealist, poor Daniel. He'd died a year ago, weakened by lack of food, and she still missed him.

The line of women shuffled forward and someone poked Sarah to make her move with them.

When a gentleman with silver hair stopped nearby, Sarah didn't at first realise he was speaking to her.

Mrs Foster, one of the lady supervisors, said sharply,

'You, Boswick! Step out of the line and answer the gentleman. He's spoken to you twice already. Where are your manners?'

Sarah moved quickly, not allowing herself the luxury of resenting the scolding, because it didn't pay to cross the supervisors – not if you wanted to eat here regularly. 'I'm sorry, sir. I'm afraid my thoughts were miles away.'

'It's partly my fault. I should have waited to be introduced to you before I spoke. I'm Simon Marville, from the town of Swindon in the south, and I'm here because my church has raised some money for the relief fund here.'

She tried to pay attention, in spite of the smell of food nearby. Sometimes gentlemen or ladies came to the north to stare at the poor starving cotton operatives. It was annoying to be treated like a wild animal on display, and it did little good that she could see. There would still be no work for those in Lancashire after the visitors had gone back to their comfortable lives.

'Could we talk for a few minutes, Miss Boswick?'

'Mrs. I'm a widow.' Sarah couldn't help looking towards the food and as she did, her stomach growled.

'Have you eaten today?' he asked, still in that same gentle tone.

'No, sir. The only food I'll eat today is what's offered here at the soup kitchen.' She saw Mrs Foster looking at her and added quickly, 'For which I'm very grateful to these kind ladies.'

He turned to the supervisor. 'Do you think we could have some food brought for this poor woman, ma'am? It'll be hard for her to concentrate on what I'm saying if she hasn't eaten anything yet.'

'Of course. If you sit down over there, I'll bring some across for you both.'

'None for me, thank you. Save it for those who need it so desperately.' He led the way to the table indicated and pulled out a chair for Sarah.

At least this visitor was treating her courteously, she thought as she sat down.

He took his own seat and was about to speak again, when Mrs Foster came across with a big bowl of soup and two pieces of bread.

Sarah's mouth watered at the sight of the larger bowl and extra bread. Clearly the lady patronesses were out to impress. She waited till Mrs Foster had gone away and looked at him, wondering whether to start eating.

He waved one hand as if giving her permission and she could hold back no longer. She didn't gobble down the food, because that would make her ill, but chewed slowly, spooning up soup in between each dry mouthful of bread. As she finished the first slice, she looked round and whispered, 'Would you mind if I put this other piece of bread in my pocket, sir? I have a neighbour whose child isn't thriving.'

'No, of course not. Though you look as if you need it yourself. You're very thin.'

'I'm managing but it's harder on the little ones.'

When she'd finished eating, he asked, 'How long have you been short of food?'

'Since my husband died last year – well, before that even.'

'May I ask what happened to him?'

'Daniel came down with a fever and hadn't the strength to resist it. He was very low in spirits, which didn't help, because he took it badly not to be able to earn a living.'

'That must have been hard for you.'

Mr Marville's expression was so genuinely sympathetic, Sarah felt tears rise in her eyes. She could cope with anything except genuine sympathy about her loss, so stuffed the bread quickly into her pocket and tried to change the subject. 'What do you wish to talk about, sir?'

'You, my dear. I'd like to find out more about your life.'

That puzzled her. What had the ladies been telling him?

'I've been charged with helping select a group of cotton lasses to go to Australia, where there is plenty of work for those willing to become maidservants. The supervisor has suggested you. What do you think of the idea?'

She gaped at him. 'Go to Australia? Me?'

'Yes. Do you know where Australia is?'

'On the other side of the world, sir. I saw it on the globe at school. But I don't know much else about it. I'll have to see if there's a book about it in the library.' It had saved her sanity, the new free library had. If you could lose yourself in a book, you could forget the gnawing hunger for a while.

'A ship going to the Swan River Colony will be leaving in two weeks. How long will it take you to decide whether to go?'

She looked round and laughed, though it came out more like a croak. 'I don't need any time at all, sir. If there's work there, I'll be happy to come because there's nothing for me here now.' Only Daniel's grave, and beside him in the coffin a tiny baby who had only lived for one day. At least he had known his mother's kiss.

'How long will you need to get ready, pack your things?'

She looked down at herself and grimaced. 'I have very

little beyond the clothes on my back. I regret that. I'd keep myself cleaner if I could.'

'A complete set of clothes can be supplied.'

'I'd be very grateful for that and I'll look after them carefully, I promise.'

He hesitated and asked again, 'Are you quite sure?'

She wasn't sure of anything, but to do something was surely better than doing nothing. 'I shan't change my mind, sir.'

'Then you may as well travel south with me when I return. I'm sure Mrs Foster will provide you with clothes for the journey and we have other clothes in the poor box at my church.'

'Thank you.' Poor box clothes. She knew what those were like, but beggars couldn't afford vanity.

'Do you have any family here?'

'No, sir. I'm an orphan.' She'd only had Daniel. At the moment she was sharing a room with five other young women, to save money. They would be jealous of this chance she'd been given, so the sooner she could leave the better.

When Mr Marville had gone, she took her platter to the clearing-up table and went to thank Mrs Foster for recommending her.

The other woman nodded then reached for a small, cloth-wrapped bundle. 'You'll need better food to face such a long journey. There's more bread here and a boiled egg. Eat it all yourself.' She held on to the cloth. 'Promise you'll not give this to anyone else like that bread in your pocket.'

She blushed in embarrassment. 'I promise. Um, could I ask why you recommended me?'

'Because you're still trying to help others, sharing what little food you have. You deserve this chance more than some.'

'Thank you.' Tears welled in Sarah's eyes at these unexpected words of kindness.

'Come back at four o'clock and we'll go through the clothing in the church poor box to see what else we can find for you.'

She'd look a mess, Sarah thought. No one gave away pretty clothing. But she couldn't afford to care and at least she'd be warmly clad. She'd been so cold during the winter.

For the first time in months, she slipped into the church on the way home and gave genuine thanks to her Maker for reaching out to help her.

2

Ellis Doyle stood by the rails, his back to Ireland, staring out across the water towards England. He didn't really want to go to Australia, but after his wife died, it seemed the only place far enough away to escape the anger of his employer, who was a mean, spiteful man.

After the funeral he'd overheard Mr Colereigh gloating to his wife that Doyle would make a fine new husband for Mary Riley and that would get the expense of her and her children off the parish.

Colereigh's wife had been kinder than him and had protested that Doyle might not want to marry her, but her husband had just laughed and said the fellow would marry her if he wanted to keep his job.

Mary was a slovenly woman with a nasty temper and

three whining children of her own. Ellis wasn't having his two sons raised by such as her. He and Shona had made such plans for their boys, saved their money so carefully. As he saw the wooden coffin he'd made himself lowered into the ground, he'd sworn to see that he'd somehow make his poor wife's dreams come true.

He watched the buildings of Liverpool show on the horizon in the chill grey light of dawn, then went to wake Kevin and Rory, who were huddled together on a hard wooden bench below decks. 'We're nearly there and it's light already. Come and look at Liverpool, boys.'

He helped seven-year-old Rory to straighten his clothes, and checked nine-year-old Kevin, annoyed that however hard he tried, he couldn't keep the lads looking as neat as his wife had.

He wondered what Mr Colereigh would say when he found that Ellis had run away while the master was visiting friends. Would he come after them? Surely even he wouldn't go so far to get his own back?

Ellis had heard good things about Australia. A man had come all the way back from there to the next village to take his family out there to live. Ellis had spent hours talking to him.

By the time they arrived in Southampton, after a long rail journey from Liverpool, the boys were bickering and complaining. Ellis was exhausted but didn't dare take his eyes off his sons.

The emigrants' hostel consisted of large rooms full of bunk beds, with whole families housed in one. After they'd eaten, he put the boys to bed, warning them sternly that if they moved away from their bunks, he'd tan their hides.

In the middle of the night he woke with a start to find Kevin standing beside him, tugging at his sleeve.

'I need to go, Da. You said not to go on our own.'

'I'll come with you.'

They used the necessary then Rory said, 'I don't like it here, Da.'

'It's just a place to stay till we go on the ship.'

'There's nowhere to play.'

'There's a yard outside. They'll let you out tomorrow after we've seen the ship's doctor.' He knew they were all three healthy, so he didn't fear failing the medical – well, not much. But they couldn't leave the hostel till they passed their medical on board. The supervisor had been very clear about that.

Ellis didn't care. He didn't want to go anywhere in England. All he wanted was to make a new start in Australia.

3

Passage was booked for the group of sixty female paupers from Lancashire on a ship called the *Tartar*. Sarah hated being labelled a pauper, but it was just one more indignity among many. They were sent to the emigrants' hostel, which was crowded with people waiting to board the ship.

They would have to undergo a medical examination and she hoped that wouldn't be too thorough. Her underwear wasn't ragged or dirty, but it was an older woman's sensible flannel clothing, washed till it was grey and matted. She should be glad of it, but with better food, vanity had returned. She hated to see her gaunt face and dull hair in the mirror. She looked years older than her age.

Most of the other women were haggard and some didn't look respectable. A few even had the cropped hair of women coming out of prison.

Sarah hesitated when she saw a young woman from their group beckoning to her from the corner where there were four bunks, before crossing to join her and her two companions. They looked better fed than most and all proved to be sisters.

'I'm Sarah,' she said to the one nearest.

'Pandora Blake. These are my sisters Maia and Xanthe.'

Maia was weeping silently and steadily, mopping up the tears with a handkerchief, then having to use it again.

From what she overheard during the next few hours, Sarah realised the sisters had been forced to go to Australia by an aunt, and were leaving behind a much-loved older sister, for whose life they feared.

'I have no one,' she said when they asked about her family.

But she had hope now, shining brightly in her heart.

The medical examination took place the next morning, quick but still embarrassing. Sarah was told that she'd passed, then sent to wait in the yard.

Some lads were there, waiting for their parents, and since two of them got into a fight, she took it upon herself to separate them.

'What will your mothers say if you tear your clothes?' she scolded. 'You want to look your best when you go on board ship.'

'Mammy died,' the older boy muttered. 'And Da's taking us to Australia but I don't want to go.'

'I do,' the younger boy said.

'Well, I don't! It ain't fair. I haven't got any friends in Australia.'

A man came across to join them. 'I hope the boys weren't giving you any trouble?'

'No, but they were bickering and needed settling down.'

He turned to glare at them. 'Did I not tell you to behave yourselves?'

They scuffed their feet and stared at the ground.

The man sighed then turned back to Sarah. 'Thank you for your help, ma'am. I'm Ellis Doyle, and these are my sons, Rory and Kevin.'

'Sarah Boswick.'

Just then there was a disturbance by the gate. As he turned to see who it was, his face turned pale. 'Dear God, the master's sent his bailiff after us.'

Sarah looked at him quickly, unable to believe he'd commit a crime. 'What did you do?'

'Left the estate after my wife died instead of marrying a woman the landowner chose.'

Sarah saw the desperation on his face. She knew how arrogant some employers could be and her heart went out to him. 'You could pretend I'm your wife. He won't have any use for you then.'

He stared at her, then nodded. 'Are you sure?' At her nod, he said, 'Thank you.'

'Put your arm round my shoulders and look affectionate. Rory, in this game I'm your new mother. Come and stand next to me.'

'I *want* to go back,' Kevin said.

'And have Mary Riley for your mother?'

Kevin hesitated then went to his father's side.

By the time the supervisor got to them, they were standing as a family group.

'This is Doyle,' the bailiff said. 'He's running away from the woman he promised to marry. Mr Colereigh wants him back.'

Sarah said boldly, 'Well, he can't marry anyone else. He's married to me now.'

'There hasn't been time.'

'We bought a special licence,' she blurted out hastily.

'I'd not have come back, even if I hadn't married Sarah,' Doyle said. 'And there's no law that says I have to.'

The bailiff leant forward. 'What if the master said you'd stolen some money? You don't have enough for a special licence.'

'You never said anything about stolen money,' the supervisor said, looking suspiciously from the bailiff to Doyle.

'It was my money that bought the special licence,' Sarah said. 'It took every penny I had.'

Doyle put his arm round her and pulled her close. 'Even if you forced me to go back, I couldn't marry Mary Riley now, could I?'

Everything hung in the balance for a moment or two, then the bailiff stepped back. 'I'd not marry her, either. It'd be better if I tell him I couldn't find you. Don't ever come back, though.'

They watched him walk away, then Sarah realised Ellis Doyle was still holding her close. She didn't dare move till both the bailiff and the supervisor were out of sight. And she didn't want to move, either. Ah, but she'd missed the feel of a man's strong arm round her shoulders.

Ellis sighed and took his arm away. 'Your quick thinking saved us. I can't tell you how grateful I am.'

'He didn't ask to see the marriage lines. He could have proved us wrong.'

'No. He's not a bad fellow, but he's caught in a trap, too, if he wants to keep his job and home.'

Rory tugged at her skirt. 'Are you our new mother? We haven't got a mother now.'

'No. We were just pretending. But I can be your friend.' Her eyes sought Ellis's for permission and he nodded.

4

As they stood there, Ellis cleared his throat. 'Um, I probably need to go and see the supervisor and explain to him that we aren't really married. Will you keep an eye on these two rascals?'

'I'm happy to do that.'

But the supervisor had come back into the yard. He walked across to them, determination on his face. 'I want the truth now. Are you two married or not?'

'No, we're not married,' Ellis said in his lilting Irish voice.

'Well, you'll need to get married if you want to travel as a family.' The supervisor studied the children. 'Looks to me as if these two need a mother.'

Sarah could feel her cheeks burning because she'd had a sudden fervent wish that she was married again. She was so tired of being alone, fending for herself.

The supervisor looked at Sarah with some disapproval. 'We don't allow any hanky-panky on board the ship, missus. They're very strict about that sort of thing.'

'It's not hanky-panky to be courting someone,' Ellis told him. 'Not that I've ever heard, anyway. And that's what we're doing, courting.' He put the arm back round her shoulders.

Sarah didn't know where to look.

The supervisor's voice softened. 'Oh, it's like that, is it? Well, I'll have to report this, but no one can stop you talking to one another on deck.'

He walked away and Ellis looked apologetically at Sarah. 'I'm sorry. I had to say something.'

'I'm really grateful. But . . . we'll have to meet and talk to one another or they'll be suspicious.'

'I know. I hope you don't mind.'

But he didn't look at her as he said that, not the way a man looks at a woman he desires. That lack of real interest would soon become obvious to everyone, she was sure.

And there would be other women on the ship who were nicely dressed, who would attract and keep the attention of a man like him. Such a nice-looking man he was.

She sighed and told herself not to be stupid. But she wasn't used to being ignored. She'd been told many times she was a fine-looking woman. Other men had wanted to court her, not just Daniel.

She wasn't fine-looking now, wouldn't have been even if she had been dressed nicely and looked better. Haggard was the best way of describing her these days.

Perhaps one day she'd attract a man again, even if not this one. She'd like to marry, have children, get a normal life.

In the meantime, she had an adventure to enjoy, a journey by ship to undertake and new friends to talk to.

The Blake sisters were well read and always had something interesting to say. She envied them their education. They must have read many more books than she had to know so much. She hoped there would be books on the ship.

5

Sarah was glad when it was time to board the ship, but sorry to find herself lodged with another group of single women, widows like herself, instead of the Blake sisters. The big cabin had a long narrow table down the middle and cubicles down the sides, each sleeping four in two pairs of hard, narrow bunks. They were placed in messes of eight people and the leader had to deal with the food for the group.

Why they chose Sarah as leader, she couldn't work out. She didn't want to be singled out in any way, just wanted to build up her health.

When they went up on deck, the matron kept a careful eye on the single women. That amused Sarah. Did they think any of the single men would want women who looked like starvelings?

She didn't see the Doyles the first time, but later the sea was choppy and a lot of people stayed below, so there was more room to walk above decks.

While his father was chatting to another man, little Rory came running towards her, smiling, and she found herself sitting there, talking to him, telling him stories, as her mother used to do with her.

Kevin stood to one side, pretending not to listen.

Ellis came across to join them, speaking politely about the weather, not staying long. She wished he had. Time was going to hang heavy on their hands for the three months or so the voyage would take.

To her delight they organised classes to help pass the time. She joined groups for reading and sewing, went to the regular weekly concert. She'd have joined the choir, but she was a poor singer, and her attempts made people wince.

She noticed that Ellis was in the choir and found the boys coming to sit with her during the concerts. Afterwards Ellis would always hurry them away.

No pretence of courting. Well, he'd never pretended it was real, had he? He probably found her repulsive with her scrawny body and horrible old clothes.

Only once did they have a real conversation.

'What did you do in Ireland, Mr Doyle?' she asked.

'I was a stable hand. I'm good with horses. But I'll do anything to make a good life for my lads in Australia.' He hesitated, then added thoughtfully, 'It must be hard, going there on your own.'

'Yes, but I have a job waiting, as a maid.'

'Will you like that?'

'I'll like eating regularly and being paid. And whatever it's like, it'll give me a start.'

'I don't have a job waiting. But I'm hopeful. People always need help with horses, don't you think?'

'Oh, yes.'

Sarah did more listening than talking at the classes, because some of the women attending were obviously above her in station. Not that it made them better at sewing or reading aloud. Definitely not.

The Blake sisters were the best readers. She could have sat and listened to them all day.

Ellis was a member of the reading group, but when he

was asked to take his turn, he read so haltingly and looked so embarrassed, he wasn't asked again. The teacher was tactful like that.

A very short woman called Miss Roswell was the best sewer. It was soon obvious that she didn't really need sewing lessons, just wanted the company. She soon began helping the teacher, who could get a bit impatient if people were clumsy in their work.

When the teacher claimed exhaustion and gave up running the class, Miss Roswell took over, which was all to the good.

One day she asked Sarah to stay behind. 'I hope you don't think I'm being too personal, but I know what it's been like for the people of Lancashire. I can see that your clothes were made for other women, and I wondered if you'd like me to help you alter them?'

Sarah felt ashamed, but she wasn't going to miss an opportunity like that. 'I'd love it. Would you have time?'

'I have all too much time on my hands at the moment.' She sighed. 'You'd be doing me a favour.'

So, gradually, Sarah's hand-me-downs were transformed into well-fitting and even stylish clothes. Oh, that made her feel so much better.

But out of perversity, she didn't wear the new ones, even though Miss Roswell had hinted that Ellis kept looking at her when he thought no one would notice.

Sarah knew that her face had become rosier, could see for herself that she was getting her shape back.

But if she had to have nice clothes for him to want her, then he wasn't worth it.

* * *

Ellis joined the reading group to while away the long hours of doing nothing. He sent his lads to another class for children, relieved that they wouldn't see how poor he was at reading. Well, when had he ever had the chance for a proper education?

He saw Mrs Boswick in the class, but when he made a mess of his reading and heard how well she could read, he felt too ashamed to do anything but sit at the back and try to escape everyone's notice.

He was glad to see her looking better, though, filling out a little, getting nice rosy cheeks. She must have been short of food for a long time. She wasn't the only woman whose appearance had changed since they set off. Quite a few of them had blossomed. But they didn't interest him. She did. He couldn't understand why.

After the second reading group meeting, the teacher asked him to stay behind.

'Would you like me to give you some extra help with the reading, Mr Doyle?'

Ellis didn't know what to say, other than, 'Why would you do that, Mr Paine?'

'Because it'll help to pass the time and because reading is such a joy to me that I like to share it with others.'

'Oh. Well. If you don't mind, I'd be grateful. I never got the chance for much schooling.'

'You can come to my cabin for the lessons. We can be private there.'

But what was he going to do with his boys? They were so lively, they needed someone to keep an eye on them. He didn't want them falling overboard.

After some thought, he asked Mrs Boswick if she'd mind

keeping an eye on them, because she seemed to enjoy their company. He was too embarrassed to explain why, but she didn't ask, just said in her usual quiet way, 'I'd enjoy that. We can play games or I can read to them.'

Rory in particular seemed very attached to her. He was such a loving child. Ellis wasn't sure whether that fondness for her was a good or bad thing and it might grow stronger if the lad spent more time with her. After all, they might never see her again after they arrived in Australia and Rory had already lost one person he loved.

But learning to read better was so very important that Ellis took the risk. He didn't want Sarah, or anyone else looking down on him in his new life.

6

The men talked quite a lot, sharing what they'd heard about life in Australia, mentioning their hopes for a better life. A few really seemed to know what it was like, because they had relatives there. And one man had lived there for a while and was going back, complete with a new wife. People hung on Martin's every word.

'Couldn't you find a wife there?' one man teased.

'No, I couldn't. There are ten men to every woman in the part we're going to. So I went home and let my aunt find me a wife. And she did very well by me. A fine, sensible woman, my wife is.'

'Do you think being sensible matters most in a wife?' Ellis asked.

Martin looked at him as if he was utterly stupid. 'Of course it does. Women are much more practical about life, including marriage, than most people give them credit for.'

That gave Ellis a lot to think about. He hadn't intended to marry again. But it hadn't taken him long before he began to think of Sarah when he wasn't with her and he knew where that could lead. Only she made him feel so comfortable and well, he enjoyed talking to her.

But if there were ten men to every woman, she'd have other suitors, a lot of other suitors, once they arrived. She could choose someone better than him, someone who could read and write fluently, who didn't sing like a hoarse crow, who didn't already have a family.

And even if he asked her, she might say no, make him feel about ten years old, as she'd done to one man who tried to get fresh with her.

But . . . he did like her.

So he had to be sensible about this and do it quickly, before someone else got in before him. He chose a moment when he could get her on his own, determined to ask her straight out. 'I've been thinking—' He couldn't get the words he'd rehearsed out. They sounded stilted.

'Thinking what?'

'Thinking we should . . . get married.' He couldn't bear to look her in the eyes. If she looked at him he'd shrivel up and die.

Her voice was cool. 'Why should we do that?'

He summoned up the main argument, the one he thought would appeal to a woman most. 'Because the boys need a mother and I need a wife. It's the most *sensible* thing to do.'

'Is that all?'

Words stuck in his throat. 'Isn't it enough?'

She shook her head. 'No, it's not enough. You didn't say you cared for me.'

Someone came along just then and he turned to look over the rail, screwing up his courage. When he turned back to say of course he cared for her, Sarah had gone.

Ellis tried several times after that to catch Sarah on her own, but she seemed to be avoiding him. Maybe that was her way of saying no.

He didn't know what to do next. He couldn't sleep at night for thinking of her.

Then he heard two of the other men joking about a bet they'd made, as to which could get Sarah to marry him. Pete and Jim had also listened to Martin, it seemed.

He got up one day determined to have it out with her, if he had to shout out his feelings for the whole ship to hear.

After breakfast he saw her at the other end of the deck and hurried along. This was it. He'd do it.

But he saw that Pete was on his knees in front of her and he knew what that meant. He'd have turned away, but she looked across at him. It seemed to him that she was pleading with him, that she was trying to pull her hand away from Pete's.

Something snapped inside him and Ellis ran across the last few yards of deck, pushing between Sarah and Pete. 'Don't do it! Don't marry him. He won't love you half as much as I do. I can't *bear* it if you marry him.'

'Hoy, you! I got here first.' Pete tried to pull him away.

He shoved Pete aside, but the man came barrelling back.

Sarah stepped between them. 'Go away, Peter Millton!' she yelled. 'Or you'll spoil it for me.'

She turned back to Ellis.

He smiled, his anxiety past now. Confidence surged up.

'I love you, Sarah Boswick. I can't think of anything else but how much I love you. That's much more important than being sensible. Will you marry me?'

'Of course I will, you fool. I'd have said yes last time but you never said a kind word to me with the proposal.'

He laughed and clapped her in his arms, kissing her soundly. It took him a while to realise that someone was tapping his shoulder. He swung round, ready to punch Pete if he had to.

But it was the matron of the women's quarters. So he gave her a big hug, too. 'She's just agreed to marry me.' Then he turned back to finish kissing his Sarah properly.

Give It a Try

Introduction

This story was inspired by our elder daughter's wedding. There's nothing like a real wedding for making you feel sentimental.

I should say up front that none of the characters is based on real people, either those at our lovely wedding, our daughter's, or our friends' and families'. Indeed, I've been happily married to my own hero for over fifty-five years now.

But I watch people everywhere I go and feel sad when some seem determined to be nasty to one another, and I rejoice when I see kindness and a sense of humour, because they're two qualities that make those people so good to be with.

So I thought I'd allow my heroine, who'd had an unhappy first marriage, to find a delightful man the second time round.

I always enjoy creating people who can love one another. It gives me a warm fuzzy feeling.

This is just a short story, a single tale, and it had to be 1,500 words the first time. This time it's about 2,400. I think it works better at this length.

Happy reading!

Give It a Try

Allie flew to Australia for the wedding, not without misgivings. She hadn't gone back there for five years, though Holly had visited her in England. But you couldn't miss your daughter's wedding, even if that meant spending time in the same country as your ex.

She was determined not to show any weakness this time. Well, she'd give it her best try. Paul wasn't going to walk all over her again.

She wept happy tears as Holly exchanged vows with Dez. He was neither tall nor handsome, but he had a smile ten miles wide. Allie had taken to him on sight. She even dared hope this marriage would last. Unlike hers.

At least the two of them hadn't rushed into it. Their little son was proof of that.

At two, Charlie was their attendant, dressed in a miniature suit and bow tie. He stood quietly, holding the bridesmaid's hand.

Once his parents started exchanging vows, Charlie grew

bored and began to play with his buttonhole carnation. Pulling it carefully to pieces petal by petal kept him nice and quiet as the words were spoken.

As the guests moved slowly out of the church afterwards, Allie came face-to-face with her ex. She'd been dreading this, but had planned to stay calm and speak civilly if she was forced to talk to him. She had no intention of speaking to his much younger trophy wife.

Paul greeted her with, 'England hasn't improved you, Al. You're looking as dowdy as ever. Why don't you get some streaks in your hair and buy some new clothes, try for a more modern look?' He turned sideways to smirk at his wife.

He'd deliberately spoken loudly enough for others to hear. Well, Allie had too much pride to answer back.

She realised suddenly that he'd dyed his hair. It had been going grey even before they split up. And he'd combed the hair over a bald patch. Unfortunately, the hair was lifting in a slight breeze, all in one piece as if stuck together with glue.

She suddenly had no trouble smiling. He must have tried to lacquer it into place. That sign of weakness made her feel much more confident about dealing with him.

He pulled his wife forward. 'You've not met Cheryl.'

'No, and I don't want to.' Allie tried to walk on.

He moved to block her way. 'You always were a spiteful bitch! No wonder you've not found anyone else.'

The piece of hair lifted again, as if encouraging her to strike back. 'Haven't I? Are you quite sure of that?'

'Who'd want you?'

'That'd be telling.' She held her head high and walked out of the church ahead of them.

The reception was in a nearby hotel, which had big, beautiful gardens. The meal seemed to go on for a long time, with too many speeches.

Afterwards the dancing started. The bridal waltz was first, with Holly and Dez leading it, then everyone else joining in, including little Charlie.

Later her new son-in-law asked Allie for a dance and so did his father. Kind of them. A really nice family.

Paul was doing some showy steps with his new wife. He danced with her and his daughter and no one else.

As the music changed, getting louder, Allie found a seat in the corner furthest from the band. The noise was getting to her, thumping through her veins. Still, the wedding had gone well. That was the main thing. She did hope Holly would be happy.

She was wondering how soon she could escape to her hotel when someone touched her arm lightly. She turned to see who it was. She recognised his face but couldn't remember his name. Some cousin or other of the groom's father, she thought.

'A few of us oldies are escaping to a quiet spot in the gardens,' he whispered. 'Want to join us? Unless you're into loud music.'

What a kind family they were! It'd be nice not to be alone. 'I'd love to.'

She followed him outside towards the back of the hotel, stopping to admire the flowers and shrubs. 'Such beautiful gardens.'

'Aren't they? I love flowers.' He'd taken off his tie and jacket, and unbuttoned his elegant shirt, which was looking nicely rumpled now.

'This way.' He led her to a patio with wooden tables in the shade. Six other people were already there, looking relaxed.

'Another refugee from the noise!' her rescuer called. 'This is Allie, everyone.'

She wished she could remember his name. He seemed a bit younger than her with his boyish smile but a couple of the people were clearly of an older generation.

'Here. Take a seat. White, red or beer?' He indicated a tub with bottles and cans sitting on some ice.

'White wine, please.'

Behind him some honeyeaters were dipping into the bright pink grevillea flowers for nectar. The flowers were bigger than the tiny birds. She'd forgotten how pretty they were.

A ring-necked parrot landed in a tree, followed by a second one. They fluttered down to the grevillea bushes and began to nip off the flowers one by one, not eating them, just dropping them on the ground.

'Destructive devils, aren't they?' Her companion set a glass of white wine in front of her then chased the parrots away. To her delight, he came back to sit beside her on the wooden bench.

Popping the top of his can of beer, he lifted it in a toast. 'Cheers.'

She clinked her glass to it automatically. 'Cheers yourself. I'm sorry, but I can't remember your name.'

'I know you're Allie, mother of the bride. You don't look nearly old enough to be a grandmother, though.'

She felt instantly better. 'All compliments gratefully received. I'm Allie Carson now. I took back my maiden name after my divorce. And you?'

'Brodie Kelly.'

'Irish?'

'Nah, Australian. Born and bred here. My grandparents were Irish, though.'

The rest of the group introduced themselves and she tried hard to memorise their names as music continued to blast out from the function room.

'Can't stand that row, even at this distance,' one man said, draining his glass. 'Are you ready, love?' He and his wife nodded to everyone and left.

Within twenty minutes the rest had gone too.

'I suppose I'd better—' Allie began.

Brodie set one hand on her bare arm and she was surprised at the warmth that flooded through her at his touch. 'Don't go yet, Allie. I'd have to go back and join the younger set and I can't face the noise. Anyway, I'm enjoying your company and I hope I'm not boring you to tears. Tell me about yourself. What do you do for a living? I gather from what you were saying just now that you live in England.'

'I buy and sell antiques, just in a small way. Buy cheap and sell at a profit.'

'Like that TV programme?'

'A bit like that. I never thought my hobby would earn me a living, but it does, and a decent one, too. I seem to have an eye for bargains. What about you?'

'I run a little company. We service garage doors for the manufacturer.'

'Interesting work?'

'Not really, but it brings in a crust. I've been doing it too long. I'll find something else one day. I'm a bit into antiques too. I collect mechanical toys. I like repairing them, seeing them march up and down.'

'I have a small mechanical dog. It's rare, worth quite a bit, but I can't bear to sell it. It's such a clever little thing.'

She found him so easy to chat to, she forgot the time.

Suddenly the loud music stopped.

He closed his eyes for a moment, smiling. 'Oh, listen to the silence! Isn't it beautiful?'

'Wonderful. I love to sit in a garden and listen to the birds.'

'Me, too. You're not driving, are you?'

'No. I'm staying in a hotel in town. I'm getting a taxi back.'

'Oh good. Have another glass of wine with me. I'm from out of town too and I'm enjoying your company.'

A waltz started up, just as loud but somehow not as jarring as the previous music. He grinned and looked down at her feet. 'You're tapping your toes.'

'I love waltzes.'

'Me too. I think they're playing our tune.' He held out his hand and tugged her to her feet.

He was a good dancer, tall enough to guide her and she gave herself up to the moment as they danced round the patio. How long since she'd danced with an attractive man?

Loud voices interrupted them and they paused, grimacing at one another, not wanting to be interrupted.

Nearby a couple were having a ding-dong argument, voices shrill, words chosen to hurt.

Brodie began to grin. 'She's really got the edge on him when it comes to arguing, hasn't she? I bet she rules the roost.'

The man said something soothing.

Allie gasped as she realised who it was. 'Oh, no! That's my ex and his new wife.'

'He sounds happy. Not.'

She began to smile. 'Definitely not. It may be spiteful, but I can't help being a bit glad. He was the one who broke up our marriage, sneering at me for—' She broke off. 'Sorry. I don't normally talk about that stuff. I have moved on. It's just that I've not seen him for several years and it brought everything back. He hasn't changed a bit.'

'I couldn't help hearing how he spoke to you earlier. Nasty type. I didn't take to him when I met him at Christmas. I could never understand how Holly could be his daughter. I can see now that she takes after her mother.'

Allie enjoyed the compliment but began to feel embarrassed as the argument continued nearby. Paul was still getting the worst of it, but she wished she didn't have to eavesdrop. However, the only way back into the hotel led right past the quarrelling couple.

'I've got an idea,' Brodie said in a low voice.

'An idea?'

His eyes were dancing with mischief. 'Yeah. Want to give old rat-face something to think about? You owe him one for the way he spoke to you earlier.'

'What do you mean?'

'Well, they're coming this way. What if they found us in a clinch, looking all lovey-dovey? Wouldn't that annoy the hell out of him on top of the quarrel?'

'I don't know if I . . .' But it would annoy Paul, she knew. Hugely. Oh, she couldn't resist it. She nodded.

'And what if we looked starry-eyed as well, a bit like our young newly-weds? Think you could manage that?'

'Maybe. Why are you suggesting it? I don't need anyone's pity. I've moved on from *him*.'

'Nothing to do with pity. Fellow feeling. My wife ran off three years ago. She was always putting me down, too.'

'Oh.' Then the memory of how Paul had sneered at her when he told her why he was leaving her for a younger, prettier, smarter woman made Allie say, 'Yes, let's do it.'

The quarrel seemed to have ended and footsteps began to crunch towards them along the gravel path.

'Here we go.' Brodie took her in his arms, smiled down at her and began to kiss her.

Allie felt stiff and awkward.

'You can do better than that,' he breathed in her ear. 'That wouldn't convince anyone.'

Terrified of looking a fool in front of Paul, she put both her arms round Brodie's neck and kissed him back. That felt better. So much better that she lost herself in the kiss and forgot why they were doing it.

'What the hell—'

She floated back down to earth and turned her head slowly to see Paul glaring at her from across the patio.

Brodie put an arm round her shoulders. 'Darling, let's go back to the hotel. I've had enough interruptions.'

He nudged her arm and she realised she had to keep up the pretence. 'Yes, let's do that.' She raised one hand to caress his cheek and gazed into his eyes, nearly chuckling when he winked at her.

As they walked slowly back through the gardens, Brodie kept his arm round her shoulders and she put her arm round his waist. That felt good, too.

Behind her, Allie heard a shrill woman's voice. 'I thought you said she wasn't with anyone. You can see how he feels about her. Why don't you ever look at me like that?'

Cheryl's remark was the icing on the cake. Allie shot Brodie a triumphant look.

As the path turned a corner, he stopped and pulled her into his arms. 'Quick! Kiss me like that again. He's coming after us.'

So she did, enjoying the touch of his lips, the feel of his soft brown hair.

When they moved apart, she looked round for Paul but there was no sign of him.

Brodie smacked a kiss on her cheek and grinned at her. 'I lied. They weren't following us, but I couldn't resist another of your luscious kisses. They're very moreish.'

'Oh.'

'Not been dating since the break-up?'

'No.'

'Fancy trying it with me?'

'I do, actually. Trouble is, I'm only here in Australia for two weeks.'

'That's enough time to see how well we get on, don't you think? If the relationship is worth pursuing, we'll find a way to continue it.'

Her breath caught in her throat as she took in the kindness and warmth in his face. He was going thin at the back, like her ex, so perhaps he wasn't as young as she'd first thought. But he hadn't dyed his hair or tried to comb it over the bald patch. She couldn't imagine him even thinking of doing that. He seemed . . . honest . . . as well as having the most gorgeous grey eyes and the softest lips.

She gave in to temptation. 'Yes. I'd really like to get to know you better, Brodie.'

'Good.' He kissed her other cheek, then her lips again.

When she surfaced, she felt dazed and happy, didn't have to pretend. This was definitely worth a try.

The Greening of Emily Baker

Introduction

This was a sequel to one of the first short stories I ever wrote, 'Kissing Emily Baker', and it's still one of my favourite tales. One day I'd like to write a novel giving the full life story of Emily, who became such a vivid character to me that I wrote three longish stories about her over the years.

Again, this was published in a women's magazine in a much shorter version than the one that follows. The other two have also been extended and published in my other collection of short stories (*Short and Sweet*).

In the first story we found out how Tom and Emily met during an era when many women were definitely not 'liberated', and 'equal opportunity' wasn't a phrase most people had heard of.

That shows you how old I am, because I remember clearly how 'unliberated' I was when I first got married – luckily to a man who has never been anything but equal in his dealings with all people.

It was a shock and an act of unfairness that made me understand and care about discrimination against anyone. I went for a job interview and was called in afterwards and told 'You're the best candidate but we can't give you the job because you have small children.' As if the children didn't belong to my husband as well! He, by the way, has never been asked whether he has children at a job interview. I was outraged by that.

So I felt it was time Emily came to understand her rightful place in the world and poor Tom had to join in. He was a lovely, kind guy but very set in his ways.

It was such fun to write this story. I join in with my characters when I'm typing at the computer, crying with them at sad patches, smiling sentimentally when they fall in love, and chuckling aloud when something amusing happens.

I chuckled a lot when writing this story and hope you'll find it amusing too.

The Greening of Emily Baker
Western Australia, 1970

Tom slammed the car door shut and walked wearily up the veranda steps. 'Em! I'm back!' The front door was locked and he stared at it in bafflement before fumbling for his key. It didn't often happen that his wife wasn't there waiting for him.

The kitchen was empty, the morning's dishes still unwashed. Suddenly afraid, he ran from room to room, but there was no sign of Em, conscious or unconscious. 'Women!' he muttered, ashamed of his brief panic.

He fumbled a cold can from the fridge and sighed with relief as the beer gurgled down his throat. It'd been a hot day, like an oven on the building site. He'd be fifty-eight next month, six years older than Em. Fifty-eight! He was the oldest brickie in the team and on hot days he really felt his age. And there were still seven years to the pension.

Well, bricklaying was all he knew and it was a living, so he had no choice but to continue working. He was proud that they'd raised two fine children and paid off the mortgage on the house without his Em ever having to go out to work. And so he'd told the young blokes he worked with, time after time. Someone needs to be there for the children and to run the house.

'It'll be one of the grandchildren,' he said aloud. Em always rushed over to help their daughter, Katie. Measles last year. Young Bill's broken leg the year before.

Tom relaxed, got himself another beer and reached for the paper. It was nice and quiet after the noise and dust of the site.

It was dark when he awoke. Took him a minute or two to remember where he was. He switched on the light and squinted at his watch. He needed reading glasses, but he hated the thought of wearing the horrible things! They wouldn't survive long on a building site. If he didn't break them, he'd lose them. He watched other fellows taking them off and putting them on, hanging them round their necks. He remembered shouting 'Speccy four-eyes!' at kids who wore glasses to school. A bit unkind, but kids never think of things like that.

And what was he doing sitting there thinking about things long past? It was nearly nine o'clock! No wonder he was hungry. He stared at the raw steaks in the fridge, but couldn't be bothered to cook one, so made himself some toast with Vegemite on and then another batch of toast with jam on.

Then he started watching the clock. Em was late. Maybe she needed picking up from somewhere. She'd been pestering him lately about learning to drive and getting her own car, but he wasn't going to be driven around by a woman. What would the blokes say? And anyway, they couldn't afford another car. Simple as that!

He rang his daughter, then his son. Neither of them had seen Em for days. A cold chill settled in his stomach. What could have happened to her? She never went out on her own after dark!

For two long, slow hours Tom prowled round the house. Every now and then he went outside and listened for footsteps. Three times his hand hovered over the phone, but somehow, he could not bear to confess to some uppity young policeman that he'd mislaid his wife.

At quarter past eleven Katie rang up to check that her mother was back and took the opportunity to scold him. 'No wonder Mum's gone out on her own! When was the last time you took her out, Dad?'

When she rang off, he went to put the kettle on, slamming the teapot down beside it.

Of course he took Em out! What was Katie talking about? Why, they'd been out to the bowling club's annual dance only a month or two ago. No, that was last year. This year he'd been too tired to go. Besides, it'd been pouring down.

He'd meant to take Em out on her birthday last month, to make up for it. But it'd been a real scorcher, just like today, and he'd fallen asleep on the sofa even before they got ready, so Em had said they'd go another time. Hard work, laying bricks on hot days. But he should have made more effort to take her out. She was a good wife, the very best.

As midnight approached, he decided that he'd just have to call the police, but before he could pick up the phone, a car screeched to a halt in the street. He ran outside, only to stop dead on the veranda, shocked rigid.

There was his Em by the light of the street lamp brandishing a placard that said SAVE OUR FORESTS! She'd just got out of a car that was full of women, and there was a piece of old sheet tied across the bonnet saying NO MINING IN OLD GROWTH FORESTS.

A fat woman in baggy trousers – what a sight she looked! – was climbing back into the car. 'See you tomorrow, Em! Down with mining companies!'

'Save our forests!' Em called back just as loudly.

Tom started forward. What would the neighbours think? That porky old biddy should be at home, looking after her family, not keeping hard-working blokes out of their beds!

Em came through the gate, humming. 'Oh, hello, love!' She planted an absent-minded kiss near his cheek as she passed.

He sniffed. She'd been drinking!

The car screamed away. Women drivers!

Tom turned to confront his wife, but she had already disappeared into the house. He stormed in after her. 'Where have you bloody well been till this time, Emily Baker?'

'Out.'

'I can see that! Where?'

'To the camp.'

'Camp? What camp?'

'The Women Against Mining Camp. You know! The one that's been in the news all week. They're trying to block the road and save the old growth forests.'

He could only goggle at her.

'I heard on the radio this morning that they wanted volunteers to help prepare food and look after the children. I was fed up of staying at home, Tom, fed up to the teeth! So I volunteered. Hannah came and picked me up.' She collapsed into a chair and kicked her shoes off. 'Ooh, my poor feet are aching! I haven't sat down once today!'

He gobbled in his throat, angry words tripping over each other. She'd deserted him and left him without any tea to go and join those loonies! He noticed her flushed cheeks. 'And what's more, you've been drinking!' he roared.

'Only one glass of white wine. It was lovely. Not like that sweet stuff you always buy me. This one's called Chenin Blanc. I'm going to buy myself a cask of it.'

She hadn't even noticed how upset he was, hadn't thought of him when she rushed off. 'Em—' His voice was pleading. He wanted his old Em back. Not this stranger who drank wine and stayed out till all hours with a bunch of crazy females.

'I just dropped everything,' she continued dreamily, 'and I went. Oh, Tom, it's been so exciting! We stopped the trucks getting in today. Didn't you see us on the news?'

'I didn't watch the telly. I was too worried about you. And I'd have been even more worried if I'd seen you on the news.'

'You weren't too worried to have a few beers.' She nodded towards the empty cans.

'It was hot today. I needed them!'

'Well, it was hot where I was, too. I needed the wine. What did you have for tea?'

'Bread an' jam.'

'Well, I'm not cooking anything for you now. I'm

exhausted! Those girls at the camp are real nice kids, but sloppy. I had to show them how to . . .'

Still talking, she began to get ready for bed.

Over the next couple of weeks, Tom learnt about the mysteries of takeaway food and twice ran out of beer, because Em didn't remind him to buy more. When she was at home, she kept ranting on about criminal governments who allowed multinational companies to destroy rainforests, not to mention her worries about the future of her grandchildren and the planet.

He lived in terror of seeing her on the telly. The blokes would never let him forget it, if they found out that his wife had turned greenie!

One day, she made him some funny sandwiches for lunch. He always had ham and cheese sandwiches! She knew he did! These had a sort of whitish paste inside and what looked like grass. He sniffed them suspiciously – nothing he recognised! – so he threw them away and bought himself a pie.

When he got home, he complained, but she just shrugged and said she was sick of the sight of ham and cheese, and why didn't he buy his own lunches from now on?

It was a poor lookout when a married chap had to buy lunch from a stranger.

He never knew whether he'd find her at home or out. What if she got herself arrested? He had nightmares about that.

Once, and once only, he tried to put his foot down. 'This has gone on for long enough, Em. I'm not having you mixed up with that bunch of freaks any more! I never know where you are. You can just stop going to those meetings and . . .'

He couldn't believe it when she stormed out of the house.

He was worried sick when she didn't come back for two whole days. He tried ringing Katie but he got such an earful of abuse that he slammed the phone down. Well, but at least he knew Em was safe!

What was the world coming to when a bloke didn't get any respect from his own family? His father must be turning in his grave.

The anti-mining camp finished and of course the big companies won. He could have told her that, but he didn't even try because she'd not have listened.

Em still went around with her new friends and came in late as often as not on those evenings.

One dreadful day he came home to find his own house full of them: weirdos, women mostly – at least, he thought they were women. You couldn't always tell. The fat one was there, wearing bright purple trousers this time and making herself at home in his kitchen. She even had the nerve to wave to him.

His own daughter was in the thick of all this.

'Hi, Dad!' yelled Katie. 'Isn't Mum great? She's been showing everyone how to make damper. Now Jasmin's showing us how to make halva.'

'This is my husband,' said Em, and the whole pack of them turned to stare at him.

He backed out of the room and onto the rear veranda, yelping in shock when he opened the door of the beer fridge. Those women had even raided his tinnies! There was only one can left.

As he poured the beer from it down his parched throat, he stared gloomily into the house. The kitchen was full of women. Two small children cannoned into his legs. There was a baby crying in a pram at the end of the veranda, a very loud baby. Probably took after its mother.

Some things you couldn't fight. He crept out along the side of the house and drove out to buy some more beer. He put it in the picnic box with some ice and retreated to the garden shed when he got back.

A child tried to follow him inside the shed and he snarled at it. He felt guilty when it ran away crying, but a man had to have some peace after a hard day's work.

During the weeks that followed, Tom tried several times to reason gently with Em, but in vain. She'd always been able to out-argue him. She started telling him about the damage being done to the ozone layer. What did she expect him to do about that, for heaven's sake?

Mostly he suffered in silence. What could a bloke do? It was her age. Women went funny sometimes at that age, the other blokes said. It couldn't last! Em would come to her senses soon and find him more than ready to forgive her.

He became quite friendly with the deli owner on the new estate where the team was working. Spiro sold the juiciest ham he'd ever tasted. They had long conversations about the peculiarities of women. Spiro had his own problems with his daughter.

Tom revised his former opinions about Greek migrants. You couldn't meet a nicer bloke than Spiro.

* * *

Winter came and Tom began to feel a bit livelier, what with the occasional wet day with no work and the fact that he'd lost nearly a stone in weight since Em cut down on baking cakes. He didn't miss the spare tyre round his belly . . . but he did miss her apple pies!

He came home one chilly day in July to find the table set with a white lace cloth. There were flowers in the middle and wine glasses at each place. He stood and blinked in surprise.

Em came out of the kitchen with her apron on and a dab of flour on her nose. His heart lifted. She'd come to her senses!

'Go and get washed!' she ordered, kissing his cheek. 'We're celebrating.'

'Celebrating?' He did a hasty calculation. No, their wedding anniversary was next month. 'What are we celebrating, then?'

'I'll tell you after the meal.'

He had a quick shower and put on his best slacks and a clean shirt to humour her, sniffing appreciatively. You couldn't beat home cooking!

'Sit down, love. Here's your soup.' Her face looked flushed and happy. She was wearing her best frock. She was still the prettiest woman he'd ever met. He beamed at her. This was more like it!

He picked up his spoon, but his hand froze halfway to his mouth. The soup dish was full of green liquid, with things floating in it. He squinted at it, trying to make out exactly what it was.

'It's just green pea soup, Tom. You like peas.'

'What are those things in it? They're not peas!'

'They're called croutons. Bits of fried bread.'

'Oh.' He stirred the soup suspiciously. 'New recipe, eh?'

'Yes.'

He only liked tomato soup. She knew that. But she was watching him and he didn't want to spoil things by complaining, so he had a taste. It wasn't too bad, actually. Definitely peas. Thank goodness it wasn't something spicy.

He'd have liked a beer with it, but she'd already poured him some champagne. He gulped it down and held the glass out to be refilled.

The next course was something with an Italian-sounding name. Pieces of veal with a mess of tomatoes and cheese all over them. And a bottle of a different wine, pink stuff this time.

He'd rather have had a nice pork chop, but Em had gone to a lot of trouble, so he didn't like to complain. He even had a second helping because the veal tasted far better than it looked.

'I knew you'd like it, Tom!'

She had a cheeky grin, did old Em. He loved her smile, couldn't help smiling back.

'One of the girls is Italian and she's given me a few recipes. I'm going to be making all sorts of lovely foreign food from now on!'

Alarm bells began to ring in Tom's head. 'Now hold on, Em! You know I don't like messed-up things! And some of that foreign stuff is muck!'

'Not when I cook it, it isn't!'

He wasn't brave enough to disagree with that! Em prided herself on her cooking. And she was good. Very good. Usually.

He turned with relief to the dessert. Apple pie with ice cream! His favourite.

When the meal was over, he could stand the suspense no longer. 'What egg-egsackly are we sh-celebratin'?' That wine was stronger than it seemed! He blinked hard and tried to concentrate.

'I passed my driving test today.'

'You . . . *what*?'

'And . . . and I bought a second-hand car. I don't know how I've managed without one all these years.'

Tom shut his eyes for a moment till the floor steadied, then asked the question nearest to his heart. 'How much?'

'Only three thousand dollars.'

'Three th—Where'd you get that much money?'

'I paid the deposit out of the holiday savings.'

'How the hell are we going to pay the rest off? I don't get much overtime in winter. You know I don't! An' what about our holidays? We've been saving that money for a holiday.'

She fiddled with her spoon, not meeting his eyes. 'You won't need to work overtime if you don't want to, love. I've – I've got myself a little job. Down at the supermarket. Three days a week. I can pay for the new car easily. And for the holidays. Besides, you've been looking a bit tired lately. You should stop doing overtime at your age.'

'I don't want you going out to work! It's a man's job to support his wife!'

'Oh, rubbish! No one thinks like that any more! And anyway, I'm fed up of staying at home.'

'I – *won't* – *have it!*'

'How will you stop me, love?'

He stared at her in silence, then got up and went to bed, narrowly missing the door post on his way out.

The next day was fine, but Tom didn't go to work.

'You all right, Tom, love?'

'Yes. Well, sort of. I just don't feel like going to the site today. Ring 'em up and say I'm sick.' The truth was, he didn't feel like facing the blokes. What was he going to say to them about Em's job? He'd always boasted about how his wife had never had to work, made a big point of it.

He hid behind the curtains and watched Em drive off to the supermarket in the new car. She backed out quite well, for a woman. Well, she was a very capable woman, he had to give her that. Anything she did, she did well.

He fidgeted round the house all day. Usually, when he stayed home, Em was there and they chatted. He missed her. She was good company, old Em was.

Time passed slowly. He thought a lot about what Em had said about him not needing to do any more overtime. So she had noticed how tired he'd been getting!

But that still didn't excuse the sneaky way she'd been behaving. Learning to drive. Getting a job behind his back like that! Spending three thousand dollars without even asking him!

Some of the blokes at work would have told him to knock a bit of sense into her, but he couldn't have hit Em. Never had, never would. Men who did that were rascals and deserved a good thrashing themselves.

What the hell was he going to do about this situation, though?

* * *

The next day was fine again and he knew Em didn't have to go to work. He looked at her across the breakfast table. 'Ring the foreman up and say I'm still sick and then we'll go out for a bit of a drive.'

Her face lit up and she gave him a hug.

He couldn't stop himself grinning back at her. Nothing warmed his heart like seeing his Em smile.

'We'll do better than that, Tom Baker! We'll drive out to the beach and have a barbecue. Like when we were courting. It's going to be fine today.'

'OK. And – er – we'll go in your new car, eh? Give it a bit of a run.'

She looked at him sideways, but she didn't say anything, thank goodness.

He kept quiet when she took a corner too closely. After a while he relaxed. She had the makings of a good driver – for a woman. Everyone made little mistakes at first. She didn't make many. Well, Em wouldn't.

The beach was nearly deserted. They went for a walk along the edge of the water. Better than laying bricks, any day.

'Do you want to do the barbecuing?' he asked when they got back. 'Or am I still allowed to do that?'

She laughed at him. 'You do it. I'll get the rest of the food ready.'

They sat and talked over their steaks. They hadn't talked so frankly in years! Why hadn't she told him how bored she was staying home once the children had left? The last traces of Tom's resentment vanished.

Of course, he'd still rather she didn't go out to work – a man had his pride – but he'd learnt years ago that when Em really set her mind on something, that was that. You just had to like it or lump it.

And the money would help a lot, not just with the car payments. They could put a bit aside for their retirement and still have their holidays.

On the way home, he asked her to stop at the shops. He felt an idiot carrying such a big bunch of flowers back, but Em only cried like that when she was really happy.

She let him drive the rest of the way home and he had to admit the new car was a beauty. Much more comfortable than his van. Air conditioning and everything! She'd chosen well. Trust old Em!

He went back to work the next day, but started taking things a bit easier. The other blokes didn't mind. No one could do the fancy brickwork as well as he could and well they knew it.

He heard them talking about him a few weeks later, saying he was beginning to show his age, getting a bit absent-minded. He let them talk. He had too much on his mind to worry about what the blokes thought.

He might have known it was all too good to be true. Women! They were never content. Always had to be changing things. Couldn't let a man live in peace.

He didn't mind Em going off with those greenies – well, not much! – or even bringing them home – if she warned him first – but he was dammed if he'd join them himself!

Calling themselves conservationists! They should be called what they were: weirdos. They should be banned! What if the blokes saw him with that fat old biddy in her baggy purple trousers? He shuddered at the mere thought.

And as for him joining a protest march, Em could forget it! His soul shrivelled at the very idea of that. He was not going on a march! Not now, not ever!

He'd told her that several times now, but she still kept trying to persuade him.

He bit into a ham roll that tasted like sawdust. Oh, hell, what was he going to do? Once his Em had her mind really set on something, she usually got her way.

Lucky Stars

Introduction

At one stage there were refugees coming to Australia from Vietnam and other places. I knew what it was like to be a migrant because we came to Australia in 1973 in our early thirties. And I'd met people who'd come here as refugees.

Even when you speak the same language it's hard to move to another country and culture – well, nearly the same language. There is an Aussie English, just as there is an American English and a South African English.

Simple things trip you up in your new country. I knew one British family who'd been invited to a party and told to 'bring a plate' and that's what they did, literally took along an empty plate. They hadn't realised everyone shared the catering.

I was upset by parties where all the men congregated at one end of the house and the women at the other. This was a group of young professional people. We'd given many parties back in England and people had always mingled. And danced.

But these were small details compared to what someone from a totally different cultural background, who didn't speak much, if any, English must feel when going to live in a new country. My heart went out to them, so of course I wrote a story.

This one wasn't published in print: it was read in a short story segment on the radio. So of course it had to be particularly strict about word count.

Lucky Stars

I walk slowly along the dusty road. Follow the others. Here is the ship at last! Don't look back! Just go on board quietly!

I keep tight hold of my new passport. I wait long time for it. Very long time. Years pass slowly in a refugee camp.

The sky is dark now. I feel very alone. The others are strangers. I look up. Ah, good! My stars are there, looking down. Far away, but old friends. I talk to them often back in the camp.

The ship is big. It will take us to Australia safely. So many small boats do not get there. Or the people are sent back.

I have a passport now, though. I won't be sent back.

I walk slowly, move where they tell me, wait and then wait again.

I have one bag. Not heavy. Still, I walk slowly. Like an old person. I'm tired. So tired. Too tired to feel the happiness properly.

I find my cabin. Very small. Four bunks. Clean, but not much space. But then, I have few possessions now.

One person lies in a bottom bunk. Face to the wall. Crying quietly.

Another lies in a top bunk. Face up. Staring at the ceiling. They do not speak to me.

I leave my bag on the other bottom bunk. I go up on deck. But I take my passport. I keep it with me all the time.

Water is dark round the ship. Other people stand by the rails. Most are in groups. A few stand alone.

I walk past them all. I find an empty space. I just stand there. Look up at my stars. Look down at the water.

Waiting. Always waiting. But this time hope waits with me.

Hours later, the ship sails. Middle of the night. I am still on deck. So are many others.

My eyes fill with tears. Even leaving the camp is a loss. Friends are still there.

My family is long gone. All I have left now is myself. But I will not let tears fall. *Stop that! You have wept enough, foolish one.*

The sea is calm. The ship slides quickly away from port. The land lights grow smaller. Soon they look like little stars. Then they vanish.

I turn away from the ship's lights. I hide my face in the darkness.

One tear escapes, then another. Cold on my cheeks. I grow angry with myself. Australia will be a good place for me. *No more crying, foolish one!*

But sad thoughts stay with me. How is my village? My old friends? Is anyone still alive from my family?

More coldness on my cheeks. But it is dark. No one to see the tears. Except the stars.

We travel for days. The ship is clean. The bunks are comfortable. Plenty to eat. I am not very hungry, though.

In the cabin we speak each other's names now. Very polite, all of us. But we each live under our own shadows.

We do not ask questions. Questions can hurt. We talk of the future. Dreams we share. Sometimes.

The past is done with. The future is a mystery.

The sad one still weeps at night. We leave that poor soul time to weep alone. But there are four of us in the cabin. We cannot always walk the decks. So we hear the weeping sometimes.

On the ship I find a library. Books are a joy to me. But these books are all in English. Hard English. Long words. I can only read slowly. I lose the story. Still, I read the words. Must improve my English. Prepare for my new country.

Some books have pictures. Like a child, I look at the pictures. Pink, happy people. Large houses. Many possessions. Very lucky people. Are you real?

Time is slow to pass. I am used to that. I have been two years in the camp. Long, slow years. I walk round the deck a lot. And most nights, I have the stars. They keep me company.

One day we see small boats. Fishermen. The captain's voice: 'Nearly there now. You'll see the coast of Australia this afternoon.'

The ship sails on. The wake drags behind, heavy with our sorrows.

Land grows on the horizon. Hope grows in us, little by little. Here we can stay. Here we can make new lives, new friends, new homes.

Families smile at one another. Some people stay on deck all night. Watching. Thinking. I stay there too.

Next afternoon we arrive. The ship moves slowly, very slowly now, into the docks. Men in uniforms come on board. Polite men. No shouting.

Nothing else happens. We wait. Hours we wait. Harder to wait patiently now, so close to stepping onto Australia.

Then, at last, a new voice. 'Will all immigrants please collect their luggage and go on deck.'

We go down to our cabins. We all say goodbye, goodbye, good luck, live long.

I probably wouldn't see them again. I hoped they would be lucky.

Slowly, slowly, the line of people moves along the deck. Not much talking. What is there to say? All been said many times before.

At last I reach the gangway. I watch the people below me. They step onto Australia. They look round, expect something different. But docks are the same everywhere.

Legs do not move properly after the boat. People stagger along. Follow the pointing hands. Nod. Smile.

I stagger after them. I nod. I try to smile. I can't.

'Move along quickly, please! Queue here, please!'

We arrive at customs. So noisy it hurts. Queues everywhere. So many people! So many loud voices.

I wait in line. *Patience, foolish one! You cannot hurry these things. Life moves fast or slow, as fate decides. Move with it.*

I watch the people around me. The old ones – will they meet their children again? The ones of my age – have they husbands and wives waiting? The children – have they any family to care for them?

Not many are alone, like me.

My turn at last. The customs officer speaks too quickly. 'Slowly,' I say to him. 'Speak slowly, please.'

'Want an interpreter?'

'No, thank you. I have some English. Just speak slowly.'

He looks at my passport, then my bag. Not much to show him. I feel shame to bring so little.

'Anyone coming to meet you?'

'No. I go to hostel.' I show him the letter.

'Right. You go through that door in the corner.'

'What door?' I see no door. Too many people in between. Taller than me. I am afraid to get lost. I cannot move. Like a fool, I stand there.

'Come on! I'll show you the way. Can't have you getting lost, can we?'

Such kindness makes me want to weep! I don't let myself.

We walk across the shed. We pass people from the boat. Some are talking and laughing. They have their families. Their tears are happy ones. How lucky they are!

But I am lucky, too. I am alive. In Australia. At last.

We arrive in the corner. The door is open.

'There you are, mate! Go through there. See that lady? She'll help you. Good luck!'

Nice man, the customs officer. Kind. I hope he enjoys long life.

In a camp, you forget how to think for yourself. I walk quickly to the lady. I am glad to leave the loud noise behind. I feel empty inside. And very tired.

The lady is kind, like the man. She gives us cups of tea. Strong. Milk in it. Not very nice – but warm. Something to do.

I sip it slowly. I say, 'Thank you. It is very good.' The lady smiles.

'Welcome to Australia!' She says it to everyone. Loudly. 'Welcome! Welcome!' She tries very hard to make us feel happy. So we smile at her. We nod when she looks at us.

You learn to hide behind a smile. To hide and wait for the time to pass. Our lives are still not our own. Not yet. But we have arrived at last.

Soon we can make a start. Australia. Lucky country.

Later the lady takes us outside. We get into a bus. We each have a seat. No one has to stand. Very comfortable. And quiet. Even the lady stops speaking. So we can stop smiling.

I look out of the window. Night-time now. City centre. Bright lights. Hotels, restaurants, shops. A world I have forgotten. All cities look alike.

But people are different here. So pink, so plump. These people have eaten well all their lives.

Then we leave the city centre. At first many cars on the road. Then not so many. Just houses to see. Warm with lights. Big gardens. Some curtains not drawn.

No fear inside. Just families. Sitting together. Blue lights of televisions. Australia. Like in the pictures we saw in the camp.

Very different from home, these houses, these people. Too different, perhaps?

I shiver. How will I fit in here? How will I find a job – meet friends – make a home? Hard to do that, on your own.

We arrive at the hostel.

The lady gets out first. She starts talking again. 'This way, everyone! Hurry up, please!'

People get off the bus. I wait. Get off last. Afraid now. The lights are too bright.

I stop for a moment. I look up. Ah! My stars are still there. Many stars, shining down.

I take a deep breath. I smile. New country. But same old friends up there in the sky.

Not that different here, foolish one!

Moving Day

Introduction

This story is based on a real life moving day of our own. Oh, boy, was that a day! My husband and I have moved several times in over fifty years of marriage, but the episode with the moth and cat really happened on one of our moves.

OK, I admit it: I freak out when big fluttery moths come anywhere near me. I know they can't hurt me. I know I'm being ridiculous. But I simply can't help shrieking and diving for cover.

And the cat incident was real, too. He stayed with us for several years after that. I've usually preferred dogs to cats, but this was a black half-Persian, very beautiful, and he behaved more like a dog – or perhaps we treated him that way and he responded accordingly. Who knows? Animals are as variable as human beings. We all loved him. He used to walk round the garden with us, stop when we stopped, carry on with us.

And the incident with the dressing gown really happened

to my husband too on this moving day. We hadn't realised how visible we'd be in a bedroom that jutted out over a valley. Great views – both ways.

Ah, moving days! There's nothing like them.

Moving Day

The day started badly. It had been after midnight when they'd finished packing, so they set the alarm to wake them at six. But for some reason it didn't go off and the removal men had to wake them up.

'Oh, no! Look at the time! You go and let them in!' Jemma rolled out of bed and dived for the bathroom.

Grumbling, George dragged on his jeans and padded to the front door.

The removal man grinned. 'I see you're ready to go.'

'I'm afraid we overslept. And the alarm didn't go off.'

'Never mind. You're up now.' Without asking permission, the man strolled into the house and started surveying the contents as if he owned them.

'Look, can you just give us half an hour and—?' George began.

The man shook his head. 'Nah. 'Fraid not. We've got another job to go to afterwards. Late booking. You should have got a proper alarm clock, mate.'

George gritted his teeth. 'Well, can you start in the living room, then?'

Again, the man shook his head. His grin said he was clearly enjoying his moment of power. 'We always start with the beds.'

Jemma poked her head into the hallway. 'Give me two minutes to get dressed. You can start in the spare bedroom. George, show him where to go, then wake the kids!'

Three-year-old Sarah had been sick in the night. George stared at the evidence in disgust, then scooped her out of the bed. 'Come on, baby, let's get you washed and dressed.' Still holding her, he strode next door and woke his son.

Paul promptly burst into tears and started pummelling his pillow. 'I don't want to go to a new house!' He'd said that on and off all day yesterday as he watched them packing the last of his toys. Still sobbing, he dived under the bedclothes.

George lost his patience and pulled the covers off Paul. 'Get up! Now. And get dressed before you come into the kitchen. The men are here already.'

'I want my breakfast first. I always have my breakfast first.'

'Well, today you're getting dressed first.'

No one could whine as well as Paul, George thought. No one. If they put whining in the Olympics, Paul would win gold every time.

Ten minutes later, he deposited a sweet-smelling daughter in the kitchen and grabbed the piece of toast Jemma thrust at him.

'I put your clothes on the bed,' she said.

'Thanks, love.'

Three hours later, the men carried the last of the furniture out, saying they were going for an early lunch on the way.

George found Jemma in tears in the kitchen, with the children clutching her skirts and wailing in sympathy.

'We've been so happy here,' she sobbed.

George put his arms around her. 'The house is too small. And you know how thrilled you are with the new one. Come on, love. This isn't like you.'

Jemma was usually the strong one, the person who sorted other people's troubles out. There was only one thing in the world she feared and that was moths, the mere sight of which sent her into instant hysterics. The rest of the time, she was the most capable female he'd ever met.

'Come on! Let's go,' he said.

When they arrived at the new house, they ate the burgers and chips they'd bought on the way, then Jemma made beds for the children on the floor of their new bedrooms with the blankets from the car.

'Have a nap,' she ordered.

They didn't even pretend to close their eyes, but they stayed there for a while, at least.

The removal men arrived in a more co-operative mood. Like two young gods, they carried the furniture inside effortlessly, without bumping the walls, seeming happy to move things again, even when Jemma changed her mind about the positioning of the heavy old piano.

By three o'clock they'd accepted a cheque for their services and left.

At some time during the afternoon a black cat entered the house, and when they shooed it outside, it sat at the back door yowling pitifully. It obviously considered this its home.

'I bet the previous owners abandoned it,' George said.

'Well, it can go somewhere else. I haven't time for a cat.' As it turned to look at her pleadingly, Jemma shooed it away.

Twice the children were found playing with the cat on the back veranda. Twice more she shooed it away and tried to distract them, before going back to unpacking boxes.

She kissed George on the nose as she passed him. 'Aren't the views over the valley fabulous? Soon have the bedrooms sorted for tonight. You go and deal with the boxes in the garage.'

George returned the kiss with enthusiasm and strolled outside, master of all he surveyed. How lovely to have a big double garage and workshop!

After a while, the cat grew tired of sneaking clumsy cuddles with Sarah and came to investigate what George was doing. It spent the rest of the afternoon with him. It was a nice cat. Companionable.

Jemma poked her head in to see how he was going. 'Not you as well! It's *not* staying.'

At six o'clock, they stopped unpacking to feed everyone then get the children ready for bed, something they always tried to do together.

'No,' Jemma told Sarah for the fifteenth time, 'teddy won't be frightened to sleep in this lovely big room. Look, he can sit on the windowsill.'

Sarah looked unconvinced, but brightened when the cat strolled in. It settled down next to the bed. Delighted, Sarah also lay down.

Jemma rolled her eyes. 'I'm too tired to argue. We'll

take it to the cat rescue people if it hangs around.'

They unpacked a few more boxes then went to bed early. George put an arm round her shoulders and together they stood staring out of the window. Their bedroom was built over the garage and had a magnificent view of the valley below them. The views were one of the things they'd liked most about this house.

'It's a pity the new curtains won't be here till the weekend. Perhaps we should have left the others up. No, they were filthy rags. They had to go.' Jemma waved to the neighbour across the road, who was blatantly staring up at them. 'We'll have to get undressed in the bathroom.'

George was just sinking into sleep when there was a rustling by the window.

'George!'

'Mmnh?'

A hand poked him urgently in the side. 'George!'

'Wassamatta?'

'George, that sounds like a moth.'

'Can't be.' He prayed fervently that it wouldn't be a moth.

The rustling was louder this time, but not as loud as Jemma's shriek. 'It *is* a moth!'

'Won't hurt you.' He'd used the same argument many times before and it'd never worked.

Jemma pushed him out of bed and dived under the covers, yelling, 'Do something!'

'You idiot! I'm stark naked and we've no curtains.' He tried to scrabble back under the bedcovers, but they were all in a tight bundle round Jemma.

'If you don't do something, I'll kill you, George Turner!'

He fumbled around the window. 'I can't find it.'

'Put the light on, then!'

'I can't. I'm not wearing any clothes.'

'What happened to your jeans?'

'I dropped them in the shower. They're dripping wet.'

The bundle of bedding was still tightly defended against him. 'Get rid – of that – moth.'

'I haven't unpacked my clothes.'

She was never sympathetic about his untidiness. 'We have an agreement, George Turner. About moths. If any get inside the house, you kill them for me. Immediately.'

'But—'

'You're not coming back to bed until you get rid of the horrible thing. My dressing gown is on the chair. Put that on.'

He picked it up. 'Hell, it's your frilly one. I'm not wearing that.'

'It was the only one I could find. And I don't care what you wear.' Her voice rose another few decibels. *'Get rid of that moth!'*

He glared at the hump under the bedding. 'I hope you're suffocating in there,' he muttered under his breath as he pulled on the frilly dressing gown.

In other circumstances it had been known to turn him on. It was a beautiful thing, black and lacy. Tonight, it had the opposite effect. It embarrassed him. He peered out to check that no neighbours were about then switched on the light.

The moth was huge. And active. Obviously in training for the Moth Championships. He crept across to the window, holding the frills together across his loins. If anyone saw him like this, they'd get a very wrong impression of his married life.

He reached out one hand carefully. The moth sat still, trembling slightly. His fingers were just closing round it when it sensed danger and fluttered upwards.

The raked ceilings were twelve feet at the highest edge. The moth sat up there, fluttering its wings to and fro gently, mocking him. If moths could laugh, it'd have been chortling with amusement.

George cursed and let go of the dressing gown, then hastily pulled it round him again. 'It's gone up to the ceiling. I can't do anything about it.'

'You're not coming back into this bed until you've caught it!'

The fact that her voice was muffled by several layers of bedding made no difference. When Jemma used that tone of voice, there was no doing a thing with her. Especially when it concerned a moth. George had hunted them in Europe, America and Australia.

As he was racking his brain for a way to reach the damned thing, his eyes fell on a string of rubber bands. He'd fastened them together as he unpacked for future reuse, a silly habit he had. His mood lightened. Maybe not such a silly habit. It would require a very accurate shot, but he'd always had a good eye for a ball.

After four pings which sent the rubber bands flying up towards the moth, he was beginning to get his eye in. 'Nearly got you then!' he yelled.

The covers lifted and Jemma peered out. 'Did you kill it yet?'

'Nearly.' He brandished his makeshift weapon.

'What on earth are you doing with those?'

'I told you. The moth's up in the top corner. This is the only way I can get at it. We haven't got a long enough ladder.'

The moth did a few practice swoops around the bedroom and Jemma disappeared with another shriek of terror.

Why was she so frightened of them? he wondered for the millionth time.

When the fearsome monster had settled down, George took careful aim and whooped with delight as he hit the target.

The moth fluttered slowly towards the ground, but it was still bobbing up and down.

'Poor little thing!' He could afford to be generous now that he'd won.

Still clutching the black lacy frills around himself, he strode across, hoping to administer the *coup de grâce* before it flew up to the ceiling again.

A black head poked round the side of the door and in strolled the cat. It took one look at the moth and pounced, chomping with great enjoyment and delicately licking up the bits of wing that fell out of the sides of its mouth.

George scooped up the cat and took up a heroic pose. 'We killed it for you. It's gone.'

Red and sweaty, Jemma crawled out of the covers. 'You took long enough,' she grumbled. She took another look at him and giggled. 'Goodness, I hadn't realised how transparent that dressing gown is!'

George looked down in horror, then his eyes caught a movement in the driveway opposite. Two of the neighbours were gaping up at him, open-mouthed. He dropped the cat and dived for the light switch.

The cat stayed, of course, a valued member of the family after that act of heroism. George christened it Galahad and Jemma fed it until its coat gleamed and its belly bulged. Fortunately, this in no way lessened its liking for munching the occasional moth.

It took a while for the neighbours to come round, but when Jemma had hysterics over a moth while Louise next door was in for coffee, the thaw started.

'Does she always freak out?' Louise whispered to George.

'Always. That's what happened the night we moved in.'

'Ah.'

'A barbecue,' Jemma decided. 'And we'll tell everyone else exactly what happened.'

The wine was flowing nicely and a good feed had been had by all when George started his tale of their moving day.

Louise chipped in with the tale of how Jemma had freaked out a couple of weeks ago over another moth.

There was much laughter and the men stopped looking wary when George got close to them to pour glasses of wine.

The next time Jemma needed a dressing gown, George helped her choose it – black velvet, ankle length.

He still had nightmares about that transparent thing.

It had lost all its sex appeal now, and the mere sight of it made him shudder.

When he sneaked it out of the house, the charity shop was very glad to take it off his hands.

Sunshine and Parrots

Introduction

There is a saying: *Everything is grist to a writer's mill.* In other words, anything that happens may be useful in a story one day.

Here is another story based on our first encounter with a neighbour who kept a parrot – well, actually, it was a galah, which is a type of cockatoo, but the magazine editor called it a 'parrot' in the story because not many people in the UK are experts at types of parrots. Galahs are good mimics and are sometimes kept as pets in Western Australia, usually in a cage outside in the shade.

It was my husband who first 'met' the neighbour across the road after we moved in. When he knocked on the door, a voice with a strong Birmingham accent said, 'Hello. How are you?' and he looked round but could see no one. He introduced himself again and got the same response, so in the end came home, saying what a weird neighbour we had.

Turned out the neighbour (who later became a friend) was out, and the galah was outside round a corner, not visible from the front door. Kathy came from Birmingham and had a very strong accent, so her galah had picked up the same way of speaking and sounded so like her, it always made us laugh during the years we were friends.

Writing the introductions to these stories is bringing back a lot of memories and I'm enjoying doing it even more than I thought I would.

Sunshine and Parrots

Penny moved into a furnished townhouse in Perth, Western Australia one hot spring day, exactly a week after emigrating from the UK to join her brother.

Fancy November being the last spring month! She was looking forward to the warm weather and had set her mind on a barbecue on the beach for Christmas, just like it said in the tourist brochures.

She was still angry at Peter for suddenly taking a job in the north of the state and leaving her to settle in alone. He'd helped her find this townhouse, then vanished.

It was a fly in, fly out job, where he spent six weeks working up north, then four weeks at home. The money was excellent, so he couldn't turn it down.

She camped out the first night in the townhouse, using the bed Peter had provided for her and a plastic outdoor chair and table. This was going to be fun, she told herself firmly. But it was rather disconcerting to find herself facing the difficulties of settling into a strange country alone. As she'd already found, there were differences, and not just the weather.

Still, she'd cope. She always did.

The following day she waited for the possessions she'd shipped out to Australia to be delivered, and was delighted when they arrived early. Well, life seemed to start earlier here than it had in England.

She still needed to buy some furniture, but unpacking the treasured possessions she'd sent ahead made the place feel more homelike.

She was interrupted by the postman. 'I've got a parcel for your neighbour. Can you take it for him?'

'Of course.' It'd be a good way of getting to know whoever was next door. After she'd closed the door, she glanced at the name: Matthew Langham. The sender was Fiona Davies. Girlfriend? Married sister? You couldn't help being curious.

She smiled at her own nosiness and put the parcel down in the hall, continuing to organise her things. Thank heavens for air conditioning! She'd come here straight from the snow of an English winter and was still learning how to deal with the heat.

She'd made the mistake the first day at Peter's flat of opening up the windows in the morning and he'd yelled at her for letting the warm air in.

At teatime she went next door with the parcel. There was still no car in the carport, so she didn't think her neighbour was home, but she knocked anyway.

A woman's voice said, 'G'day!'

'Er – hello.' She'd feel foolish saying 'g'day' back, so an English 'hello' would have to do. She looked round, wondering where the voice came from. Perhaps that open window.

'G'day!' repeated the woman.

Penny frowned. Was someone mocking her? 'I already said hello.'

'Go away! I'm busy.'

She blinked in shock. This was sheer rudeness. 'I have a parcel for Matthew Langham.'

'I'm busy.'

Furious, she took the parcel back home. What a rude woman!

She heard a car draw up next door after she'd gone to bed and remembered that she'd not left a note about the parcel. Well, it'd have to wait till tomorrow. She wasn't getting up again. She was exhausted.

Penny woke early and went out into the back courtyard to enjoy the coolest time of day. She'd intended to take the parcel round after breakfast, but the car drove away from next door at seven o'clock. The guy was definitely an early starter.

She didn't have time to worry about the parcel. She was starting her new job today.

When she got home that evening, a man drove into the next carport at the same time as she entered hers. She sat in her car, feeling suddenly nervous of introducing herself to her neighbour because he wasn't at all what she'd expected. He was drop-dead gorgeous. How come someone like that was living with such a bad-tempered woman?

He came towards her, smiling, hand outstretched. 'Hi!

You must be my new neighbour. I'm Matt Langham.'

She shook hands, feeling a bit flustered. 'I'm – um, Penny Kerr.'

'I've been a bit busy or I'd have introduced myself sooner. But this was the last hellish day, thank goodness. The project is now finished.'

'Yes. Right.'

'I believe you have a parcel for me. There was a card in my letter box from the postie.'

'Yes. I brought the parcel round yesterday, but some woman shouted to go away. She said she was busy.'

He frowned slightly, then began to grin. 'She's like that. Come and meet her.'

She looked at him in puzzlement, but found herself following him to his front door.

'G'day!' said the same woman's voice.

'How are you today, Gus?'

Gus? The voice had sounded like a woman.

'Go away! I'm busy.'

Matt looked at Penny, eyes dancing in amusement. 'Let me introduce you.' Instead of going into the house, he led the way round the side, gesturing towards a huge cage in which sat a pink and grey bird.

'A parrot!' she exclaimed. 'Oh, I do feel an idiot.'

'Not a parrot, a galah, which is a sort of cockatoo.'

He put his fingers into the cage and began stroking the bird, which rubbed its head against him. 'No trouble today?' he crooned.

He smiled at Penny. 'There's a new neighbour two houses along with a cat. It comes round to torment poor old Gus. It can't get at him, but he's a gentle old soul and he gets upset when it paws the bars of his cage, so I chase it away. I'm hoping it'll take the hint.'

She watched the two of them for a minute, smiling. 'I'll go and get your parcel.'

Matt didn't follow her but when she brought the parcel round, the front door was open, so she knocked.

'Come in!' he yelled.

She went into a house that was the mirror image of hers and found him in the kitchen, pouring some white wine into two glasses.

He held one out to her. 'Unless you prefer red?'

'I like either.' She clinked glasses with him.

'Welcome to Australia.'

'How did you guess I was new?'

He grinned. 'Pommie accent, thought a galah was a parrot, rosy English complexion, no suntan. Easy peasy.'

'Oh.' She felt flustered so sipped her wine.

'How are you settling in?'

'Fine. My brother was supposed to help me. He's been in Perth for over a year, you see. But he's got a new job up north, and a four-hour plane flight is a bit far to nip to and fro. I can't believe how big Western Australia is.'

'It makes up about a third of Australia in land mass.'

They chatted for a while, then her stomach rumbled, so she set down her empty glass. 'Must go and get my tea.'

'I'm going down to the local Chinese restaurant. Do you want to join me?'

She definitely did. Evenings could get a bit lonely when you didn't know anyone.

They had a lovely evening, a great meal, then he said goodnight at the door.

She wished he'd acted as if they were on a date, but he didn't. Well, there you were. You couldn't win prizes all the time in the dating game.

Even without her brother's help, Penny felt she was making a good job of settling in. People at work were friendly and they took her out for a drink on Friday evening.

And there was Matt next door. During the next few weeks they went out for the occasional meal or shared a drink in the evening. He called that a sundowner.

He was . . . nice. More than nice. But he hadn't made any attempt to kiss her.

Of course, if she were truly a liberated woman, she should be able to kiss him first. But she didn't dare do that.

On the way back from their next visit to the Chinese restaurant, she tripped over some uneven paving.

Matt caught her and kept hold, bending his head. The kiss was long and sweet, but afterwards he frowned. 'It's not good to get too close to a neighbour.'

She blinked at him in shock. After a scorching kiss, this was the last thing she'd expected to hear.

Then he smiled ruefully. 'It's a bit late to say that, isn't it? Especially as I'm about to repeat the misdemeanour.'

She went to bed in a haze of happiness. Could life get any better? All this sunshine and a gorgeous man.

The following day, when she went round to invite Matt for a drink, Gus called out, 'Welcome, Fiona!'

Penny stiffened. She'd not heard it say that before. Who was Fiona? An ex-girlfriend?

But though Matt's car was there, he didn't answer the door.

She slept badly. What was going on? Who was Fiona?

Above all, why hadn't he answered the door?

There was a rush on at work and she was late getting home. As she sat in her car, gathering her belongings, which included some tinsel and a few Christmas decorations, another car drew up in Matt's drive.

A woman got out, about Penny's age and very pretty. She banged on the door and when it opened, she hurled herself into Matt's arms.

He picked her up and swung her round and round. 'Fiona! You're back. Give me a big cuddle! I've missed you.'

As they disappeared into his house, his arm was round her shoulders. They were both laughing.

Tears welled in Penny's eyes. She felt used. This woman was obviously more than a friend. She'd seen Matt's face, absolutely radiating happiness.

She got herself and her shopping into the house, not letting the tears fall. It'd only been a few weeks and he'd not made her any promises. But still . . .

She started to put up the tinsel, but that made her feel worse, so she pulled it down again and dumped it in a corner.

Unable to settle to watching TV, she went to bed early with a good book.

Tried to read the book.

Failed.

She couldn't help listening and the other car didn't drive

off. It was still there at midnight when she fell asleep.

It was still there in the morning, too.

After work Penny drove cautiously home. Matt's car and the other one were still there. She felt like driving past, not wanting to run into him. But that would be cowardly, so she turned into her carport as usual.

Matt came out of his house, turning towards her with a smile. There was a loud squawk from the other side of his house. Gus. The squawks sounded frantic.

Matt hesitated, then waved to say he'd be back and ran round the side of the house.

Penny took the opportunity to hurry inside and lock the door.

When the doorbell rang, she peeped out from upstairs. Matt. She was tired, didn't want a row, hated rows, so didn't answer it.

She didn't go out to get her mail from the letter box at the end of the drive until she was sure he and his visitor were sitting outside in his rear courtyard.

She'd received some Christmas cards from England. The mere sight of them made her feel homesick. Only two weeks to go to the holiday. She'd sent all her cards a while ago.

The cheerful messages from her friends upset her. She dumped the cards on a side table, tore the envelopes to tiny shreds and kicked the tinsel under the table for good measure.

This was going to be the worst Christmas ever.

She'd have to hide how she was feeling from her brother, who was due back soon after working double shifts for the money. He was saving for a deposit on a house. Which was good, admirable in fact.

But oh, she wanted very much to see him again. With their parents dead, he was her closest relative in the world.

The following evening Matt was waiting for her outside his house, arms folded. She couldn't, just couldn't face him, so she drove past and didn't come back for another hour.

He wasn't there then, thank goodness.

She was stupid enough to wish he had been.

But she grew angry at herself for wishing that when she peeped out of her bedroom window and saw the other woman sitting outside in the courtyard, laughing and clinking her glass of wine against Matt's.

He was looking thoughtful and it was Fiona who was doing most of the talking, gesticulating wildly.

Penny grew angry at herself for staring longingly out of the window at a man who didn't give two hoots about her and had brought another woman to live with him, without warning her that he wasn't serious about their relationship. All right, potential relationship.

How pitiful she was, dwelling on that. She should get on with her life, find another guy. There was one at work who'd been chatting to her a lot. Only she wasn't attracted to *him*.

Neither car was next door when Penny got home from work the following day. Good. She could unload her shopping in peace. Christmas food. Her brother was coming down to Perth soon and they'd be able to spend Christmas together. It'd be fun.

She was determined to have fun.

Somehow.

But as she was going into the house, she heard the parrot squawking again. Then there was a crash and the squawking reached desperate levels. She couldn't leave it at that, not if the bird was in distress, so she dropped her shopping and ran through Matt's carport and round the side of his house.

The cage was on its side on the floor, with seed spilt everywhere. A huge cat was poking its paw through the bars. Gus stopped squawking and risked a jab of its beak at the cat, which yelped and backed off, fur standing on end.

'Get away!' Penny yelled. 'Go on! Scat!'

The cat scampered off over the low wall to the next house.

Penny set the cage upright, speaking soothingly, hoping Gus wouldn't bite her hand. 'It's all right. I've chased that nasty old cat away. Let's get your cage sorted out.'

'I'll do that.'

She jumped in shock as Matt spoke from beside her. 'Oh! I didn't hear you coming.'

'You wouldn't with Gus squawking like that. Was it the damned cat again?'

'Yes. I chased it away.'

'Thanks. Penny, I—'

'I've got to get home and—'

He caught hold of her arm. 'What did I do to upset you?'

She tugged her arm away. 'You have another woman living with you! You kissed and cuddled her when she arrived. I can take a hint.'

'Fiona?'

Penny nodded.

'She's my cousin.'

As he spoke, Fiona drove up. 'Hello! You must be the elusive neighbour. Matt's been trying to introduce us for days.'

Penny shook hands then backed away. 'Got to go. I dropped my shopping to rescue the parrot and I've got frozen stuff thawing out.'

Matt didn't follow her. What did that say?

But as she carried the second lot of shopping into her house, he came out and took it from her. 'Let me. We need to talk.'

'Do we?'

'I hope so.'

She waited in the kitchen, feeling breathless. He did that to her.

'Fiona's been away overseas for a year. That's why I was so happy to see her. She's my favourite cousin and she's staying with me till she gets a place of her own. Her fiancé will be joining her at Christmas. They were working overseas together, only his contract has another couple of months to go. They're going to get married at Easter.'

'Oh.'

'Does that explain the situation?'

She felt such a fool, could feel her cheeks heating up. 'Yes. Sorry.'

'Will you join us for a sundowner? I have some very nice white wine.'

She had been such a fool, jumping to conclusions, but Matt was smiling at her anyway. 'I'd like that.'

'And can we resume our friendship, see where it leads?'

'Yes.' She couldn't help adding, 'Thank goodness for your parrot.'

'It's a galah.'

'Sorry. He still looks like a parrot to me.'

'He's a hero today. I must give him a piece of apple as a thank you for bringing us together again. See you in a few minutes.'

Penny danced round the kitchen after he'd left. She knew where she wanted their friendship to lead.

It was going to be a wonderful Christmas, she was sure. And if she had her way, they'd have a barbecue on the beach, too.

Sunshine and parrots . . . well, all right, galahs . . . and perhaps love. What more could a woman want?

Dress Sense

Introduction

Most of my short stories are romantic or (I hope) lightly humorous, but not this one.

It was one of the first short stories I ever wrote and was broadcast on the radio. I learnt so much from writing it – and rewriting it a dozen times at least!

The story was inspired by a drama on TV about spies. I wasn't interested in the guns and fighting side of things, but in the human element, which set me wondering what would happen to an ordinary woman caught up in one of those cases.

What if it was no longer safe for her to stay around? How would she cope?

As I have done with most of the short stories in this book, I've added more details to this version.

Dress Sense

Heather had always been nervous after dark, for no reason that she or her parents could work out. Her father used to laugh at her, as gently as he'd done everything else. She wished he were still alive to mock her fears tonight.

She carried her shopping into the house and closed the outer door. When a draught of cold air crept round her neck from another direction, she spun round, a shiver of fear rippling down her spine. There shouldn't have been any draughts, because she'd locked up her father's house very carefully indeed that morning.

As she turned back towards the kitchen, someone grabbed her by the arms. A hand covered her mouth. 'If you scream, we'll shoot you.'

There were two men. Big men, who towered over her. Men with masks over their faces. She had no hope of fighting back.

They hauled her out to a chair and dumped her on it.

She didn't dare scream. Her heart was pounding hard as every woman's worst nightmares came true.

'Good girl,' said a soft voice. 'You don't want to cause us any trouble, now do you? That might make us very angry indeed.'

'Answer him, girlie!' It was the hoarse voice that had haunted her nightmares for the past month, ever since someone had tried to grab her in a dark street – and had very nearly succeeded. Thank heavens for observant passers-by who'd come to her aid!

One man poked her hard on her upper arm. 'Answer him.'

'No, I don't want to cause any trouble,' she said hastily.

Another masked man came out of the shadows in the hall. He stood over her. 'Tell us where your father kept his notes.'

'The police took all his papers away. There weren't many things at home.'

'We know he kept some rather special papers here. It wasn't allowed, so he must have had a hiding place somewhere. The police haven't got the ones we want.'

'I don't know anything about that.'

One man shook her hard, then slapped her face.

'I don't!' she cried desperately. 'Dad never told me anything. He always said his job involved boring mathematical stuff.'

The eyes of the third man, who seemed to be the leader, narrowed and his lips thinned with anger.

She waited for them to kill her. And she didn't even understand what this was all about. Her father couldn't have been mixed up in conspiracies.

'Well, boys, I think we'll have to look for some clue in

her memories. God knows, it's a long shot, but she may just have seen something. Give her an injection.'

A needle jabbed into her arm and the scene around her faded into a blur. Voices shouted at her. Question followed question. She answered as best she could, but it didn't seem to be what they wanted.

Someone kept sobbing. Some poor woman. Muffled, agonised sobbing and moans. She felt so sorry for that poor woman.

After a black eternity, she could feel the drug starting to wear off. She was surprised at how hoarse her voice was, and when she moved, pain stabbed down one arm.

A voice cut through the confusion in her mind. 'She obviously knows nothing. Shoot her and let's go.'

'Is that really necessary?'

'Yes. She's heard our voices, seen our bodies.'

Fuelled by terror, she managed to take them by surprise. Jumping to her feet, she started running across the room, trying desperately to get away from them.

'Shoot, damn you!'

The bullet slammed into her back with a force that tore one scream of anguish from her before the floor came up to hit her in the face and the lights started to fade.

A shadow crossed her face and as she half opened her eyes, a voice echoed in her ears from a long way away. 'Heather, wake up! We haven't long. Dammit, girl, wake up!'

It was a colleague of her father's, one she had never liked. 'Mr Jones! Are you dead, too?'

'No one's dead.'

She took a deep breath and managed to focus on the

room. Two men by the door, handguns at the ready, another standing beside her.

Mr Jones took hold of her chin, making her yelp with pain and focus on him. 'Sorry. But I need you to concentrate. What happened here, Heather?'

'Some men broke in.' She forced more words up the sandpaper tunnel of her throat. 'They wanted Father's papers.'

'Tell me what happened! Every detail.' He was as urgent in his questioning as the others had been, and only marginally more gentle.

Her thoughts kept wandering off. After the funeral, Mr Jones had advised her to move out of the house and she had refused. Her father had always said she was pig-stubborn, just like her mother. But why should she have to leave? She loved that old house.

Well, now she knew why. What had her father been working on, for heaven's sake?

'Some men – I don't know how they got in. They were just – there suddenly. How should I know who they were? They gave me an injection. Then they questioned me.'

'What did they ask you?'

'About Father's papers. I can't remember clearly.'

'Try.'

'I can't remember! And then they shot me. They killed me.'

'Stupid bitch!'

The man beside her spoke. 'It'll have been one of the new relaxant drugs, sir. She really won't remember much and it'll take her a while to regain proper focus.'

Heather looked down at herself. She could see no blood, but her back was a mass of agony and it hurt her to draw breath. 'They did shoot me,' she insisted. 'In the back. Why am I not dead? Am I dying?'

Mr Jones stepped back. 'Find out why she isn't dead, for Christ's sake, then maybe she'll talk sense!'

The man with the kind voice tried to move her carefully. But it hurt, dear heavens how it hurt!

'She has a bulletproof vest on, sir. Her back's badly bruised and I'd guess she's got a cracked rib or two, but the bullet didn't penetrate. It must be a damned good vest.'

'Bulletproof?' Heather grabbed his arm. 'What do you mean – bulletproof?'

'You're wearing a bulletproof vest. Surely you knew that, love?'

She started to laugh, but the pain was too sharp and the laugh turned into another moan. 'No! I didn't know. I was just cold. I saw Dad's quilted jerkin and put it on.'

Mr Jones leant over her again. 'Well, you've just saved your own life by wearing it.'

'Why should my father need a bulletproof vest? What was he doing?'

'You really don't need to know.'

Tears were trickling down her cheeks. 'No. I don't need to understand any of this, do I? I just have to act as a living target. After my father's accident—'

'Murder,' he corrected.

She always had trouble saying the word 'murder'. The father she knew was a gentle, loving man. Why should anyone want to murder a mathematician? Whatever Mr Jones said, she had been sure that it was all a mistake, a horrible mistake.

Until now.

'What am I going to do now?' she whispered. 'I can't stay here any more.' Tears made chill tracks down her cheeks.

'No, you can't. They don't usually leave living witnesses. You did see them, didn't you? Good. At least you'll be able to help us make up digital pictures.'

'Yes. I saw them quite well, actually, because the masks slipped when they were thumping me.' Nausea roiled round her stomach as she realised that the intruders had made little attempt to hide their faces once they were inside the house. They must have intended to kill her all along.

'What can I do now?' she whispered. 'They'll come back for me.'

'You'll have to vanish.'

'Pardon?'

He spoke slowly, as if to an idiot. 'You're going to have to vanish, Heather. Permanently.'

'You mean – like in the spy movies?' Surely not? Things like this didn't happen to ordinary people like her.

'Exactly like that. We'll give you a new identity, then find you a home and a job in another country. Australia is the usual choice. Or Canada. You'll settle in there and carry on with your life.'

'And plastic surgery, too?' she joked. She would not, could not believe this was real.

'Yes, of course.' His voice was impatient. 'You don't want anyone to recognise you, do you? Good thing your hair's a nice mousy brown colour. If it'd been an unusual colour, you'd have had to dye it.'

The dark man cleared his throat. 'We can't delay much longer, sir.'

'You're right. Call the ambulance.'

One of the men watching the door slipped outside.

Helen stared up at Mr Jones's cold face. 'What was my father doing? I demand to know.'

'You're in no position to demand anything. Besides, a dedicated greenie like you wouldn't like it if we told you.'

'But—'

'Let well alone, you silly bitch! Just accept our offer gratefully if you want to continue living.'

'My father wouldn't work on anything that would damage our planet,' she said stubbornly.

'Your father was a patriot. Let's leave it at that, hmm?'

'Then who were those men?'

'Terrorists. From an organised group, not noble bloody amateurs like your sort.'

She lay back, too tired to argue. Her fingers rubbed against her father's vest. She looked down at it and started laughing, in painful jerky gasps.

'What the hell's got into you now?' Mr Jones snapped.

'The bulletproof vest,' she told him, still laughing.

'What about the damned thing?'

'I only chose this one because I liked the colour. It matched my new jeans, you see. I always did have good dress sense.'

The two of them stood staring down at her, faces expressionless.

'You must see how funny that is.'

But they didn't laugh.

She was still smiling when a woman gave her an injection and the world began to slip away.

The last thing she heard was Mr Jones's voice.

'Cover up her face! We want her to look nice and dead when we carry her out.'

After that, it was a very long time before she laughed again.

And even longer before she found the everyday happiness she'd taken for granted before.

Play Along

Introduction

I started off my career as a novelist by writing historical romances in the style of Jane Austen and Georgette Heyer. I soon moved on from there into my own style of writing – they call it a writer's 'voice'. My husband says he could tell a piece I'd written anywhere because he knows my voice.

I'm now writing historical sagas and modern tales, but in the past I've written fantasy stories set on imaginary planets and romances both modern and historical. I've also had over twenty poems published, numerous articles about writing, and about fifty short stories.

My first novel published was *Persons of Rank*, a Regency romance, and it won a big prize in an Australian writing competition. More importantly to me, it won me my first publication of fiction. (I had nine French textbooks published when I was a teacher, but no one ever reads a textbook for pleasure, so it's just not the same joy for the writer!)

I'm rather old, or as I like to say, I'm turning into 'a

valuable antique'. I began my career pre-computer. Yes, there was such a time! In my early days of writing we didn't have much choice of how we got published. No Internet. No word processing. No easy way to self-publishing. You just kept trying until a publisher 'picked you up'. Or you kept waiting and hoping.

A few writers make huge money, but most don't, especially at the beginning of their careers.

I started writing short stories for women's magazines because it was a way of supplementing my income, which had dropped drastically when I gave up work as a human resources officer. I found romances were more likely to be accepted, but not so much historical ones, so I moved on to modern love stories.

Writing is a business, after all, and unless you're that rare creature, an instant bestseller, it takes a few years and a few books published to earn a living. I had no problems with writing romantic short stories. I'm happily married myself, so I like to create warm fuzzy encounters and endings!

I thought of this story idea as I was doing the family shopping in a big echoing shopping mall. I didn't look where I was going and turned into a dead end where the lifts were – as you do when you're a working mum and are rushing round trying to do ten things at once.

Stories spin into my head at the oddest times. I've had characters wake me in the night to show me scenes, I've had ideas occur to me while my husband is driving us along a motorway, and they've even dropped into my mind as I sit miserably in my plane seat flying to and from England. It's putting it mildly to say I'm NOT a happy flyer, so the latter flash of inspiration has always surprised me.

The idea for the start of this story came to me as a young woman ran past while I was struggling to turn my heavily loaded shopping trolley round to get out to the car park. She was running towards the lifts . . . and there you were . . . she ran into my story as well.

Play Along

Nell skidded to a halt at the edge of the shopping centre and risked a quick look back. The man was still following her, even though she'd run away from him.

She didn't know his name, but she knew what he'd been up to and when she'd been investigating that, he'd come after her. The mere sight of him made her feel threatened.

She heaved in another lungful of air and set off again at a brisk pace, expecting to find an exit, but instead finding herself in a dead end facing a group of lifts, all in use.

No way out.

'Oh, no!' She groaned aloud and stared up at the indicators. One lift was coming down. She looked behind her. The heavy footsteps were getting closer, sounded to be just round the corner.

'Hurry up!' she muttered as the lift left the first floor and continued down.

A light started flashing as it arrived. She looked behind her. The man came into sight and stopped, a gloating smile on his face. He knew he had her cornered. And there was no one else in sight. If he tried to touch her, they'd both find out whether her self-defence classes had taught what they claimed.

Before he could reach her, there was a bell tone and the lift door opened. Another man stepped out of it.

Nell darted forward and desperation lent her the courage to do something which would normally have made her curl up in horror. 'Darling!' she exclaimed loudly and threw herself into a complete stranger's arms.

As he opened his mouth to protest, she began to kiss him, stifling his exclamation of shock with her mouth. She could see his eyes widen in surprise, feel his body stiffen in protest.

She drew her mouth back for long enough to hiss, 'Please, play along with this! Please! I'm desperate to escape that man.' She couldn't tell him the whole truth, so she added, 'I don't know why he's following me, but I didn't feel safe. I don't know what I'd have done if your lift hadn't opened just now.'

He stared at her face then at the man, who was standing nearby, arms folded, watching them.

'I don't like the looks of him, either.' Suddenly he grinned. 'My pleasure to help you. Let's make him think you've got a permanent protector.' He dropped his briefcase and took charge.

Before Nell could move a muscle, a warm soft mouth took possession of hers and a hand yanked her body firmly against his. It was a long time since anyone had kissed her like this, far too long.

When he pulled his head away, she could only cling to him dizzily.

'Am I playing the game correctly?' he breathed into her ear.

'Y-yes. Thank you.' She gazed up into his smiling brown eyes and threw a quick glance over her shoulder. *He* was still there, watching her, waiting, but frowning now. 'He's still there!'

'Want some help to get away?'

'Would you?'

He held her at arm's length and said loudly, 'You look wonderful, darling!' adding under his breath, 'Promise me that you've not been doing anything illegal. I'll not help a thief.'

She stroked his cheek with a loving fingertip. 'I'm definitely not a thief!'

'Then if you want to escape, it's your turn to play along with me.' He put his arm round her shoulders, saying loudly, 'Let's go home now, darling.'

Only then did she notice that another man had left the lift and was hovering protectively behind them, as if he were a bodyguard. He'd already picked up the briefcase dropped by her rescuer.

Surely if they moved away together, the man chasing her would go away? But no. He kept following them.

She stole another glance at her companion. There was something familiar about his face, but she still couldn't place him.

Outside, he stopped next to a waiting limousine. A chauffeur held the door open.

'Do get in, darling.'

Nell hesitated, but the guy was still behind them, as if checking up on her. Taking a deep breath, she got in, slinging her handbag down on the seat, not caring how it bounced about, just wanted to get away from *him*.

The bodyguard got into the front beside the driver.

'Take me home, please, Bill.' The stranger switched the intercom off and turned to Nell. 'I think you owe me an explanation now, so let's start with your name.'

He had changed from the handsome stranger play-acting to protect her at the lift into a rather forbidding man very much in charge of the situation. His fingers were tapping impatiently on the seat beside his leg and the sleek business suit couldn't hide the fact that he had a hard, muscular body.

'My name's Nell Dawson.'

'Go on!'

She fumbled for her ID, but her bag fell on the floor. 'I – I'm a journalist for the *Weekly Star* magazine and—' The expression on his face made her freeze and wish people really could click their fingers and vanish in a puff of smoke.

'I might have known it was a trick! Stop the car, Bill!'

'Can't stop on the freeway, sir. Give me a minute.'

Her rescuer folded his arms, ignoring her. She tried desperately to think of something to persuade him that she hadn't been trying to interview him. Who was he, anyway?

They turned off the freeway and the car came to a halt near a group of industrial units.

Her rescuer reached across to throw the door open. 'Out!'

'Look, I—'

'It's certainly a novel ploy, but you didn't think it through. I never give casual interviews, not under any circumstances. Now get out.' He made a gesture and the bodyguard reached inside the car and dragged her out.

She only just managed to grab her handbag. She watched the car drive away, muttering, 'Well, thank you very much!'

Her handbag felt lighter than usual, so she checked it. Her mobile phone was there, but her purse was missing. She fumbled desperately through the bag again, but there was no purse.

She was stuck out here in the suburbs with no means of getting home.

She phoned for a taxi, but had to go back to work and get someone to pay her fare. She felt such a fool.

There had been a whole series of mishaps since she'd started work here and she had to confess to her editor that she'd failed to get the story she'd been sent out for.

Steve rolled his eyes. 'You're not doing well, Nell Dawson. You said you were up for a challenge and I gave you one.'

'That was too much of a challenge.'

'Well, I couldn't very well send a man on a job like that, could I?'

She'd hoped her rescuer would at least return her wallet, but three days passed and he didn't. She still couldn't place his face, so had no way to contact him.

In the end, she had to waste hours reporting her credit card missing and signing up for a new one.

Worst of all, her editor had transferred her to cover social events while Danny Gratski was on holiday. She felt she'd reached rock bottom. Celebrities and who was getting a divorce left her totally cold. She'd become a journalist because she wanted to make a difference to the world.

Unfortunately this job had been the only one available when she returned to Australia from backpacking round the world. It would look bad if she quit after a few weeks so she had to stick it out for a few months longer.

The desk phone rang. 'Golden wedding today, Nell,' Steve said.

She took down the details and set off. They were a sweet older couple, very much in love still, but this wasn't exactly cutting-edge reporting.

A few days later, Steve called her into his office. He was grinning as if he knew something and she didn't, but she didn't challenge him. She'd learnt by now that he couldn't be pushed into revealing anything till he was ready.

'Go and cover the charity lunch at the Royal Aztec Hotel, will you.'

Nell brightened. 'Oh, goody, free food.'

'It sure is. Enjoy.'

The waiter showed her to a press table at the side, where she met a couple of people she knew.

A murmur by the door cut their conversation dead and they all turned round to see who had arrived.

Nell gasped. It was him! Just as tall and distinguished looking as she'd remembered. She nudged her neighbour. 'Who's that?'

'Harry Gilson. Surely you recognise him?'

'I recognise the name and the face, but not together.' The famous playboy turned philanthropist and the man who'd helped her. No wonder his face had looked vaguely familiar, though he usually tended to shun the press. She shrank back. Perhaps, if she was very careful, he wouldn't notice her. She didn't want him throwing her out.

By this time the place was full of glitterati, cooing acidly at each other, and using the word 'Darling!' with nauseating frequency. Nell dutifully recited the names and descriptions of outfits into her phone.

Harry Gilson was making triumphal progress across the restaurant, stopping here and there on his way to the top table to shake hands and smile at people. It was disgusting the way they were all fawning over him.

Before the meal started, he got up on the podium and made a short gracious speech thanking them for their attendance and for their generous donations to the hungry street kids of the city.

'Never mind the street kids, I'm famished,' Nell muttered to her neighbour. 'When do they bring out the food?'

He gave her a startled glance, then a slow grin crept over his face. 'Any time now.'

Waiters began offering baskets of bread. Nell grabbed a piece. Carafes of water were brought out. She nudged her neighbour. 'Ask the waiter for some butter, will you?'

'Someone's been kidding you along, honey. This is a famine lunch. Bread and water only.'

Her stomach rumbled. Just wait till she got back. She'd kill Steve!

For an interminable two hours, Nell sat watching people toy with pieces of bread and sip daintily at elegant wine glasses of water. She ate several pieces of bread. It stopped her stomach making noises, anyway, even if it didn't please her taste buds.

She sighed in relief as people started to leave and followed them out.

As she was passing an alcove, someone grabbed her arm, yanking her aside so quickly she had no time to do more than yelp in surprise.

She found herself staring into the eyes of the bodyguard. 'Get your hands off me! I'm here quite legally!'

'Mr Gilson wants to see you.'

'Oh, does he? Well, I'd like to see him, too.' She intended to ask him what pleasure it had given him to steal her wallet.

Outside, the same limousine was waiting, with a shadowy figure sitting in the back. The bodyguard opened the car door.

'If you want to speak to me, you'll have to get out. I'm not getting inside that thing with you again!'

Gilson stared out at her. 'I have a business proposition for you. A scoop. Either you come inside and listen to it, or I'll find someone else.'

'I'm not going anywhere until I've got my wallet back.'

His lips curved into a sneer. 'That was a cheap ploy to get my attention.'

'That was no ploy. The wallet had all my money and credit cards in it. I had trouble getting home after you shoved me out of the car, had to go somewhere where I could get the fare paid for the taxi I'd called.'

He had the grace to look a bit ashamed. 'I'm sorry. At the time, I thought you were trying to wriggle your way into an interview.'

'At the time,' she mimicked his tone, 'I didn't even know who you were, Mr Gilson.'

'So your editor said when I complained and Steve has never lied to me before.' He smiled ruefully. 'That's why I'm apologising. Please get in. I promise to drop you anywhere you like after we've talked.'

You didn't look a gift horse in the mouth or upset a celebrity. She got in, but sat on the edge of the seat, as far away from him as she could manage. To her annoyance she was still attracted to him. It was only physical attraction, she told herself. Mentally, he was a rat and who liked rats?

He handed her the wallet and smiled at her again. 'I'm sorry about this. Bill didn't find it until several days later. It'd slipped under the seat.'

'Oh, very well. Let's call it quits. After all, you did save me from that brute the other day.'

'Why was he chasing you?'

She could feel herself blushing. 'Because I was trying to find out if he really was pressuring women into serving topless at his boss's special parties.'

'And was he?'

'Yes.' Her face grew still hotter. 'He was . . . horrible. He cornered me and tried to take my top off to see if I'd suit, he said, and he wouldn't stop. So I hit him over the head with the nearest thing – which just happened to be a vase. Then I ran away. Only he came after me. I don't think he is used to women saying no.'

Her stomach gurgled loudly and Gilson reached forward to open a compartment. 'Are you hungry? I have a picnic here.'

'Of course I am. Dry bread isn't very filling. Isn't it cheating, though, for you to have this waiting? After all, you've just been telling everyone how worthwhile their sacrifice was.'

'Possibly, but most of the people who were there today

will be feeding their faces now. Anyway, the famine meal wasn't my idea. I can't see what good it'll do for rich people to miss one meal.'

'Why did you go, then?' She accepted a chicken leg and bit into it hungrily.

'Because for some reason, my presence usually doubles the contributions, and it is a worthwhile cause.'

For a moment there was silence as they both ate the chicken and crudités, going on to cheese and olives, followed by chocolate croissants.

'I like a woman who enjoys her food,' he murmured, wiping his fingers on the linen napkin and reaching for another piece of fruit.

She bit into her apple. 'I'm lucky. I don't put on weight. So what's this business proposition of yours?'

'I offered your editor an exclusive on my work and he snapped my hand off. You're the one who's doing the piece.'

She gaped at him. 'Steve gave that sort of job to me? But I'm only a junior reporter there.' The blush returned. 'And I haven't done very well at the challenges they've set me so far.'

'They shouldn't have set up someone as pretty as you with that topless story.'

She could feel the warmth creeping back into her face and changed the subject back to the exclusive interview. 'I can't believe Steve would give a story like this to me.'

'I said I'd only do it if you were assigned to the story.'

'Oh? Why?' She looked at him suspiciously.

'No tricks about it. I wanted to make amends for jumping to conclusions and dumping you like that. And . . . well, I wanted to get to know you better.'

She looked at him suspiciously. 'So what does this special assignment involve?'

'Spending a week with me, seeing what sort of a story you can make from it, all with an eye to helping some worthwhile charities.'

If he was setting her up for a naughty week, he was in for trouble. 'I think you'd be better with another reporter.'

He was still smiling at her, so she decided it was best to be blunt. 'I don't go to bed to get my stories. Not with anyone.'

His smile faded. 'Very flattering. I don't have to bribe women into my bed, thank you very much. Are you always so mistrustful?'

'Yes. I'd like to check with Steve first.' She pulled out her mobile phone and looked at him.

He waved one hand. 'Be my guest.'

Steve made it very plain that this was a scoop of major proportions and that if she did anything – anything at all – to spoil it, she would be looking for another job.

She put the phone away in her bag. 'Very well, Mr Gilson. Give me your address, tell me what time you want me to turn up in the morning and I'll be there.'

'It's a little more complicated than that, I'm afraid.'

'Complicated? What do you mean, complicated?'

'Well, I have an appointment in Western Australia tomorrow, which necessitates us flying out from Sydney this afternoon. All right with you?'

'Flying?'

He raised one eyebrow. 'Anything wrong with that?'

She gulped. 'No, of course not.' Which was a lie. She hated flying.

'Look, I promise to be on my best behaviour. No more jumping to conclusions about you. As long as you don't make a habit of throwing yourself into the arms of strange men in shopping centres, that is?'

She had to smile. And she had to take the offer. 'Very well. Just let me go home and pack my things.'

'We'll drive you there on the way to the airport. My things are in the boot already.'

Of all the embarrassments, he insisted on coming up with her to the tiny studio flat. Then he washed the dishes while she packed. Her kitchen had never looked so tidy.

At the airport, she found they'd be flying in a private jet. Which was marginally better. But she still had to force her stiff legs to walk up into the plane.

She let a stewardess settle her and tried to look nonchalant. But it was no use. As the engines began to roar, she gulped and clutched the arms of her seat.

A warm hand covered hers. 'Not comfortable flying, Nell?'

'No.' She clutched his hand gratefully and closed her eyes. If she didn't look out of the windows, if she didn't see them taking off, she could manage – just – to control her fear.

Once the plane was airborne, she let out a breath in a whoosh. 'Thank goodness that's over. And . . . um, thank you for holding my hand.'

She tried to let go, but he held on to her hand tightly. She found it hard to breathe. And the way he was looking at her said he was affected too.

He gave her one of his gorgeous rueful smiles. 'That's why I wanted you to do this assignment. I couldn't stop thinking about you and our mock kiss in the shopping centre. Only it didn't feel like a mock kiss.'

She shoved his hand away. 'You're just sweet-talking me.'

'I'm telling the simple truth. Look, if I promise not to touch you again without your permission, could we just see whether our mutual attraction leads anywhere?'

She looked at him doubtfully. Either he was the best actor on the planet or he was sincere. But how could a rich guy like him fancy someone like her, who was always tripping over her own feet or getting into trouble?

'Steve thinks well of you – and no, I didn't ask him directly. He says you're not the most skilful journalist but you have a good heart.'

'Oh.'

'Will you give me a chance, Nell? Will you play along with my hunch that we're meant for each other?'

What could she say but yes?

But she also intended to prove that she was a damned good journalist and make Steve eat his words. Talking of eating, the stewardess was holding out a tray of hors d'oeuvres. She took a few to put her on till she got a proper meal.

He chuckled.

She had to laugh at herself.

And suddenly the world seemed brighter and she didn't even mind flying.

The Lady of Silverbrae

Introduction

This is one of my favourite short stories of all, if not THE favourite. It was written one Christmas, when I was just starting the tradition I have of giving myself a few days off my normal writing to do something different for pleasure – a busman's holiday, but I love it.

It's very different from the sort of story I write most of the time. It was first written under my Shannah Jay pen name. I wrote fantasy novels for a while as 'Shannah' and they're still for sale as ebooks. I loved writing them and creating whole worlds out of my imagination. But the historical stories were selling better, making more money, so I pursued that avenue. And anyway, I love writing them too.

Writing is, as I've said in another of these preambles, a business. Should it be? I don't know. People have to make a living, after all. And if you write purely for yourself, you're missing the joy of giving other people pleasure. I love putting pleasure into a world where there's increasing violence and mayhem.

Anyway, back to this story: it's best described as a spoof fairy tale for adults, written with tongue deeply embedded in cheek. I did it for sheer fun one Christmas. I chuckled as I wrote – and I chuckled all over again recently as I polished and extended the story for this collection.

I've always thought 'The Lady of Silverbrae' would make a good Walt Disney movie. I certainly 'saw' it with that sort of animation as I wrote it. I'm a very visual writer, and I always 'see' the scenes my characters are living in very clearly as I write.

I hope you enjoy reading it. It is definitely not meant to be taken seriously.

The Lady of Silverbrae

Through the eyes of his magical shadow self, the wizard watched Annora ride through the forest on the most beautiful white mare he'd ever seen. He had heard so much about the young woman and was intrigued to find her even more beautiful than they said. If he could have gone to her family's castle, he'd have seen her sooner. But he could only go there by invitation. Now that he had seen her, he knew what he must do.

She was demurely clad in a flowing blue velvet cloak over a white silk gown with a high neckline and long sleeves. But she didn't look demure, because the gown clung to her body so closely it showed her delightful womanly curves. Her slender waist was encircled by a sword belt bearing a weapon in a gilded leather scabbard. Her skirts were carefully draped to hide her legs, but rumour said they were exquisite too.

Gavyn took a deep breath and told himself to concentrate. But it was hard to because a strand of silver-blonde hair escaped from her filmy white veil at that moment and she brushed it away impatiently with one slender fingertip.

Her eyes were glorious, of a vivid green in colour. Young men wrote poems to those eyes. Sickly stuff, that poetry. It could never do the real thing justice.

As he watched, it seemed as if she looked straight at his shadow self and knew he was watching her. No, she couldn't have known. No one could penetrate his invisibility spell.

Behind her rode a huge ox of a fellow, completely hairless, dressed in studded leather and carrying several weapons. No jewels on his scabbard, only deep gouges from previous battles.

Gavyn's shadow moved along beside them, eavesdropping when they spoke, which wasn't often.

'Beautiful countryside, eh, Otho?' she commented. 'I don't know why my father was so insistent that I keep away from Upperlea.'

'This forest is dangerous for the Silverbrae family. You should have let me fetch the mage to you.'

The wizard snapped his fingers in scorn. As if anyone could have coerced him to do that!

Her voice was low and musical. 'He wouldn't have come at your bidding, Otho. I'm the only one left with the right to compel him, now my father's dead.'

She spurred the mare on, to hide the tears that welled in her glorious eyes.

Was she really weeping at the loss of her father? It showed a proper respect, but he'd been a nasty, suspicious fellow. Gavyn knew that from personal experience.

Rumour said Annora Silverbrae was shrewd and heartless, not soft and womanly in nature as she seemed to him. It would be interesting to find out where the truth lay.

He'd let her reach his home before he did anything.

He brought his shadow self back and dispelled it with a certain phrase repeated thrice, before going to stand by a window that overlooked the entrance. He wanted to watch her enter his domain.

He was, he admitted reluctantly to himself, intrigued by Annora, far more intrigued than he'd expected to be. Who would not be drawn by such exquisite beauty? This quest he'd set himself would be a pleasure to pursue.

Annora reined in her mare just inside the gateway and stared round. The habitation was picturesque, not exactly a castle but not a humble dwelling by anyone's standards. Scarlet thornflowers climbed its aged stone walls. These plants had the longest thorns and the most vivid flower cups she'd ever seen. Heavenspur thrust up blue spears in shady corners, its stems caressed by an abundance of misty green fronds.

An elderly hound lying across the threshold raised one eyebrow at them, uttered several deep coughing barks, and continued to stare at the visitors.

As Otho dismounted, the hound stood up abruptly, waist-high and muscular. It raised its head and howled, a long pulsating challenge that echoed round the courtyard.

But still, no one came to the door to greet the visitors.

'Ho there!' roared Otho, looking annoyed at this slight to his mistress. 'Attend your door, Wizard! You have company.'

The wizard sent his voice echoing round the visitors. 'Go away or I'll change you into a frog.' In fact, he almost did that to the man-at-arms to see how she'd react.

'Knock again!' ordered Annora, fingers tapping impatiently on her scabbard.

Otho's fist crashed against the door several times. 'We're not going away! Come out, damn you!'

The wizard sighed. Well, perhaps it was time. But he'd been enjoying watching her, he had to admit.

He flung the door back on its hinges and strode out, sending Otho staggering back to the side with one touch. He ignored the man and concentrated on the woman, wanting to see her reaction to him.

He kept himself in good trim, if he said so himself. He was tall and well-muscled. A fine figure of a man, his mirror always told him. Today he'd chosen to wear a pair of tight black breeches, which left little to the imagination, and a sleeveless leather jerkin over a full-sleeved white shirt, open at the neck.

His hair was dark as midnight, with one silver streak along the right temple. It fell back from a peak and was tied back loosely at his neck by a leather thong.

Ah, thank goodness! He was having his usual effect, making this woman stare at him as others did. He hadn't been quite sure about that. She was, after all, a Silverbrae, if not an outright enemy, definitely not a friend. And that could cloud your vision.

'Don't you know it's dangerous to disturb a wizard at work?' he demanded, posing carefully at the top of the stone steps to accentuate all his best points.

Annora was betrayed into a gulp and was immediately annoyed with herself. She'd never even seen a wizard before, because they were banned entirely from Silverbrae. She could see why now. Oh my, yes!

Wizards, her father had always said, were nothing but trouble. And they consorted with unicorns, which were even more trouble. Jasper Silverbrae wasn't breeding either his mares or his daughter to such creatures.

As Gavyn of the Forest walked slowly to the top of the stone steps and stopped there, Annora's breath caught in her throat and a pang of longing shot through her belly. In her experience, men like this were only to be found in dreams. The man her council wanted her to marry was a spindly fellow, given to reciting bad poetry to her at the drop of a hat – poetry so appallingly bad that she'd been hard put not to laugh.

The wizard scowled across at her from the same level as she was on her horse. '*You* must be a Silverbrae. No one else has hair that colour. What do you want here?'

She took a deep breath and followed her plan, though it was an effort to appear unmoved.

Swinging her leg across the saddle, she deliberately allowed her skirt to ride up and display the creamy flesh of her legs. She saw his eyes linger on them and regained some of her confidence. *Look your fill, Wizard,* she thought. *Take the bait I'm offering.*

Slowly, slowly, she slid down from her horse and took up the pose she'd practised in front of her mirror.

'I have come here today to claim your help,' she said, in as sweet a voice as ever sang. She had spent even more time practising that sweet tone, and very hard it was to get it just so.

* * *

Gavyn was surprised by how her voice affected him. It took a huge effort to tear his eyes from the tender swell of her bosom. Then a sudden pang of conscience struck him, because she was still so young. 'Lady, I wish you personally no harm – no red-blooded man ever would – but you would be wise to ride on or I cannot be answerable for my actions.'

'I'm not leaving till I've got what I came for. You owe my father one favour and I'm here to claim it this very day.'

Well, he'd tried to do the decent thing.

He leant against the doorpost, allowing his expression to show only boredom. But as his eyes flickered over her body, breath whistled softly into his mouth. Something about her appealed to him more than any other woman ever had. Not only was she lovely, but she was spirited too. He had never liked meek women. And that long fall of silver hair – ah, how it gleamed in the sunlight, making him itch to run his fingers through it.

'I owe the favour to your father, not to you.'

'My father's dead. I'm the only Silverbrae left. Therefore I require and demand your help.'

He flicked an imaginary speck off his sleeve. 'You could find a hundred swordsmen willing to lay down their lives for you, lady. Why come to me? I'm not the most skilful wielder of swords.'

'I can defend myself against mortal flesh.' She patted the hilt of her sword. 'But I can't fight against magic.'

'You're that good a swordswoman?' he mocked. 'Please don't take me for a fool, lady! A woman hasn't the strength to best a man.'

She moved forward up the steps to stare him in the eye. She was tall for a woman. He liked that about her, too.

'Will you keep your family's promise and answer Silverbrae's need, Gavyn of the Forest, or will you break your word? My father saved your father's life once.'

He sighed. 'I suppose I do owe you something, then. But I'm right in the middle of a fascinating new spell to summon wood nymphs. Very friendly creatures, wood nymphs.'

With a quick wave of his fingertips he made sure Annora could feel his breath on her cheek, and that it burnt her like a lover's kiss. She took an involuntary step backwards, staring at him, breathing rather more quickly than before.

Gavyn let the silence lie heavily in the air between them before continuing. 'A man can get lonely sometimes, you see. And wood nymphs can be delightfully playful.'

He hid a smile as he saw his visitor's tongue flick across lips gone suddenly dry. 'Well, lady, tell me your need quickly. I'm a busy man.'

'We have ogre trouble at Castle Silverbrae.'

'Get your knights to kill the damned thing. Ogres aren't that hard to dispose of. It'll only cost you a knight or two.'

'At first there were several ogres. And we did kill them. How do you think my father lost his life? But after we'd driven them away, a black ogre came in their place.'

'Aaah. Now, that *is* a problem. It's a long time since I've dealt with a black ogre. It might be . . . interesting.'

'So you'll help us?'

He waited, watching her lean forward slightly, so eager for the answer. 'Well . . .'

'Well, what?'

'I'll come and rid you of it.'

He put his fingers to his mouth and whistled. Out of the woods came his unicorn, a tall white stallion with a wicked glint in its eyes and a huge jutting horn on its head, as well as the usual masculine appurtenances below. It took one look at the mare and trotted over to nuzzle her.

The mare stood still, trembling slightly.

'I'm not having that – that *thing* in my castle, upsetting everyone. Look at what he's doing to my mare.'

'He's just greeting her. Perssim's a tame unicorn, very polite with other steeds,' Gavyn said mildly.

'I've heard the tales. No unicorn is that tame. And no mare is safe from them.'

'He doesn't get the urge to mate all the time, you know, just every now and then.'

'That's still too often for me.'

Gavyn folded his arms. 'Either I ride my unicorn to your castle or I don't come.'

Annora lowered her lashes to cover the triumph in her eyes. 'Well, in that case I'll have to put up with him. But you'd better keep him away from my mares while you're there. I want no unicorn blood tainting my breeding stock.'

'He's not in the mood for an orgy at the moment. You'd notice it if he was.'

She couldn't help blushing at that. She had, after all, been raised a lady.

'But I have to warn you that if Perssim grows hungry for one of your mares, not even I will be able to stop him satisfying that hunger.'

The way the wizard's gaze ran up and down her body made heat run through her.

'And . . . like master, like man,' he murmured softly.

She had to make a huge effort to speak briskly. 'Well,

you'll both starve in my castle, then. Only my husband will ever touch *my* body!'

He didn't allow himself to smile. He didn't want to frighten her off. 'Let's go, then.'

She went back to mount her mare.

Gavyn hid a smile as he leapt up on his unicorn's back. He was going to enjoy himself.

'Not yet, Perssim,' he murmured.

His steed tossed its head.

'It'll be worth the wait.'

He didn't even try to stop Perssim leading the way.

Nor did Annora.

One of Silverbrae's four towers was smoking, its famous silver-grey stone blackened and chunks of it missing from one corner.

Annora reined in and pointed. 'As you can see from the state of our castle, Wizard, we've had a hard time of it. Even your powers may not be enough to defeat that black ogre.'

'We'll see. But I can't do it from the back of Perssim.'

She watched him dismount, wondering why Otho hadn't come to help her get down. She couldn't in all politeness refuse the wizard's help when he came to help her instead.

His hands behaved in a gentlemanly fashion, but his eyes were sending another message entirely.

She could feel herself blushing and breathing rather too deeply, so turned away from Gavyn to see Otho shaking his head as if to clear it. What was wrong with him?

She summoned the head groom and gave crisp orders

for the separate housing of the unicorn. The unicorn didn't allow anyone to touch it but at least it followed the groom towards the stables.

And her mare followed Perssim eagerly. Oh dear.

As she led the way towards the great hall, she was still too aware of Gavyn's lithe body beside her, in spite of the danger they were about to face.

A fully armoured knight clanked forward to greet them, but an attempt at a full court bow nearly made him fall over.

'Oh, Thurstan!' Annora tried to be patient with the idiot, who was some sort of distant cousin, heaven help her. 'We haven't got time for all that protocol stuff. How is the fight going?'

'We've lost another knight and the ogre's gained another chamber, my lady.'

'Damnation!' She turned to Gavyn. 'If *you* can't deal with it, I'll lose everything.'

'You're asking rather a big favour, considering all your family ever did was give my father shelter one winter's night.'

'In the depths of winter, with my uncle raging after him, what my father did saved his life. Or did he fancy being chained to a spellproof stake – outside – during the wildest blizzard of the century?' She had the satisfaction of seeing him shudder at that image.

'Your uncle had some nasty prejudices against wizards. One of the worst Silverbraes ever born, he was. I hope you'll choose a husband carefully, Annora. You need to breed some sense into your family. The men keep getting themselves killed.'

She had already chosen a husband, and for that very

reason, but she wasn't going to tell him that. 'I'll be breeding nothing unless you are able to remove that ogre.'

Gavyn untied the strings of his cloak and let it billow to the ground behind him. Rubbing his hands briskly together, he made a few passes in the air, spun round three times and muttered an incantation. 'Right, that's the preparations completed. But sending a black ogre back to the netherworld is hard work. I'll need your help.'

'I'm at your service, O Wizard.'

'I can think of nothing I'll enjoy more.'

She glared at him. 'In this matter only. What shall you do?'

'My plan is to distract the ogre with my magic and let someone else hack it to pieces.'

'You have only to say the word, O Mighty Wizard.'

'Don't start all that flowery talk when there's a battle ahead. It makes me want to puke.'

She blinked. 'Very well, then, *Gavyn*. My knights will assist you and—'

'Those tin rattletraps! They can barely assist themselves to stand upright.'

'Otho is a doughty fighter. Perhaps he can—'

'No, it must be you. A swordswoman will take the ogre by surprise. You *can* use that hog-sticker of yours?'

Her eyes flashed. 'Yes, of course I can.'

'You must be the one to help me, then. But afterwards I'll be very weak, so I want two promises from you, else I'll not do anything. First, you'll not let a healer near me afterwards.'

'But what if you're hurt?'

'No healers! One of them dosed me up after I killed

my first ogre. Took me weeks to recover from his potion. Impure ingredients, badly chosen and just as badly mixed. And the taste. Ugh!'

'Very well. No healers. And the second promise?'

'That you'll nurse me better with your own fair hands, O Lady of Silverbrae.'

A flush warmed her cheekbones. 'I've no experience in sickrooms.'

'I shan't be sick, just weak. You can keep me entertained, talk to me, spoon broth into my mouth.' He winked at her. 'And provide any other little services I happen to need.'

She drew herself upright. 'You can just forget that sort of service. I'm a certified virgin.'

He shook his head with mock sadness. 'So suspicious, Annora. I wasn't intending to take your virginity.'

'You'd better not try. I'm saving myself for my husband.'

'He'll be a lucky fellow, whoever he is. You have the body of a wood nymph yourself.'

She flushed scarlet, glancing around to see if anyone had heard. The habits of wood nymphs were a scandal in the land. Her father had never let them into the castle.

Gavyn leant closer. 'You will look after me, Annora, won't you? With your own fair hands? Afterwards.'

Her voice was faint and just a trifle wobbly. 'I tell you, I have no skill in the sickroom!'

He began to tap one foot. 'Are you going to stand here quibbling all day, woman? I'm not asking much, when you consider how this job is going to deplete my astral forces. Do you want me to help you get rid of that creature or not?'

The ogre's roar shook the whole building.

She shot an anxious glance towards the tower. 'I promise to do as you wish. Word of a Silverbrae.'

Gavyn raised her hand to his lips to seal the bargain, and that sent a trail of fire scorching up her arm.

She pulled away and breathed carefully through her mouth till her pulse had settled down again.

He flourished one hand. 'Right, then. Lead me to your ogre.'

The clanking knight led the way upstairs with much puffing and panting, followed by two more mailed swordsmen. One of these tripped and lost his balance, rolling down with a series of clangs and bumps, and yelling loudly enough to awaken all the demons in the netherworld.

As the other knights rushed to right their fallen companion, Gavyn chuckled softly.

Annora couldn't stop herself smiling.

'Do we really need those inbred fools?' he whispered. 'We have a castle to save here.'

She turned to the swordsmen. 'Sir Melesh, will you and your companion guard our rear from the bottom of the stairs?'

The noise of his salute with mailed hand against helmet echoed around the hall, but Annora was used to that and merely gritted her teeth till the vibrations had died down.

At the base of the stairs, Sir Thurstan drew his sword and brandished it wildly, drawing sparks from an iron torch holder on the wall.

'Tch! Tch!' Gavyn made a casual gesture with one hand. Sir Thurstan froze in place.

Otho rumbled with anger and took a hasty step forward.

The wizard scowled at him and started to raise his hand, finger pointing towards Otho.

'Do you have a suitable spell for the ogre, O Mighty Wizard?' Annora said hurriedly.

'Of course. And I keep telling you: my name's Gavyn, not "O Mighty Wizard", thank you very much.'

'It seems – more suitable, somehow. Especially now.'

'O Noble and Luscious Lady, let's not get into semantics. Let's just find that damned ogre and get rid of it.'

The two of them tiptoed up the curving stone staircase of the tower itself, with Otho following a few paces behind. Threads of black, evil-smelling smoke wafted around them as they got near the top.

'Such destructive fellows, black ogres,' murmured Gavyn. 'They can never resist a bonfire. Right, Annora, stay outside the door and *do not* follow me in until I call. But come quickly then and make sure your sword is drawn.'

He made a few sweeping gestures and muttered another incantation. Something crackled in the air and a nimbus of blue light began to flicker around him as he strode through the black smoke and vanished into the room.

Annora and Otho moved closer together, exchanging nervous glances.

A roar of fury rent the air and more smoke came rolling out of the door. Loud shrieks and booming sounds assaulted their eardrums. A stray bolt of lightning zipped out of the doorway and had them ducking for cover as it ricocheted around the landing.

Inside the room, Gavyn set a spell on the door to prevent anyone entering and sat down on a couch, while the ogre took his ease on the bed. Occasionally, one of them would launch a bolt of lightning or send thunder booming through the smoke near the door.

'Well?' asked the ogre. 'Have I done as you wished, O Wizard?'

'Not another one!' Gavyn groaned. 'If I've told you once, I've told you a million times, my name's just Gavyn.'

The ogre winked one of its three eyes. 'For a wizard of your rank, you're ridiculously coy about your title. Anyway, have I discharged my debt to you?'

'Nearly. You did well to tell me of this attack by the other ogres. I've been looking for an excuse to get into this castle for years. I'm sick of living on my own in that damp and gloomy forest.'

'I'm yours to command, O *Mightiest of Wizards*.'

Gavyn ignored that deliberate provocation. 'I need you to vanish with a bang when she attacks you. How about blasting a wall out as you leave?'

The ogre scowled. 'Only beginners are so clumsy.'

'Yes, but Annora won't know that.'

'My family will, though. They'll tease me about it for decades.'

Gavyn started twiddling the dull black ring on his finger.

The ogre tensed and moaned in pain. 'Oh, very well!'

'When I call Annora, let her run her sword through you a few times, then do something spectacular and vanish. All right?

'Yes, O Wizard.'

Gavyn jumped up off the couch and as they took up fighting positions, he removed the spell from the door and yelled, 'Now, Annora!'

* * *

Coughing in the smoke, she rushed through the doorway with drawn sword. She gasped at the sight of Gavyn grappling with the ogre.

Then the struggling pair turned so that the ogre's back was towards her, and she took a deep breath before starting to slash it. Her sword master would be proud of her, she was sure. But she found the thick trickles of black blood from the various wounds made her feel rather nauseous.

The ogre roared loudly, then moaned piteously and vanished in a clap of smoke and thunder. One wall of the chamber blasted outwards, spraying chunks of rock everywhere.

The silence seemed deafening.

'Gavyn?' Annora advanced through the haze, stumbling over something and seeing him lying unconscious at her feet. Falling to her knees, she examined the magnificent body. No gaping wounds met her tentative fumbling, but there was a bruise on one side of his head.

She allowed herself to touch his hair lightly, then stood up and dusted down her skirts. In control of herself – just! – she gestured imperiously towards Gavyn. 'Have the wizard carried to my bedchamber, Otho.'

Once they reached the next tower, Otho laid Gavyn on the bed and said pleadingly, 'It isn't right for him to be here, lady.'

'I promised to care for him. He kept his promise to save us, so I must now keep mine.'

She turned quickly back to the invalid, who had just groaned.

His eyes flickered open. 'You'll look after me?' His voice was husky, his hand clasping her wrist was warm and his velvet dark eyes were very beautiful.

'I'm a Silverbrae,' she said proudly. 'I always keep my promises.'

'I was – rather counting on that.'

He sank back against the pillows and gave her a faint smile. 'Lady—'

'Otho, you are dismissed.'

When she turned round she caught a smile on Gavyn's face as he opened those beautiful eyes.

'I'm so weak and yet I feel quite safe with you, Annora.'

She felt guilty. She'd brought him to this, used him, put him in danger. 'I will look after you to my last breath,' she vowed.

He reached out for her hand and took it to his lips.

Nothing had ever made her feel like this before. And it definitely wasn't part of her plan. But still, it was a good feeling so she'd just see what happened. After all, a Silverbrae never broke a promise, whatever it entailed.

Annora rather enjoyed the next few days. Otho kept people away and she spent hours chatting to the convalescent wizard. Gavyn had some fascinating tales to tell, tales which made her feel even more dissatisfied with her own humdrum life. Being a virgin was greatly overrated, she decided.

On the tenth day, Gavyn seemed so much better that she invited him to dine in the great hall that night.

'I don't think your knights would appreciate that, Annora, my pet.'

'They'll do as they're told.'

'Well, tomorrow, perhaps, though I really should go home. If you can call that hovel a home.'

'Wait until you've fully recovered.' He raised her hand

to his lips, which always sent shivers through her body. She rather liked the feeling, but hoped she hadn't betrayed that.

'Annora, this has been the happiest time of my whole life. And you are the most beautiful woman in the world.'

She couldn't help blushing, really blushing; he was so very handsome and attentive, not to mention interesting to be with.

Gavyn sighed. 'I shall miss you sadly.'

'Will you?' She fiddled with the edge of the counterpane. 'Will you really?'

'Of course.'

'Couldn't you – stay here, then?'

'Ah, if only I could!'

'We Silverbraes have never had a court wizard before, but—'

'*A court wizard!* My dear girl, certainly not! I'm a Wizard of the First Rank. I'd be thrown out of the Wizards' Guild if I accepted such a lowly position.'

His voice took on that husky tone that sent her pulse racing as he added, 'Whatever my own feelings.'

'Oh.'

'In wizard terms, that's the same as being a prince, you know,' he added casually.

'Is it?'

As if she didn't know. She really should have carried out the rest of her plan by now, but had been enjoying herself so much that she'd delayed. Before she could do anything, she heard something and stilled.

What was that?

In the stables, the unicorn felt the wizard's need, stamped his feet, then shrieked defiance at the stable boy. One sharp white hoof smashed through the door as if it were made of parchment. The stable boy ran for his life.

Outside in the meadow Annora's mare began to whinny. As the unicorn led the way eagerly towards the forest of Silverbrae, the mare followed just as eagerly.

Before entering the green shadows the unicorn raised his head and shrieked his lust.

Sitting on the sofa next to Annora, Gavyn stiffened. 'That's Perssim.'

'Is he doing what I think he is?'

'Yes, Annora. My dear one, I'm afraid he's about to mate with your mare.'

'Oh?' A tingle began to creep along her veins, a feeling that was definitely forbidden to a certified virgin, though it was rather a nice feeling and was what she'd been planning and hoping for. 'But you said no one could stop him once he'd—'

'Alas, no. And he and I are closely linked. Will you ever forgive me for this?'

As Perssim started nipping the mare's neck, Gavyn drew Annora to him. 'You said your family had bred all the unicorn out of your horses.'

'Yes. I did, didn't I?' A dreamlike languor filled her limbs. 'It was my father's rule. He would never explain why.'

'This is why. They're linked to some humans. In this case, Perssim has linked to you as well as to me.'

When the wizard began to kiss her, she sighed and melted into his embrace, murmuring, 'I forgive you.'

As the unicorn mounted the silky white back of the mare, Gavyn laid Annora on the bed. 'You,' he murmured in her ear, 'have bewitched me.'

'Me?' For a moment, she strained away from him, then

the unicorn called again and she fell back, a smile curving those perfect lips. 'I'm no witch.'

No, he thought, as he kissed the delicate curves of her eyelids. *But they didn't quite breed all the magic out of your precious family, did they? Look how you're reacting to Perssim. And our children will have even fuller powers.*

His loving smile held more than a hint of triumph.

And so, he thought, as he rained kisses on her tender flesh, *Castle Silverbrae is taken at last. I hope your father is turning in his grave.*

It was a perfect revenge against the Silverbraes – or it would have been, had Gavyn been able to tear himself away from Annora once he'd had his wicked way with her. But he never could, because she was infinitely more attractive than those wood nymphs.

And Perssim had taken quite a fancy to the castle mares, especially the new ones which Annora had purchased just before going to seek the wizard's help. They were an insatiable bunch.

In the end Annora suggested they get married. Which simplified things considerably. Though it took a while to persuade her council to agree to it. She had to get Gavyn's help with that.

She thought it best not to tell him that she had planned for this all along.

Though she hadn't realised how entranced she would be, how consumed by his love. No, she hadn't even known it was possible, so could not have planned for it.

And anyway, Silverbrae did need an heir. And a few spares.

*   *   *

With her and Gavyn overseeing how things were done, the estate began to prosper as it hadn't for decades. And Silverbrae horses sold for much higher prices than most others, they were so beautiful.

Annora had done her duty to her inheritance and found the most wonderful husband for herself. What more could a lady ask for?

And it turned out that they lived happily ever after, extremely happily. Well, if a wizard can't arrange that, who can?

Gracie

Introduction

This is another story that began life as a magazine serial. I love writing about the 1920s, it was such an interesting era.

There was the beginning of a depression in Britain and other countries, yet not all of Britain suffered so deeply. It was also the beginning of all sorts of developments on a human scale now that the war was over. These included a more liberated life for women, not only politically but emotionally and technologically.

New gadgets were being invented and improved to make housework easier: electricity, washing machines, refrigerators, vacuum cleaners and radios to keep people in touch with the broader world some of them had met during the Great War.

And of course, lots of people emigrated to Australia, as I did myself fifty years after this era.

I hope you enjoy Gracie's story as much as I enjoyed writing and extending it for this collection.

Gracie

England, October 1920

Gracie Bell had a very good job as head housemaid in London. She was walking out with Joseph, a footman who worked in a nearby house. They went dancing together and to the cinema. She really enjoyed her life and was in no hurry to get married.

Then her master died suddenly, her mistress fell to pieces, helpless in her grief, and the widow's whole household was moved by the son and heir to the family's country estate in Wiltshire, while he and his family took over the townhouse and installed their own servants.

Joseph asked Gracie to marry him and leave her job. He was starting to talk about having children but she didn't want to settle down and bring up their children on her own while he continued working as a footman, hoping to become a butler one day.

No, she didn't want to marry yet. Like many others, she'd lost her girlhood years to the Great War and she wanted to catch up on some of the pleasures she'd missed before she settled down.

'Next year,' she pleaded. 'We'll think about getting married next year.'

Her friend Pamela said she was mad not to accept a tall, good-looking fellow like that, but Joseph didn't suggest them getting engaged again and Gracie didn't change her mind.

She wasn't so sure she'd made the right decision when she got to Wiltshire. It was a big disappointment in many ways. The countryside was beautiful when the sun shone, but there was no cinema nearby, and the village market consisted of half a dozen stalls selling food, so Gracie couldn't even enjoy a stroll round the shops.

Today was her afternoon off. With the rain beating down on the nearly leafless trees, everything looked bleak and she felt down in the dumps. And this was only autumn, not even the beginning of winter.

She reread her sister's letter, the third one Jane had written begging her to go out to join her in Australia. Gracie had pulled a face at Jane's first suggestion of this. There was no way she was going to live in Australia.

A second letter from Jane hadn't changed her mind, though it was smudged with her sister's tears and she shed a few of her own as she read it. She did long to see Jane again.

But now, things were different. The rambling, old-fashioned house hadn't even got electricity, so she couldn't use one of the wonderful new suction cleaners to do the carpets and had to go back to damp tea leaves and brushing the carpets by hand. So old-fashioned! And back-breaking.

Perhaps she should have said yes to Joseph, but she wasn't going to admit that to anyone else.

She paced up and down the attic bedroom she shared with another maid. She had to do something, couldn't stand this quiet life for much longer. Should she try to find another job in London or should she – daring thought – join her favourite sister in Australia? Her other two sisters lived in Newcastle still, near their widowed mother. She wasn't as close to them and they'd boss her around and expect her to care for their mother in her old age if she moved up there. Not that her mother was failing. She was still a strong woman and Gracie hoped to be like her at that age.

She was still hesitating about what to do when a letter from a London friend arrived. She told Gracie that Joseph had been seen walking out with another girl and he'd been looking all lovey-dovey.

Gracie felt furious. No wonder he hadn't written for a while. He might have had the decency to tell her and break things off.

That made up her mind! She went up to London by train on her full day off and booked a passage on the next ship to Western Australia.

When she gave notice and told them she was going to join her sister in Australia, the other servants said she was mad.

She laughed confidently. 'I'm really looking forward to a cruise through the Suez Canal and sunny days in the tropics. It'll be like a long holiday.'

She wasn't nearly as confident in the dark hours of several sleepless nights, but it was too late to draw back now. She'd used up a large chunk of her savings on the fare and didn't intend to waste it.

Besides, Jane had written about sunny days, parrots flying around the gardens and how pretty the port town of Fremantle was. Gracie was looking forward to living at the seaside in a warmer climate. Who wouldn't enjoy that?

Best of all, she and Jane would be together again. That meant a lot. Gracie had missed her next sister dreadfully and still couldn't understand how Jane could have decided so quickly that she was in love with an Australian and gone off with him.

Gracie hadn't thought that much of Tommy, who was a real bossyboots. Joseph had been a much nicer man.

Perhaps there was something wrong with her? Perhaps she was destined to stay a spinster.

Western Australia, January 1921

When the ship carrying the migrants from England arrived at Fremantle, Gracie was up on deck with the others, eager to see her new home more closely. She stared at the town with a sinking heart.

Fremantle wasn't at all pretty. In fact, the port looked downright scruffy – what she could see of it, which wasn't much from the ship. Near the docks there were several larger stone buildings and what looked like warehouses. Beyond them was an untidy collection of tin roofs, some distinctly rusty.

It was summer in Australia and the weather seemed even hotter than it had been on the ship when they crossed the equator. Sweat was trickling down her face and even down the backs of her legs. She hoped she'd get used to the heat.

She'd had time to think on the ship, and had decided she

wasn't going to work as a maid in Australia. She intended to find a more interesting job. It was so old-fashioned, going into service.

During the Great War she'd worked as a conductress on a motor omnibus in London, and she'd loved that, even in the cold weather. But once the war ended, she'd lost her lovely job to a returned soldier and had to go back to being a housemaid.

Jane had said she was sure to meet a nice fellow in Western Australia. Even though Gracie hadn't emigrated to look for a fellow, she might enjoy walking out again. But she still wasn't getting married for years. She didn't want to spend her life doing housework and raising children, and if that was selfish, so be it.

All her married friends in England worked like slaves, always short of money, not to mention having one baby after the other. Joseph had wanted six children. Heavens! The mere thought of it made her shudder. Maybe two or three would be OK. She liked children, but no more than that.

She didn't think it'd be any different in Australia. How could it be? That was what life was like for most women.

When she came out of customs, Gracie found her sister waiting for her, looking very pregnant, hot and weary, with her husband, Tommy, beside her. Her brother-in-law had grown fatter in Australia, and now reminded Gracie of an overstuffed pillow. *He* didn't look at all tired.

The two sisters hugged, then hugged again, and Jane burst into tears, so it was a while before Gracie could chat to her brother-in-law.

'Welcome to Australia. I hope you'll be happy here.'

'Thank you.'

Tommy eyed her up and down as if she was an animal he was thinking of buying. If he hadn't been her sister's husband, she'd have told him to pull his eyestalks back in. He even nodded as if in approval. Cheeky devil!

He loaded her luggage on the rack at the back of the Model T Ford.

'Is this your car?' she asked, trying to make conversation with him, because Jane was still sniffling and murmuring things like, 'I missed you so', 'I can't believe you're here', 'Oh, it'll be so lovely to have you living nearby'.

Tommy patted the car bonnet. 'No. I borrowed it from my friend Bert. He and I work together.'

'We live in Perth now, not Fremantle,' Jane said brightly. 'That's miles up the river. Wasn't it kind of Bert to lend us his car?'

'Yes.' She saw from her brother-in-law's expression that gratitude was also required from her and added, 'Very kind indeed. Why did you move to Perth?'

'My Tommy got a better job. He's doing ever so well. We're buying our own house. It's in a suburb called Leederville.'

As soon as they set off, Tommy dominated the conversation with tales of how he'd got the house cheaply, thanks to Bert, and how he and Bert had built a spare bedroom for Gracie by enclosing part of the back veranda.

Had Tommy always been this bossy and full of himself? Gracie hadn't got to know him well in England, because it had been a whirlwind courtship and the week after the wedding, he and Jane had left for Australia.

She tried to keep a polite expression on her face, but what she really wanted was to talk to her sister, find out if Jane was truly happy, just . . . chat to one another.

When Gracie mentioned her own hopes for the future, Jane gave her a warning look and shook her head slightly, which surprised her. What was going on here?

The house was small, made of wood with pressed tin ceilings. It felt rather stuffy after the heat of the day, but she duly admired it. After all, it was wonderful to be able to buy your own house. Not many people managed that.

After their evening meal, they chatted for a while, then got ready for bed ridiculously early.

Jane giggled as the two sisters hugged goodnight. 'You'll get used to early nights here, love. We get up at five o'clock so we're in bed by eight-thirty at the latest.'

'I'm used to getting up early, but not at five o'clock, well not since I was a junior housemaid and had to light the fires.'

As Gracie went into the tiny spare bedroom, a cockroach crawled from under her bed and she stamped on it. Ugh! She hated the horrid creatures, but Jane said they were part of life in a hot country.

It was still quite hot so she lay on top of the covers and opened the curtains a little so that she could look out across the moonlit garden. The lights were out in all the nearby houses. Did everyone go to bed early?

She sighed. She was wide awake, itching to go out and explore Perth, which was the capital city and surely *that* didn't shut down at eight o'clock?

Oh well, no doubt they'd go for a walk tomorrow.

The next day being Sunday, they went to church in the morning, which gave them a very short walk.

Back home, Tommy worked in the garden. Gracie couldn't believe how many tomatoes there were, just growing in the sunshine, not needing a greenhouse. She'd never eaten them newly picked before, or had fresh peaches either. They were much nicer than tinned ones.

They had cold roast lamb left over from yesterday for lunch.

'Tommy likes to have our roast on Saturdays and Bert usually comes to tea on Sundays,' Jane told her.

She spent most of the day baking a cake, an apple pie and some scones, getting red-faced in the heat, rubbing her aching back from time to time.

'Couldn't you have put Bert off on my first full day here?' Gracie asked.

Jane looked over her shoulder and whispered, 'You and I will go out together during the week. There are some lovely shops in the city. But Tommy likes things to be just so on Sundays, and Bert's his best friend, so if you don't mind helping . . . ?'

'No, of course I don't. Just tell me what you want doing.'

They were to sit out on the veranda after tea, so Gracie swept up outside and dusted all the furniture there. She tidied up indoors as well, which consisted mainly of picking up after Tommy. Didn't that man ever carry his own empty teacups back into the kitchen, or put away the pages from his daily newspaper?

Jane gave her a hug when she'd finished. 'It'll be such a help having you here when the baby arrives.'

Gracie looked at her warily. 'I don't mind doing the housework, but I don't know anything about looking after babies, I warn you.'

'You will by the time you've lived with your niece or

nephew for a while. Oh, there's the door knocker now. Bert's always on time. Come and meet him.'

'Let me just tidy myself up. I'll join you in a minute.' Gracie changed her blouse, gave her face a quick wash with cold water and combed her hair.

Bert was much better-looking than Tommy but he too was fond of the sound of his own voice. In fact, during the tea party, conversation was mainly between the two men.

Jane sat quietly, looking exhausted. Gracie tried to join in, but the men talked about things she didn't know, and sometimes they laughed openly at the mistakes she made about Australia, so she gave up.

And all the time he talked, Bert stared at her in the same assessing way as Tommy had, only worse. Bert's gaze lingered particularly on her bosom and that made her feel uncomfortable, as if she had no clothes on. If he hadn't been her brother-in-law's friend, she'd have told him off for looking at her like that.

Jane and Tommy insisted on clearing the table and making another pot of tea for their guests, which left Bert and Gracie alone on the veranda.

'You're so pretty.' He leant across and grabbed her hand, pulling her towards him and surprising her by planting a big moist kiss on her lips. She tried to get away, but he dragged her to her feet and tried to kiss her again, pressing his body against hers.

She wasn't having that. Stamping her heel on his foot, she scraped her shoe down his shin, causing him to yelp in pain, then she retreated to the other side of the table.

'Why did you do that?' he asked indignantly, rubbing his leg. 'What's wrong with a man kissing a pretty girl?'

'Do you grab every strange girl you fancy, without so much as a by your leave?'

He shrugged. 'Jane's told me so much about you, I felt as if I knew you.'

'Well, you don't know me. And I'll do worse than that if you ever try to take liberties with me again.'

'Aw, come on, Gracie. Don't be stand-offish. I'm almost family, me and Tommy are so close. I've been dying to meet you. You're even prettier than your photograph. You can't blame a fellow for getting carried away.'

Dying to meet her? Told him so much about her? Alarm bells rang in Gracie's head.

Just wait till she got her sister alone. If this meant what she was beginning to suspect, she'd put a stop to it straight away.

'Isn't Bert nice?' Jane said brightly next morning after Tommy had left for work.

'No. Well, he's not bad-looking, but he never stops talking, and he kissed me – ugh! – when you and Tommy were in the kitchen.'

Jane looked so guilty, Gracie knew her suspicions were correct. 'Did you invite me to Australia to pair me off with Bert? *Jane?* Answer me.'

'My goodness, it's going to be hot again today. I'd better go and water those tomatoes.'

Gracie barred the doorway. 'You did, didn't you?'

'I invited you to Australia because I wanted us to be together again. But I thought it'd be nice if you lived nearby, if we could see each other nearly every day, which we would if you got together with Bert, because he and my Tommy do everything together.'

'I'm surprised you didn't have a minister waiting at the docks to marry us.'

'Don't be silly. It's just . . . well, that's what girls want, isn't it? To get married. Mum's been ever so worried about you, what with your first young man being killed during the war. And then that Joseph walked out with you for ages without getting engaged.'

'He asked me to marry him. It was me who didn't want to get engaged, not him.'

'Then he can't have been the right man for you. Bert's a really good catch, you know. He'll be the next foreman after Mr Minchin leaves. The boss has already told him.'

'I don't care how much money he earns. He's boring, can only talk about himself and I never did like men with yellow hair. I've always preferred dark-haired men, you know I have.'

Jane was silent for a while, then said suddenly, 'Don't say that to Tommy, *please*. Let's see how things work out. Bert must have fallen for you straight away to kiss you. It's so romantic.'

'It's only romantic if you fancy the fellow and want to be kissed.'

Jane's lips trembled and she looked close to tears. 'Please give Bert a chance, Gracie. For my sake.'

Jane was clearly set on this, so Gracie said, 'I'll – um, think about it.'

She was glad Jane was happy with Tommy, but that also meant she couldn't enlist her sister's help in finding a job, because she didn't want to cause trouble between them. But she hadn't at all taken to Bert, so she needed to find some way of escaping from Perth.

While her sister was resting, Gracie read the job adverts in the *Sunday Times* newspaper. Lots of adverts for general maids and – aha! – the address of an employment bureau. She cut it out carefully, hoping no one would notice.

When Tommy came home from work that evening, he went on and on about his good mate Bert, and how they'd all four go out together on Saturday night. With Jane giving her pleading looks, Gracie managed not to say what she thought.

In the end, she pretended tiredness and was the first to bed, where she lay fuming and uncomfortable because it was hot in that sleep-out.

Travel in comfort and see the world, the steamship adverts said. All she was seeing was her sister's house and the corner shop. And Bert, if Tommy had his way.

There was nothing for it. She would definitely have to get a job and move out, and the sooner the better. Which would upset her sister.

She'd make it up to Jane later. If Tommy let her.

The following day, ignoring Jane's protests that there was no need to hurry into anything, Gracie put on her smartest clothes and her best hat, nodding approval when she looked in the mirror.

The hat had an upturned brim at one side, decorated by a fabric flower, and was worn pulled down to the eyebrows. It showed off her eyes, she felt, and she'd loved it so much when she tried it on, she'd paid thirty shillings for it, a huge extravagance.

Following Jane's reluctant instructions, she caught a tram into Perth from Leederville. She found the hard wooden seats very uncomfortable and it was hot again today. Even the nights weren't all that cool.

She had no difficulty finding the employment bureau and marched straight in, refusing to give in to the butterflies in her stomach. She didn't know why she was so nervous. She was usually very confident. But she'd only been in the country a few days and she didn't know exactly what sort of job she was looking for.

Maybe she should have waited to do this, but she knew her dislike of Bert was going to put Jane in an awkward position.

She was shown into a comfortable office, where a matronly woman questioned her about her experience then offered her a job as a housemaid.

Gracie stared at her in dismay. 'But I told you: I *don't* want to work as a maid. I want something more interesting.'

'There aren't many other jobs for young women without clerical skills, so it's either work as a maid or in a shop. They pay maids well here, better than in England.'

Gracie had a quick think. If she worked in a shop, she'd have to pay for lodgings and she'd never save any money. Of course, she could stay at her sister's, they'd made that very clear.

But that would mean putting up with Tommy's bossiness, and *she* wasn't in love with him. It'd also mean facing Bert's leers and fumbling hands every Sunday. She'd met his type before. They never took no for an answer.

With a sigh, she agreed to consider a live-in maid's job, promising herself it'd only be for six months. She'd save her wages and look around for something more interesting once she got used to Western Australia.

'I have a vacancy on a country homestead in the south-west, an hour's drive from Bunbury, working for Mrs Gilsworth. She's an excellent employer, pays top wages and provides the uniform. Or I have another job on a station inland from Geraldton. That pays more, because it's quite isolated.'

Gracie was puzzled. 'They need a housemaid at a railway station?'

'Dear me, no. It's a *cattle* station, like a big farm.'

'Are either of these places near towns?'

The woman laughed gently. 'A station is out in the middle of the bush, which means the countryside. It won't be near any settlements at all, let alone what you'd consider a town. It's like a little world in its own right.'

It sounded even worse than the depths of the country in Wiltshire. 'What about this place in the south-west? Is it cooler there than in Perth?'

'It's always cooler to the south. It's the opposite way round here to the northern hemisphere.'

'And is there a town nearer to Mrs Gilsworth's than Bunbury?'

'Oh, yes. Not a big town, just a pleasant little country town, but they have a cinema showing every Wednesday and Friday, and dances once a month.'

That sounded more like it. 'I'll take that job, then.'

'When can you start? Mrs Gilsworth is rather desperate for help and she's such a good customer that we'd like to oblige.'

'Would tomorrow be too soon?'

'I'll telephone her and find out. Please wait outside for a few moments.'

* * *

When Gracie got home, her elation must have shown because her sister took one look at her and burst into tears. 'You found a job, didn't you?'

'Yes.' She tried to tell Jane about it, but all her sister could do was worry about what Tommy would say, and weep because they were going to be separated again.

That upset Gracie, too, but not as much as the thought of staying near Bert did. He had such a stubborn look to him.

She hugged Jane. 'I'll come back and visit you regularly.'

'It won't be the same as living nearby.'

'No, dear. But at least we're in the same country now. Can't you take comfort from that?'

'I'll hardly ever see you. Please stay with us and look for a day job nearby.'

'I've given my word now. If I break it the agency won't find me anything else.' She went to finish repacking her trunk, feeling both guilty and relieved.

Tommy said a great deal that evening, tossing words like 'ungrateful' and 'taking advantage' at his sister-in-law as he chomped his way through an overloaded plate.

While the two women were washing the dishes, Jane begged her once again to reconsider.

This upset Gracie but she still refused. Apart from anything else, Tommy was starting to get on her nerves. She couldn't understand why Jane loved him.

And they were both so thrilled at the thought of having a baby that when Tommy wasn't talking about Bert, he was talking about his son, quite sure it was going to be a boy.

Gracie couldn't help hoping it would be a girl.

She was glad when it was bedtime and she could escape

the chilly atmosphere and angry remarks from Tommy.

But she found it hard to sleep, tossing and turning in the narrow, creaking bed. She was more than a bit nervous about going to live over a hundred miles away from the only people she knew in Western Australia.

And she would miss Jane, of course she would.

The next morning Gracie followed the porter into Perth railway station and watched as her trunk and suitcase were loaded onto the train. Jane had insisted on coming with her in the taxi and even at this late stage, was trying to persuade her to change her mind.

'For goodness' sake, stop nagging! I've taken this job and that's that!'

'But you came all the way to Australia to be with me and—'

'To make a new life *near* you! What's more, if I ever want to get married, the man will be *my* choice, not yours and Tommy's.' She hugged Jane again. 'Don't let's quarrel.'

'What good would it do? You've always been headstrong.' But Jane hugged her back.

As the train chugged out of Perth station in a cloud of steam, Gracie felt very alone. She stared out at the countryside, which was very different from England. The grass had been burnt beige like straw by the hot Australian sun and the trees had dull green foliage. She should have looked for a job in London.

Well, you couldn't go back, could you? You just had to make the best of things.

It was so hot, she took off her gloves, folding them neatly in her handbag, then took off her hat and fanned herself with it. There weren't many towns or villages to see once they left the city and she was alone in her compartment, with only her own thoughts and worries for company.

The train arrived at Bunbury, a hundred miles to the south, in the early afternoon. She got out and made sure all her luggage was unloaded, then stood looking round because they'd said she'd be met.

A tall man dressed as a chauffeur strode across to her. 'Miss Bell?'

'Yes.'

'I'm Finn, chauffeur and general factotum at Fairgums. Mrs Gilsworth is waiting for you in the car, over there in the shade. Is this your luggage? I'll see to it.'

His gaze was admiring but *he* didn't stare at her bosom. Even so, he made Gracie feel rather flustered. He was nice-looking, with dark hair, twinkling blue eyes and a very upright way of holding himself, like many ex-soldiers.

The car looked lovely, an Essex Super Six touring model. She liked looking at pictures of cars in magazines and imagining herself riding in them. This car looked shiny and well cared for, its canvas roof raised to give shade, but the sides left open.

Mrs Gilsworth was plump, amiable and expensively dressed. But why did her eyes narrow as she looked Gracie up and down? It was as if something about her new maid displeased her. 'I'm glad you arrived safely, Bell. I hope you'll be happy with us.'

'I'm sure I will be, ma'am.'

Finn came back just then, followed by a porter wheeling her trunk.

Gracie waited while he helped his mistress back into the car, fussing over her, then tied the trunk and suitcase on the rack at the back.

'She'll want you to sit in the front with me,' he whispered.

On the way home Mrs Gilsworth talked about the things she had bought at the shops in Bunbury and the dinner party she was giving next week. To hear her, Bunbury was a big town. It had seemed small to Gracie as they drove through it and they were right out in the countryside within five minutes.

The roads seemed to get narrower and dustier by the mile. Every now and then they passed through small clusters of houses, but no towns or villages.

Oh dear! What had she got herself into? Talk about coming to the ends of the earth!

'Here we are,' Finn said.

They turned off on a long drive and stopped in front of a sprawling, wooden one-storey house surrounded by verandas, with a lot of farm buildings clustered behind it. Gum trees shaded the buildings, their leathery leaves hanging stiffly in the hot air.

Gracie swatted a fly that had immediately begun pestering her. 'They said at the agency there was a town nearby,' she whispered to Finn. 'I didn't see one.'

'It's on the other side of the farm. Stay in the car.'

He opened the door for Mrs Gilsworth, fussed her and her parcels into the house, then got back into the car and drove round to the rear.

He had the good manners to open the car door for Gracie, then took off his chauffeur's cap and tossed it on the front seat, rubbing the mark it had made on his forehead. 'Welcome to Fairgums, Miss Gracie Bell.'

'The agency didn't tell me how far out in the country this place was.' She turned in a circle, studying her surroundings. 'Is there a bus into town?'

Finn laughed. 'There are no buses at all out here.'

'Then how do we go anywhere on our days off?'

He looked disapproving. 'You haven't even started work and already you're talking about days off.'

'I like going to the cinema. I used to go every week in London.'

'Well, we do get films shown here, in the church hall.'

Her heart sank. Church hall, not a proper cinema. 'How big is the town?'

'Population 273. It'll be 274 when Mrs Bates has her baby next month. There are other people on the nearby farms, of course.'

She stared at him in dismay. 'That's not a town. That's not even a village!'

'We call it a town. Anyway, think about the good side of living here. You can save most of your money in a small place. Nothing to spend it on.'

He studied her. 'I like that hat. Makes your eyes look big and mysterious. Come inside and have a cup of tea, Gracie. It's a good place to work, honest.'

This compliment was so unexpected, she could feel herself flush slightly and didn't know what to say.

He led the way inside, where he introduced her to Cook, a large motherly woman whose hands never stopped working as they talked.

'I'll take your luggage into your bedroom, Gracie,' he said.

'Thank you.'

'Nice obliging fellow, Finn,' Cook said. 'I'm very pleased to meet you, dear. You look like a cheerful lass. The last housemaid we had was a real sourpuss, but she still got herself a husband.'

'I'm not looking for a husband, thank you very much.'

Cook laughed. 'You won't have to look for them, they'll come looking for you. They're short of women in the country. Finn, you couldn't nip outside and pick me a couple of lemons, could you?'

'Of course.'

She wiped her hands on a cloth and moved across the room. 'I'd better show you your bedroom and the amenities, then you can come and help me.'

The room was large and the single bed had a mosquito net over it. A maid's black and white uniform was laid out on a chair and there were some maid's caps on top of the chest of drawers.

Cook pointed towards the uniform. 'That should fit you nicely. *She* likes the servants to dress up all fancy when we have guests. Waste of time if you ask me. Just a print dress and apron will do the rest of the time, but she does like her maids to wear a cap.'

Gracie sighed.

Cook smiled sympathetically. 'I know. Young women today don't like caps, but she's a bit old-fashioned. She's all right otherwise, not stingy with the servants' food and gives us plenty of time off as long as the work's done.'

'Are there any other staff?'

'The gardener and his wife. She comes in mornings to do the rough work. She's a good worker. Then there's a woman from town who comes out to do the washing every fortnight.'

When she was alone, Gracie went to stare out of the window. Only cows and fields to be seen. She'd expected there to be other farms nearby, at least. She had a little cry then scolded herself for being silly and changed into a print dress, sighing as she pinned on the starched white cap. She hated the dratted things.

In the late afternoon Cook told Gracie to ring the bell on the back veranda then take the weight off her feet for a few minutes.

An elderly man came to join them and was introduced as the gardener. Finn followed, his shirt sleeves rolled up, his collar open, looking very manly and energetic. Taking a piece of cake, he sat on the other side of the table and winked at Gracie. 'I prefer the hat.'

She ignored that and sipped her tea, grateful for its familiar warmth. 'What's the town called and how far away is it?'

'Beeniup and it's five miles away.'

She stared at him in shock. 'You said there was no bus. What am I going to do on my days off?'

There was silence, then Cook said in her comfortable voice, 'We forget how different it is here for Poms. You'll find we know how to enjoy ourselves, Gracie. We all go to the cinema on Wednesdays, unless the mistress has people coming, in which case we usually go on the Friday instead. The missus lets Finn have the car to drive us into town for it. I do love a romantic film.'

'Especially one that makes you cry,' he teased

'Better than that horrible *Dr Jekyll and Mr Hyde*. Gave me nightmares, that one did. I was glad we couldn't hear them speak.'

'Well, you liked Douglas Fairbanks in *The Mark of Zorro* and you wept buckets over the wedding of him and Mary Pickford when they showed it on the Pathé News.'

Cook sighed sentimentally. 'I do love a good wedding. She made a beautiful bride. Oh, and there's a church social one Saturday a month, Gracie. You just missed one but there'll be another next month. All the young folk go to that, which means you and Finn. I'm too old for dancing.'

'Nonsense.' Finn pulled her to her feet and twirled her along the veranda and back. Cook pretended to slap him for cheek and he pretended to be afraid of her.

He turned to Gracie. 'Do you like dancing?'

'I love it.' She knew all the latest dance tunes. But she wasn't sure she wanted to go to a social event with Finn. He was more than a bit cheeky, if you asked her.

She did more listening than speaking. If there was one thing she understood, it was to tread carefully when you were new to a place.

Gracie soon got used to the different ways of doing housework. There were a lot of bare boards to mop. They were nicely stained and varnished, but would show all the dust. When sweeping them, she could open up a little trapdoor at the back of the hall and brush the dust through, because the house was raised on stumps.

There was a lot of dust in such a long dry summer. It hadn't rained for two months, Cook told her. The living room furniture had to be dusted twice a day. Mrs Gilsworth was fussy about that.

Sylvia, who came in to do the washing, was very good, and took care not only of the family's clothes but the servants'. It was really easy to get things dry in this climate. What you had to watch out for, Sylvia said, was fading. 'Turn your blouses and tops inside out when you take them off, or you'll get a sun stripe from where they hang over the line.'

Mr Gilsworth remained aloof from the rest of them. He was out most of the day, supervising the farm workers. When she commented on how little they saw of him, Cook said he was a quiet man, who liked best to be left in peace or to spend time with old friends.

He had a nice smile, though, and once stopped Gracie to ask if she had settled in now.

Gradually she got used to Finn's ways and relaxed with him. Everyone liked him. He made people laugh, but he also seemed to notice when she was feeling homesick, or when a letter from Jane upset her, and made an effort to cheer her up, even if it was only by challenging her to a silly game of tiddlywinks.

He didn't pester her for a kiss, thank goodness. Didn't lay a finger on her, or even brush against her. Which was a relief after Bert. She wouldn't have minded an occasional compliment, though.

To her surprise, Finn was a thinking man beneath that light-hearted exterior, interested in the wider world, asking her about the changes in post-war England. He'd been stationed there for a time during the war, so could talk about London too.

After nearly four weeks at Fairgums, she was looking forward to the monthly dance. They'd all been to the cinema every week but arrived late and rushed home afterwards.

It'd be nice to make some women friends in Beeniup, too. She hoped to meet some at the dance.

On the day of the church social Gracie put on her best summer dress, calf-length in soft voile trimmed with white lace. It was the same blue as her eyes.

Finn was waiting for her in the kitchen, looking very spruce in a dark suit, waistcoat and white shirt, his skin rosy and newly washed. He smelt of shaving soap and fresh air.

He let out a long, low whistle at the sight of her. 'We're in trouble,' he told Cook.

Gracie looked down at herself in puzzlement. 'What do you mean?'

'Mrs Gilsworth will have a fit when she sees you in that outfit.'

She went across to study herself in the mirror. 'What's wrong with it?'

'Nothing. It's a lovely dress. But you look so pretty, she'll start worrying about you getting married. She's lost three maids that way in the past eighteen months.'

Feeling flustered by his compliment, Gracie picked up the plate of small iced cakes Cook had prepared, because women had to take a plate of something for supper, it seemed. 'Well, are we going or not?'

'Your carriage awaits, mademoiselle.' He flourished a bow and opened the door.

As she passed him, their eyes met and her heart skipped a beat. He was a *very* attractive fellow.

Good thing she was only staying six months.

* * *

At the doorway of the church hall Gracie hesitated, feeling suddenly nervous.

'Come on! I'll show you where to put the plate and introduce you to a few people.' Finn offered her his arm and led the way inside, nodding and smiling, seeming to know everyone.

He left her with two young women her own age and she enjoyed chatting to them about the latest fashions in England.

Then the music started and fellows crowded round them. There seemed to be twice as many young men here as women. She stood up with a different fellow for each of the first three dances, enjoying the fuss and attention, even though none of them was a good dancer. They didn't have much to say for themselves, either.

Finn met her as she came off the dance floor the third time, elbowing another man aside. 'My turn, I think. Fancy cooling down outside, Gracie?'

'That'd be lovely.'

As they walked out together she could see heads turn their way. 'Why is everyone staring at us?'

'Oh, they always watch newcomers.'

A few couples were strolling up and down the scruffy, sunburnt square of grass behind the hall. The night air was cool and the moonlight bright. Finn made her laugh and they stayed out there for two whole dances.

As they went back inside, he put one hand on his heart. 'Am I allowed to ask you for a dance, Miss Bell?'

'Why certainly, kind sir.'

It was a waltz, her favourite, but being held closely by Finn made her feel breathless. He was so tall, his teeth white in his suntanned face, his smile for her alone. He was an excellent dancer and she relaxed, securely held by his strong arms.

'Our steps match well, don't they?' he murmured as the waltz ended. 'Fancy another twirl round the floor?'

'That'd be lovely.'

Just before the supper break she went out with another girl to the lean-to at the back of the hall to use the convenience.

'You certainly didn't waste any time,' the other said.

'What do you mean?'

'Getting Finn for your fellow. I'd give a week's wages to have him smile at me like he does at you. He's never picked up with a girl before, you know.'

'*What?* He's not my fellow. Why did you say that? We just work together.'

'But he took you walking outside. Round here, that's a sign that you're courting.'

Fury sizzled through Gracie. The sneaky rat! She wasn't letting Finn get away with tricking her like that. They weren't courting. He hadn't shown any special feeling for her over the past month. He'd just been . . . friendly.

She went back inside the hall and he didn't see her coming. The man next to him was teasing him about stealing a march on the other fellows.

'Wouldn't you? Just remember she's mine.'

That made her even angrier. Finn turned and held out his hand to her. His, was she? She'd show him.

She said loudly, 'I'm finished with you, Finn O'Connor! I never want to speak to you again.' Then she stormed across to get some food. She didn't look round at him as she forced down a piece of cake that tasted like sawdust and chatted brightly to another young woman.

'What did Finn do to upset you?' her companion whispered.

'Never you mind. How can I get back to Fairgums without him? Does anyone else go out that way?'

'No, and it's five miles. You'll have to drive back with him. You can make up your quarrel then.'

Gracie scowled across the hall at Finn, who shrugged and winked at her. What a nerve! She elevated her nose and looked away.

When the dancing began again, she saw him start towards her and slipped outside. Grimly determined not to drive back with him, still furious at him for tricking her, she stood in the shadows near the hall, thinking hard.

Five miles wasn't all that far, she decided in the end. She'd walked five miles many a time. She didn't have a coat to retrieve, not in this heat, and was carrying her handbag. She wasn't going back for the empty plate. She'd pay for it out of her wages if necessary.

Anger carried her along the one and only street of Beeniup at a cracking pace. Apart from the church and its adjacent hall, the town consisted of one general store, a place advertising stock feed and farm supplies, and twenty or thirty houses. She didn't consider this a town, whatever the locals said!

She walked quickly towards the homestead. Easy enough to find her way, because the road was a continuation of the main street.

A few minutes later she heard the sound of a car engine behind her and her heart began to pound. She looked round in panic for somewhere to hide. But there were only open fields with wire fences, so she kept on walking, head held high.

Finn stopped the car.

'Leave me alone!' she yelled, not even turning round.

'Get in, you idiot! Even if I did upset you, there's no need for you to walk home.'

She turned, arms akimbo, glaring at him. 'I'm not going anywhere with you from now on, if I can help it. How dare you make people think we're courting?'

He looked at her pleadingly. 'Because I knew if I didn't do something, the other blokes would be all over you. I could see the way they were looking at you and . . . well, I wanted you for myself.'

All the air seemed to vanish from the world. Gracie tried in vain to stay angry. Couldn't.

He stopped the engine and got out.

She couldn't move, not a step. In the moonlight, Finn was even more handsome than her favourite film star, Douglas Fairbanks. Why hadn't she noticed that before?

For a moment she wavered, swaying towards his outstretched hand, then she forced herself to turn and start walking again, terrified of what she might do if he got too close.

He took her by surprise, scooping her up into his arms, laughing softly as she pounded half-heartedly on his chest.

'Let go of me!'

He tripped and she held on tightly as he righted himself, her arms round his neck now. It felt more comfortable like that, so she kept them there.

'I'll never let you fall, Gracie,' he said as he set her down gently by the car, helped her inside and closed the door on her side. He got in next to her but didn't start the engine, just sat staring ahead, fiddling with the steering wheel.

He surprised her again by asking very quietly without that masterful tone, 'Am I so bad?'

'I – don't know what you mean.'

'If you say you don't fancy me, can *never* fancy me, I'll stop pestering you, Gracie. Only – I thought we were getting on well. You're so pretty and lively, and . . . I can't stop thinking about you. All day you're in my thoughts. I walk past the kitchen a dozen times a day just to catch sight of you.'

It was her turn to stare into the distance. He was right. They did get on well. And the more she got to know him, the more she liked him. But it was too soon to do anything about it. Far too soon, only a month.

He took her hand and heat flooded through her body.

She should have pulled hers away, but somehow she couldn't. He had such warm, capable hands, always busy, always fixing things. She loved to watch him working.

'Gracie?'

The way he said her name sent more shivers through her body.

'You should have *asked* me before telling folk we were going steady, Finn.' She couldn't stop her voice wobbling.

'Yes, I should. I'm real sorry about that. Will you forgive me?'

She felt her anger start to fade. 'Perhaps.'

The silence was charged with tension. She didn't dare look at him.

'You don't . . . dislike me?'

'No.'

'Can I kiss you? Please?'

He didn't wait for an answer, but pulled her close and kissed her long and hard. No other man's kisses had sent such longings running through her. When he moved his head away to stare at her, she gazed back at him dreamily.

'We Aussie blokes don't waste time when we want something. Soon as I saw you, Gracie, I knew.'

'Knew what?'

'That I wanted to marry you.'

'Oh. Oh, my goodness!'

This was the last thing she'd expected him to say. They took things more slowly where she'd grown up and a fellow courted a girl for months or even years before proposing.

But she hadn't met any men like Finn in England. He was – special. And she wanted him to kiss her again, wanted it very much, could still feel the taste of him on her lips.

Instead, he raised her hand to his lips and kissed it gently. Even that made it hard for her to breathe properly.

'I've got plans for the future, you know, Gracie. I'm not staying a chauffeur for much longer. Only I haven't said anything about that to the others because I don't want the Gilsworths to know yet. But it's only fair to tell you.'

Hope flared up in her. 'What are you planning to do?'

'Start my own garage. Not in Beeniup, in a bigger country town. I'd do car and bicycle repairs, sell and repair tractors and cars, and sell the petrol for them, too. Cars are the coming thing. One day every family will own one, not just rich people. Years I've been saving for my garage, all through the war. I'm nearly ready to get started now.'

She liked the ambition in him, but if she hadn't fancied him as a man, his plans would have changed nothing. Only she did fancy him.

She looked at him, thinking hard. She owed it to him to be as honest as he'd been with her. She'd had dreams too, and she wasn't like her sister, content to stay at home and just be a wife.

'I don't want to be shut up in the house all day after I marry. Would there be a place for me to work in that garage of yours? I could . . . learn to do the accounts and help sell petrol, maybe sell other things, too. I worked on a motor omnibus during the war. I know quite a bit about motor vehicles already.'

'Most women wouldn't want to get their hands dirty. They want the man to provide for them after they're married.'

'I'm not most women.'

He stared at her, a little frown line furrowing the middle of his forehead, then one of his wonderful smiles lit up his face. 'No, you're not like anyone I've ever met. And yes, you can work with me. As long as it won't stop you having children.'

'No, it won't. I don't want a lot of children, though. Two or three would be enough. It's no fun having babies, you know.'

Another of those considering looks, another nod. 'I agree. Are we on, then? Will you marry me?'

She gaped at him. Could it be that easy?

'Well? You haven't said yes yet, Gracie Bell.'

It was such an enormous step to take, she still hesitated. She'd known him for such a short time. People would say she was mad. But she and Finn had spent a lot of time together during that month, seeing each other every day. He listened as much as he talked, so he knew her, too.

His voice was low, his eyes challenging. 'Go mad, Gracie! Say yes.'

She stared at him. If you couldn't go a bit mad on a moonlit night with the most handsome fellow you'd ever kissed proposing to you, when could you go mad?

Excitement ran through her and something else, some elemental response to Finn the man, Finn who intended to make his fortune, Finn who wouldn't lock her away inside the house. She looked at him, was lost and took the biggest chance of her whole life. 'Yes.'

'You mean – you will marry me?'

'I just said yes, didn't I?' She smiled because now he was the one who seemed stunned.

'I didn't think it'd be so easy. It's the first time I've ever proposed to anyone, you see. I've been practising what to say out in the paddock, asking the cows what they thought.'

He pulled her closer. 'I'll do my best to make you happy, Gracie, and—'

Something occurred to her suddenly and she couldn't help chuckling.

He broke off, staring at her in surprise. 'What are you laughing at?'

She put up one hand to caress his cheek. 'Not you, Finn. Never you.' She could feel him relax. 'I was thinking of poor Mrs Gilsworth.'

His grin showed his instant understanding and they spoke in a chorus.

'She'll have to find herself another maid.'

As they sat in the car, cuddling close, staring across the

fields, he let out a huge happy sigh. 'I'd have done whatever it took to persuade you. I could never have let you go, Gracie.'

'I just needed a few minutes to get used to the idea. You Aussies are such fast workers.'

As he bent his head to kiss her again, she strained towards him eagerly, sure that the moonlight was brighter than it had ever been before, the night breeze softer and more richly perfumed – and her days as a housemaid numbered.

What more could a modern young woman ask of life?

Time for a Change

Introduction

This story was first published by a magazine in a much shorter format (about 2,000 words). But even after that, the characters wouldn't go away, and I found myself writing and rewriting the story.

It got a bit longer, then longer still, with more details creeping in until gradually I realised I had to turn it into a novel and tell the story properly. There was so much I could say about the heroine.

I always find that either a title for a new novel comes to me quickly or I agonise for ages over finding a suitable one. There doesn't seem to be anything in between. 'Time for a Change' didn't feel to be the right title for the novel, because the story itself had changed quite a lot.

This was such a difficult title to find that I set up a three-person think tank about it, with my lovely husband and a dear friend. She quickly suggested that since it was about a heroine inheriting a vineyard we had that word in the title. Simple. Why hadn't I thought of that?

But Karen's Vineyard didn't have any 'music' to it. Maybe it's because she's Scottish originally that my friend suggested Kirsty for the heroine's name instead. Kirsty's Vineyard. Why did that sound 'right' and the other one not? Who can tell? It just did.

What follows is a longer version of the short story that started all this off. I've kept the original title but the story more than doubled in length and is now about 4,800 words. I hope you enjoy meeting Karen and seeing her lose her diffidence about the world.

And if you want to read the novel, *Kirsty's Vineyard* is still in print and you might enjoy seeing what I made of my original idea.

Time for a Change

Peter Ward stared at his younger sister, so astounded it was a while before he spoke. 'I can't believe it.'

Karen smiled faintly. It made a change to shock Peter. Usually he knew everything and didn't hesitate to tell you so.

'Mr Duncan has left me his house,' she repeated. 'It's in Australia and there's an income to go with it. There is a condition, though.' She hesitated. He wasn't going to like it.

'Go on! What condition did he set?'

'I have to live there for a year before I can sell anything or return to England. If I don't, it all goes to a charity.'

She was still reeling from the shock of it all. She had never even won a raffle and now she'd inherited a fortune. Well, it seemed a fortune to her. Librarians didn't earn huge salaries.

There was a moment's stunned silence, then Peter began making plans to accompany her to Australia.

And nothing she said would deter him from that. 'You may be twenty-five,' he declared, 'but you're a timid sort of person and you've never travelled, so you'll need looking after.'

She wasn't timid, just quiet, but she didn't argue. It never did any good to argue with Peter. Besides, she hated arguments.

To her great delight, Peter got a promotion before he could carry out his threat to come with her. There was no way he could take a holiday as soon as he started the new job. He was needed.

As she packed, she wondered yet again why Mr Duncan had left her the money, and why he had made those conditions. Such a nice old man. She'd helped him fill in forms, talked to him, been sad when he stopped coming to the senior citizens' centre.

The flight seemed to go on for ever, but Karen managed to sleep for a few hours. She got through customs quickly and wheeled her suitcase to the taxi rank.

The heat in Perth was a shock, so hot it was like walking into an overheated room. She'd come from an icy February day into the Australian summer, so was wearing far too many clothes. People around her were complaining, but after the English winter she welcomed the warmth of the sun on her face. Exhausted by the twenty-four-hour flight, she went straight to the hotel and to bed, forgetting to ring her brother as she had promised.

When the phone woke her up three hours later, she looked at the green numbers on the clock radio, feeling groggy.

'Karen? Is that you?'

'Uh. What? Peter?'

'Why didn't you ring me when you arrived? That was very selfish of you. You might have known I'd be worrying.'

'It's night here. You must have known that. I was fast asleep and you woke me!'

'Yes, but I needed—'

It was always about him. It wasn't often she lost her temper, but she did now. She slammed the phone down on him and told reception to hold all calls.

It was late morning, Perth time, when she awoke naturally. The breakfast tray was on the floor outside her door, the advertised 'continental breakfast' consisting of a sad-looking roll with one little packet of butter and one of jam, plus a banana. There was tea-making equipment in the room.

With the food came an angry message which must have been dictated by her brother over the phone. She was to ring him immediately she woke up. 'No, thank you,' she said aloud, screwed up the note and threw it across the dingy room, missing the wastepaper basket. Well, of course she missed. She'd always been a rotten shot.

She looked round, taking in details she'd been too exhausted to see when she got here. It was a horrid place, furnished in dark brown and beige. Peter had booked it because it was cheap. She began to smile. No way was she staying here, not on her first visit to Australia.

As soon as she had finished breakfast, she packed all her things and checked out of the hotel, asking the taxi driver to take her to a better one. There she booked a luxury room with a view of the river. Peter would have been apoplectic at the thought of her wasting so much money, but just for once she wanted to live elegantly, in the way she'd read of in books.

'Cinderella, watch out!' she murmured as she sat on the small balcony sipping a cup of excellent coffee and staring at the boats on the river. People were strolling along a grassy stretch of land that ran alongside it. She would make her way there later.

It was like something in a book. All it needed to complete the picture was a handsome hero. As if! Reading romances was her secret vice, but she'd never met a potential hero in real life, just a couple of pleasant but unheroic men.

She loved to read about tall, dark heroes and the courageous heroines who deserved to be loved, as they always were in the end. And the sexy scenes made her sigh in longing for a man to hold her in his arms and melt her very bones with his kisses.

If only she wasn't so shy. If only she could meet someone special. He needn't be as handsome as the heroes in the books. Attractive would do.

After a walk along the river during the afternoon, for which she bought a wide-brimmed sunhat, she slept soundly. She hadn't rung Peter, so he couldn't disturb her. Serve him right if he was worrying.

She smiled wryly. Oh, how brave she could be when she was away from him!

The next day she went out to start her new life. There was a terrifyingly large amount of money sitting in her new

Australian bank account, and the fatherly manager advised her to get a car before trying to visit her new home. 'You do drive, don't you, Miss Ward?'

'Oh, yes.' But would she dare to drive here?

Yes, she would! she decided in a sudden surge of determination. Here in Australia she was going to stop being so cautious about everything. She had enough money to live as she wished, for once. She sighed in bliss.

Another daring idea crept into her mind. She would buy some new clothes as well as a car, *and* have her hair restyled. If any of her heroines had inherited money, they wouldn't stay in a cheap hotel and wear a two-year-old skirt. She realised that the manager was still speaking.

'You won't be able to manage without a car here, Karen. Anyway, Mr Duncan's estate is in the country, in the south-west wine country. There won't be any public transport at all down there.'

In between sightseeing and shopping, Karen took a driving lesson to get used to the local traffic rules, and then she took possession of the car. A slightly larger car than she usually drove, only a couple of years old with air conditioning and everything. She hadn't been able to resist its sheer comfort.

As she was getting ready to leave, she decided, reluctantly, that she'd better ring her brother. She was eight hours ahead of him here, so waited till Australian teatime to call him. He'd have got up but not yet gone to work.

'Hi, Peter.'

'Where the hell have you been, Karen Ward?' he roared down the phone. 'I nearly called the police, I was so worried.'

'I moved to a nicer hotel.'

'Give me your number now, before you forget.'

'There's no point, Peter. I'm just off to my new home.'

'Then give me the address there. You even forgot to do that before you left England. Trust you! I don't know how you're managing without me to look after you.'

She frowned at the phone. She was a grown woman and managing quite well, in her opinion. But she didn't say that. Peter never listened to what she said. He treated her with loving tyranny, but tyranny nonetheless. 'I'll email you when I get there and set myself up with a computer. Bye.'

For the second time in her life she put the phone down on her brother while he was still speaking and told reception not to put through any more calls. 'Goodness!' she said aloud. 'What have I done?'

But she was filled with amusement at his reaction, as well as excitement – and apprehension about the coming drive to her new home.

Taking a deep breath, she picked up her luggage and went to check out.

She got out of the busy Perth traffic, thanks to the car's satnav, and found herself on the freeway heading south. It was busy at first. Traffic roared past her, huge trucks, coaches, cars galore. The whole world seemed to be heading south. But gradually the traffic thinned out and she stopped for a drink and to stretch her legs.

A few hours later she arrived, tired but triumphant at how she had coped. The sign over the gate said 'Duncan House'. Karen turned in and stopped to look at her inheritance. A wide drive led to a long, low house. It was so Australian that it made her beam with delight. A one-storey house with a tin roof and verandas all round it. And the fields nearby looked like – they were! – vineyards.

'What're you doing here?' demanded a loud voice. 'This is private property.'

Karen jumped in shock as she turned to find a man glaring at her. She stared at him, then blinked and stared again. He was rather good-looking, or he would have been, if he hadn't been scowling. Tall, with brown curly hair and blue eyes fringed in long lashes. Wow! He looked like a cover hero in a romance.

'I asked what you're doing here,' he said loudly, speaking as if she were half-witted. 'Have you lost your way?'

The pleasant tingle faded. 'Don't you dare speak to me like that!' snapped the new Karen. 'And if it's any of your business, I own this house.' She waved the key in his face.

'Ah.' The way he looked at her was distinctly unfriendly. 'You're the Pommie who soft-soaped old Charles.'

'I beg your pardon?'

'He always was a sucker for a pretty face, poor Charles was. Enjoy your loot.' The man gestured to the house then turned to go, tossing over his shoulder, 'I've been looking after things. Your bank manager rang to say you were coming. I've got everything switched on.' Before she could answer, he had disappeared behind the trees.

How dare he talk to me like that! I've never soft-soaped anyone in my life. But he had also said that she had a pretty face. She smiled to herself. She was glad he'd noticed that. She rather liked her new hairstyle herself, shoulder-length and swinging free, not tied back in a neat ponytail.

She stared around, sighing with happiness. Her own house and money in the bank. She'd never even dared dream about having so much.

The house was very old and made of wood, painted white. It was clearly a while since anyone had lived here and it was in need of some TLC.

She went inside, feeling like an intruder, stopping in the wide hallway to look down a corridor whose floor was of varnished wood, old floorboards not veneered chipboard.

But he didn't need to say that about me, she added mentally, still indignant. *I didn't even know Mr Duncan had any money, let alone try to soft-soap him.*

She walked down to the end of the corridor, exploring to find the kitchen. It was old-fashioned but had a nice view of the untidy garden. And not only were the phone and electricity switched on, but someone had thought to stock the fridge with a few necessities. It must have been the bad-tempered man. She examined the loaf and the other foodstuffs, but could find no price labels. She owed him money. And gratitude for his help.

You could have fitted Karen's whole flat into the huge kitchen.

She came back along the corridor to explore the two large living rooms to either side of the front door. One of them had two walls full of bookcases, to the delight of her librarian's soul. Between the one to the right and the kitchen, a long narrow corridor led off revealing bedrooms on either side. 'Six!' she gasped aloud, when she had explored them all. 'What on earth shall I do with six bedrooms and two bathrooms?'

She looked round guiltily. She was talking to herself as people who lived alone often did. When she caught herself at it, she tried to stop. It was so – pitiful.

Why on earth had Charles Duncan chosen to return to England and live so simply, when he had a huge house here? He said he'd been born in Northumberland and had missed it. But what a lot he'd given up to go back!

Dusk was falling as she finished unpacking. She decided to make do with cheese on toast. She couldn't be bothered to drive out again. There would be no walking to the shops from this house.

As she pulled the loaf out of the fridge, a car drew up outside, a large four-wheel drive. A young woman in jeans jumped out of it, followed by a rather pregnant dog. The woman was carrying something wrapped in a tea towel.

Karen went out to greet her.

'Hi! You must be Karen Ward. Luke said you were here.'

'Luke?'

'I think you met him when you arrived.'

'Oh, the bad-tempered man.'

The visitor grinned. 'Yes, that's Luke. But his bark's much worse than his bite. He's quite a softie, really. Just don't let him bully you.'

'I won't.' Karen didn't intend to let anyone bully her from now on, not even her own brother. It was wonderful the confidence a bank full of money gave you.

'I'm Penny Jamieson, Luke's cousin. My partner Tom and I live on the next block.' She held out the bundle. 'I thought you might like a casserole for tea.'

'Oh, how kind! Do come in! Are you farmers?' Karen asked, trying to understand her new world.

'No. We have a smallholding. Tom works in a vineyard not far from here. And I do typing from home. And we grow a few vines, make our own wine.'

'And your cousin? What does he do?'

'Luke? He's a writer.' Penny grimaced. 'Well, he's just getting started as a writer. His first novel came out last year. He only scrapes a living at the moment, but he's had a second novel accepted, so one day he might be rich and famous. Not for a while, though.'

'What sort of novels does he write?'

'Whodunnits.' She glanced at her wristwatch. 'I'll stay longer next time but I have to feed my chooks.'

'Chooks?'

Penny grinned. 'Chickens, hens. I sell the eggs.'

Three days later, the feeling of guilt could no longer be denied. Karen owed Luke Jamieson money for the groceries. However rude he was, she ought to pay him back. Especially if he was so short of money. Perhaps he had spoken sharply to her because he was still upset about his old neighbour's return to England and sudden death there. Penny said he had been fond of the old man. Or perhaps he'd expected to inherit, since Douglas hadn't any close relatives?

She rang up Penny. 'Er – could you tell me where your cousin lives?'

'Luke? Are you in the mood for a quarrel, then?'

Penny's voice was teasing, but Karen's heart sank. 'I dislike quarrels, but I owe him some money.'

'What on earth for?'

'He stocked up my fridge with groceries.'

'Oh, there's no need to worry about that. He won't.'

'I prefer to pay my debts.'

'OK. Got a pen?' When she'd finished giving the address, she said, 'Good luck. Got to go now.'

Luke Jamieson's house was only a few hundred yards away down the narrow dirt road. It was quite small, though the block was ten acres, Penny said. That seemed a huge amount of land to Karen, who'd grown up in a terraced house in Gateshead.

There were various outbuildings next to the house, most of the walls and roofs made of corrugated iron. They looked as if they were held together with sticky tape and rust. As did the car that stood near the house.

Definitely not the home of a man with money to spare. She'd been right to come. Karen knocked on the front door before she lost her courage.

'I didn't expect to see you here,' a voice said behind her.

She turned round. He was scowling at her again. She scowled back. 'Do you always creep up behind people and make them jump?'

'I was working on the garden. Do I have to go into the house and open the door to you before we can talk?'

'No. But it wouldn't hurt you to be polite.'

Luke's brows rose, and he opened his mouth as if to shout at her, then he clamped his lips together and breathed deeply. 'What can I do for you?'

'I owe you some money, Mr Jamieson.'

'You owe me nothing.'

'Yes, I do. For the groceries.'

'It was only a few dollars, for heaven's sake.'

She set her hands on her hips. 'I prefer to pay my debts, thank you very much.'

He looked at her sideways, a calculating expression on his face. 'Are you any good at sewing?'

'Pardon?'

'Sewing. I need some sewing done. That's how we do things here in the country. We help each other out. We don't count coins.'

'Oh. Well, yes, I can sew.' She was stuttering like an idiot. Why did she react to him like this? She pulled herself together – sort of.

'Come inside.' He took her agreement for granted and led the way indoors, so she followed.

He pointed to a piece of canvas on the table. 'That cross-stitch sampler is fraying in one corner. My grandmother did it. I've tried putting in a few stitches, but I made a mess of it. And Penny's worse than me, absolutely hates sewing. She just throws things away when they get holes in them, or else she wears them with holes. *Can* you embroider?'

Karen picked up the canvas. 'Yes, I can. This is lovely and I'll be happy to mend the picture for you.'

And that was the start of their friendship. If you could call it a friendship, because Luke spoke his mind on every topic and Karen gave him back as good as he dished out. Well, most of the time, anyway. It took time to make such a big change to oneself, but she was feeling more confident every day.

He mended her pump.

She cooked him a meal.

He fixed her side gate.

She lent him a few books she'd brought from England. She liked whodunnits, as well as romances. It formed a bond between them.

Her brother continued to ring her up from England every week and harangue her about not wasting her money. A bit later, after she'd mentioned Luke in a couple of her letters, Peter started warning her not to let people take advantage of her generosity. She should remember that a rich woman was a prey for all sorts of scoundrels.

Luke came round one evening when her brother was lecturing her. He saw how upset she was. 'Your brother again?' When she nodded, he took the phone out of her hand and yelled into it. 'Leave her alone. She's perfectly capable of managing her own life.' Then he slammed it down.

She should have been angry, but the thought of what Peter's face would look like at the moment betrayed her into a giggle, then suddenly the two of them were roaring with laughter.

'Oh, I wish I could have seen his face!' She wiped tears of laughter from her eyes.

'I'm glad I couldn't see his face, if that photograph of him is anything to go by. Ugly brute, isn't he?'

And she was laughing again. Peter was ugly, not because his features were mismatched but because of his attitude to life, always looking for things to go wrong, people cheating him, products not doing what the adverts had promised. Anything and everything upset him.

'Don't let your brother bully you,' Luke said later, as he left.

*   *   *

One day Luke drove her to the coast for a barbecue on the beach. It was a glorious day. She didn't think she'd ever been so relaxed.

Greatly daring, she took him out in return, asking Penny which was the best restaurant in the neighbourhood. It was part of a tourist complex.

'A bit pricey.' Penny pulled a face.

'That doesn't matter. I feel like giving myself a treat.' Karen loved the vineyards, and had driven round to several of them, wine-tasting and buying a few bottles, but she hadn't been out in the evening once. Penny said that there was a small dance floor at the restaurant. Karen rather hoped that if they danced together, Luke would keep his arms round her afterwards. She drifted away into a dream of romance on a balmy, star-filled evening.

She didn't tell Luke where she was taking him. Obviously the surprise was not a pleasant one. He took one look at the menu and became very stiff.

'What's wrong?' she asked, as they walked back to her car after a miserable time, during which he had not once asked her to dance and had ordered only a main course. When he didn't answer, she said, 'Please tell me what I did wrong, Luke.'

He looked at her, seeing the tears trembling in her eyes. 'Oh, dammit, Karen, I didn't mean to upset you.'

The tears escaped and trickled down her cheeks. She got out of the car and stumbled towards the house.

He caught her hand and pulled her into his arms. 'Come here!' He kissed her nose then wiped the tears away with one rough fingertip. Suddenly he was kissing her properly. And she responded properly too, flinging her arms round his neck and kissed him right back. Her whole body came alive in a way it had only done in her dreams before.

A little later, as they sat together on the veranda, she asked softly, 'What made you so angry tonight, Luke?'

'I can't afford to take you to restaurants like that.' His voice was gruff and she could sense the tension in him.

'Oh, is that all?'

'What do you mean, "all"?'

'I don't care two hoots about expensive restaurants, Luke. I'll cook you a meal myself next time.'

But the money lay between them like a ghost and they trod carefully whenever they were together, which took some of the pleasure out of the encounters.

Worst of all, he didn't kiss her again.

Four months after her arrival, Karen saw a taxi pull into the drive and her brother Peter got out. 'Oh, no!' She thumped the table in frustration. Why could he not leave her alone?

She gritted her teeth and went to answer the door, trying to look as if she were happy to see him. 'What a surprise! Why didn't you tell me you were coming? How's your new job?'

'Fine. I've got the staff all sorted out now, so I thought I'd take my holidays. I was still worried about you, so I decided to see how you were going.'

Before she knew it Peter had taken charge, reorganising the house and garden quite ruthlessly. She tried to stop him, but her new-found independence was still too fragile. He even took over the driving – after he had given her a lecture on how she had wasted her money buying a big, petrol-guzzling car like this.

As she could have predicted, Peter and Luke took an instant dislike to one another.

'He's a fortune hunter,' said Peter scornfully. 'That's all he is. He wants someone to subsidise his writing.'

'Your brother's an out-and-out bully,' Luke hissed at her when Peter's back was turned. 'Why do you let him do this to you?'

She didn't know why. But the habits of years slid back into her behaviour so quickly that she was ashamed of herself.

Then Penny called to deliver the puppy she had promised Karen, which was now old enough to leave its mother.

'She doesn't want a mongrel like that!' Peter stated. 'She can afford to buy a pedigree dog. And anyway, you can't take a dog back to England without a lot of quarantine fuss. You'll have to keep it.' He picked the little creature up by the scruff of its neck, making it yelp.

Penny turned to Karen for confirmation.

And at that moment something snapped within Karen. 'Don't you dare take her away, Penny!' She snatched the pup from Peter and the feel of its warm wriggling body seemed to increase her courage. 'Thanks, Penny. Er – would you mind leaving us now? My brother and I have something important to discuss.'

'Good luck!' Penny whispered, then drove away.

Karen turned to Peter, swallowed hard and said, 'You'd better book your flight back. Or – or go and be a tourist in Sydney or Melbourne.'

'*What?*'

'I need to get on with my own life now, Peter. You can see that I'm very comfortable here.'

'Just for this year, till you're allowed to sell the place, surely?'

'No. I like it here. I'm going to apply to be an Australian citizen when I can.'

'You can't mean that!'

'I do.'

'I won't *let* you.'

'You can't stop me. You've bossed me around all my life and it's more than time that stopped. Just book your flight and I'll drive you to the airport.' And she would do the driving herself, she vowed, not let him take the wheel.

Several times he brought up the subject again, starting to argue, not seeming to hear her answers, so she snatched up the car keys and the pup, and took off. Inevitably she found herself driving round to Luke's.

He was sitting on the rickety veranda. 'Isn't your dear brother with you? Don't you need protection from a fortune hunter like me?'

'Go and put the kettle on and stop talking such rot!' She pushed him into the house. The puppy wriggled out of her arms and ran round the kitchen exploring. They faced each other across the table.

'You kept the pup, then?' He bent down to stroke it.

'Yes. Why shouldn't I?'

'Penny rang and said he told her to take it away again.'

'Peter's leaving.'

Luke switched on the gas ring. 'Good.'

'I told him to leave.'

He turned to beam at her. 'Really? Oh, that's wonderful.'

'It was about time I stood up to him.' She stared at Luke. She had missed their times together, even if he hadn't kissed her again.

A daring idea formed in her mind as she looked at him. A very daring idea, worthy of the most spirited of romance heroines. And she was suddenly sure that it was what Charles Duncan had intended when he left her the house.

'Come and sit down for a minute, Luke. Never mind the tea. I have something to ask you.'

He slouched over to a chair, looking at her warily. 'If it's to do with your brother . . .'

'It's not.' She took a deep breath. 'It's to do with us.'

'Oh?'

'Luke, will you please marry me?'

He goggled at her for a minute, then scowled down at the fists clenched in his lap. 'No.'

'Why not?'

'Because I'm not a fortune hunter.'

It took several deep breaths to gather some more courage, but then she marched round the table and sat down on his knee, twining her arms round his neck, so that he couldn't push her off. 'You will, you know.' She was unable to resist giving him a big hug, then a long tender kiss.

When they resurfaced, he was smiling. 'Oh? Why will I?' His voice was gentle and he was looking at her as if he cared. Well, he did care. She knew that.

'You'll marry me because I can be as much of a bully as my brother if I let myself.'

'I'm so terrified I'd better say yes.'

When he began to kiss her, she sighed happily and ran her fingers through his beautiful curly hair, pulling his face back for another kiss. And another.

Neighbours

Introduction

We had a dog which was also an escape artist. She was a golden Labrador and very intelligent. No wonder they use them as guide and assistance dogs.

She was inventive about her escaping too. Her favourite excursion was when a neighbour was having a barbecue with friends. If she suddenly went missing, we'd follow our noses and find her chatting up the neighbour and eating their offerings.

She died several decades ago – why do dogs have such shorter lives than humans? We still miss her so much.

We've had several friends who're artists and my husband is one, too. He does the most incredible paintings, full of busy little people doing the most ridiculous and impossible things. He can be sitting watching TV and suddenly get an idea, so creeps out into his studio and adds a bit of fun to his visual tale.

The latest painting has a dinosaur rescue centre in it,

with families taking them home as pets. Which is how we got our dog, from a rescue centre.

So, that's how I came by the two themes that form the basis for this tale. And I called the dog by our dog's name. Let's face it, I'm sentimental and not ashamed of it.

Neighbours

'Hey! Is this your dog?'

The voice sounded so angry that Mel's heart sank as she turned round. She stared at Ellie's muddy nose, then looked up and blinked in shock. The most gorgeous man she had ever seen was scowling at her as if she had just committed a major crime. Tall, with brown wavy hair, blue eyes and a lean body, he looked out of place in a muddy country field. *Wow!* she thought. *Is he real? Maybe I'm dreaming.*

He poked his face close to hers and snapped, 'I asked if this was your dog.'

No. It wasn't a dream. What could poor Ellie have done to upset him so? 'Er – yes. She is.'

'Then kindly keep her under control in future. That damned animal has dug up my stakes. They'd been carefully surveyed and now they'll have to be put in again.'

'Oh. I'm sorry. I didn't know anyone had moved in here yet.' She held out her hand. 'I'm Mel Gilby.'

He was already turning away. 'James Carling.' He strode off across the grass, which was just turning green again after the first winter rains – where it wasn't muddy.

'Pleased to meet you, too!' Mel returned to her painting. She had a commission for three matching landscapes for a hotel foyer, her biggest so far. It would pay her rates and enable her to live here a little longer without going back to work for someone else.

Maybe it was because she was so engrossed in the paintings that she didn't manage to keep Ellie under control – or maybe it was because Ellie had taken an enormous fancy to James Carling. Five times during the next three days Mel's new neighbour stalked across from his block, with poor old Ellie trotting beside him at the end of a rope, wagging her tail and swiping licks at his hand.

By that time, he was beginning to see the humour of it. Well, his eyes were twinkling.

What was he doing on a country block in Western Australia, anyway? Mel began to weave a fantasy around him, that he was a millionaire hiding from publicity. No, a millionaire wouldn't live in a tumble-down shack.

After a week of winter sunshine, she woke to the sound of a lone kookaburra shrieking with laughter and rain sighing against the windows. She could hear the ocean crashing on the nearby beach. The surfers would be out in force today. She loved to sit and watch them. In fact, she loved everything about living here, even the scrimping and making do.

After breakfast, she realised that Ellie was missing again. 'Oh, no!' It was still early. If she were lucky, she would find her dog before her neighbour did.

She was not lucky.

'I'm sorry, James. I don't know how she got out.'

The sky chose that moment to pour water all over the landscape, and thunder groaned in the distance. Ellie was first to flee to the porch, standing there grinning at them as they dashed through a solid wall of water to join her.

Of course, Mel was so busy avoiding touching him that she had to trip as they arrived at the veranda. *Nice one*, she thought, as she started to fall. *Impress him, why don't you?*

Then he grabbed her and she stopped thinking clearly.

He reached out to touch a stray curl on her forehead and she was lost – mesmerised, paralysed with anticipation. Would he kiss her? Yes. Oh, yes.

His fingers lingered on her hair. His voice was husky. 'I have a thing about auburn curls.'

His lips were cool and moist with raindrops. Passion flared between them. *In capital letters*, Mel thought dazedly, *with neon lights flashing. PASSION!*

When he drew his head back for a breath, she leant against the steel circle of his arms and beamed at him. 'Wow!'

'Wow, indeed! Can I persuade you to stay for a cup of coffee?'

'I'd love to. Here on the veranda?'

'Mmm. It'd be prudent, given Ellie's muddy legs. Sit down. It won't take a minute.'

As the door swung to behind him, Mel fell onto the nearest chair and let out her breath in a long whoosh. By the time he returned with the coffee, she was in control of herself. Well, more or less. A bit less than more, actually.

'So – what do you do for a living?' she asked brightly. She was itching to get hold of a pencil and sketch him.

'I'm a property developer.'

'Oh? Are you going to build a new house here?'

'A tourist complex, actually.'

'What?' The neon lights switched off and she regained full and instant control of her hormones. 'You mean – you're going to put up tourist accommodation? *Here?*'

'Yes.'

'But you'll spoil everything, the peace, the wildlife!' She glared at him. 'You'll *ruin* things!'

He looked surprised. 'But the area is zoned for tourist development.'

'What?'

'They changed the zoning a couple of years ago. It's all perfectly legal.'

No one had told her. She'd been working in the Arab Emirates then, earning good money and sending some home to her brother to pay the rates.

'Oh, I'm sure it's legal! They always say that as they ruin our native bush.' She whistled to Ellie before he could see the tears in her eyes. Half-blinded by them, she stormed home and slammed the door behind her.

When he followed her, she yelled at him to go away, *go – right – away,* and take his damned development with him. When he tried to shout something through the door, she turned the radio on full.

She expressed herself even more forcibly the following morning and evening when he tried again. And kept the radio blasting for several excruciating hours.

After that he stopped coming. And she wasn't disappointed. Well, not much. Well, all right, she was, but she could live with that, couldn't she?

She had a little area at the side of her house with a bird bath for the dry season, and a few bushes of the sort native birds liked. They'd be driven away by earthmovers and building.

She couldn't be driven away, because she couldn't afford to go anywhere else. She'd just have to endure the interruptions and keep her mind on her painting.

During the next two weeks she could not avoid meeting James occasionally at the local store, where Ben Harper sold all the basic necessities and none of the frills of life.

The first time James looked across at her and hesitated, but when Mel turned away, he scowled and left her alone.

At home, she guarded Ellie so well that the dog did not escape again. But she whined and pawed at the door sometimes.

To distract herself, Mel worked furiously on her canvases, not stopping until she couldn't see straight at night. They weren't the peaceful rural scenes she had planned to concentrate on, because she'd sold one or two and it was good to pay the bills.

The first one was a big stormy landscape, then a lush rainforest oozing with water and with flowers cascading everywhere, followed by a scorching panorama of coloured desert that socked you right in the eye.

Day by day she peeped through her window and watched angrily as her neighbour and two helpers surveyed his whole block, setting out stakes here and there.

Tears filled her eyes on the day a portable office was set up on the far side of his old beach shack.

* * *

The following day, just before noon, someone knocked on the door. When Mel opened it without thinking, she found James standing there, with a bloodstained towel wrapped around his hand.

'I'm sorry to disturb you, but I've had an accident and—'

She gestured him inside. 'Let me see.'

'If you'll just ring for a taxi, I'll go to the doctor's and get it stitched up. I haven't had a phone put in yet and the battery's flat on my mobile.' Both batteries. He'd been thinking of *her*, damn her! She was getting between him and his work. Not just her hair, but her firm sun-tanned legs and slumberous green eyes. He drew in a deep breath and concentrated on his hand.

'Let me look at the injury first.' When he started to refuse she said curtly, 'I'm a trained nurse.'

'*You are?*'

'I'm not working as a nurse at the moment.'

'I can see that.'

As they stood by the sink, rinsing off the blood, she was suddenly conscious that she hadn't brushed her hair that morning and was wearing a very old paint-spattered sweatshirt and rather tight shorts with frayed edges.

The cut was deep and jagged. She cleaned it carefully. 'Yes, you do need stitches. I'll drive you down to the doctor's.'

'I can get a taxi. You won't want an untouchable like me in your car.'

'Don't be stupid. You're injured. And anyway, there aren't any taxis round here.'

They drove there in complete silence, sitting as far apart as possible. Which wasn't very far. It was a small car.

Two hours later, she drove him back, by which time his hand was neatly bandaged and he was looking white and weary. The doctor, assuming that Mel was James's girlfriend, had given strict instructions that James was not to drive or do anything with the hand for a couple of weeks.

'Do you – er – have enough food in the house?' she asked as they bumped along the track to his front door.

'No. I'll get something sent in.'

'Ben at the store doesn't deliver. There's nowhere else close enough. I'll make you up a couple of casseroles and get you some shopping in tomorrow when I do mine.'

He was still stiff. 'I can't impose on you like that.'

'You don't have much choice. And anyway, that's how we do things round here, we help our neighbours.'

'Well – thank you, then.'

Ten days later – ten very long days fraught with careful encounters – she drove him to have the stitches removed. He thanked her and sent her some flowers. If he'd brought them in person, she'd have made up the quarrel on the spot, but he didn't. He sent one of his assistants and that annoyed the hell out of her.

Only she was annoyed to find how much she missed him.

'Why did he have to be a land developer?' she asked the moon as she lay awake at night staring through her bedroom window.

The moon only winked at her and continued to smile knowingly.

'Stop grinning!' she yelled. 'I can forget him. I can!'

She couldn't, but at least *he* didn't know that.

A few mornings later, Ellie went missing. Mel searched frantically, but couldn't find her anywhere.

Hearing her calling, James came out of his shack. 'Something wrong?'

'Have you seen Ellie?'

'No. Not since yesterday. Let me help you search.'

They checked all Ellie's old haunts, but there was no sign of her. Then, as they were walking back along a track through the bush, James suddenly stopped. 'Is that something over there?'

It was Ellie, lying unconscious with a bloodied head.

Mel's eyes were so flooded with tears she couldn't see straight. Ellie had been her best friend for ten years.

'She's still breathing,' he said softly, bending down. 'Looks like a dead branch fell on her, the way they do sometimes.' He led the way back, carrying the dog carefully. 'We'll take my car. There's more room for you to hold her.'

Mel sat on the back seat and let him pass her the dog. Within minutes they were at the vet's, by which time Ellie was stirring and trying to raise her head and Mel was in tears again, tears of relief.

When they got back home, leaving Ellie in overnight for observation, Mel turned to James. 'Thank you so much!' She smiled as she added, 'I guess land developers aren't so bad after all.'

He got out of the car, strode round to her side, pulled her out and kissed her, which somehow she couldn't protest about.

When they drew apart, he said fiercely, 'If you'll only let me explain, show you the plans, you'll see that I shan't be spoiling anything – on the contrary! What I'm building is an eco-tourism resort, a small one where we *preserve* the bush, teach people to care about it, run classes in conservation.'

'Oh.' She sagged against him, feeling an utter fool – but a deliriously happy one.

'We won't discuss the details of that just now. I have something else in mind for tonight, and for a lot more nights to come.' He tucked her arm under his and led her inside his shack, locking the door carefully behind them.

'I'm thinking of getting into this interesting development deal – stepfather to a big furry mutt. Now what are you crying for?'

She sniffed. 'Because I'm so happy.' She grabbed his hair and pulled his face towards hers. 'And if you won't stop talking and kiss me again, I'll have to keep kissing you.'

His voice was muffled. 'I surrender.'

They both surrendered to the attraction.

A couple of months later, they also surrendered to Mel's mother, who had been dying to organise a wedding, if only her children would find someone to marry.

Later that year, Mel won a big prize for one of her paintings. 'Full of passion', said one critic. 'Naked emotion', wrote another.

'It's you,' she told James, 'filling my nights—'

'And an occasional day,' he interrupted, smiling sweetly and taking the brush from her hand.

'—with love,' she sighed, as she led the way into the bedroom.

* * *

Outside the door, Ellie sighed and went to sleep. It was time for her dinner, but she knew better than to interrupt when her humans started this game. And they hadn't even left the front door open so that she could go out and see what the strangers had done today.

Lucin the Timid

Introduction

This is another of my fantasy stories – more of a fable than anything else. It's a gentle story about a gentle young man.

It's another tale from my early days of writing in the mid-1990s, and was originally published under my Shannah Jay writing name.

If you're not used to reading fantasy tales, give it a try – come with me to visit another planet and experience another way of living. There are humans living there – probably long-ago colonists from Earth, wouldn't you think?

I'm rather fond of Lucin, who might be timid but is a very kind and talented fellow. And I've always felt as if I could see the scene he painted with the waterfall in it.

Naturally, I've polished this tale again, so it's a bit different from the original version. That one appeared once in an anthology of fantasy tales.

Lucin the Timid

1

Lucin frowned as he inspected the pieces of work: wobbly drawings, smudged paintings, poor choice of subject matter. These three apprentices were not gifted. Perhaps he ought to scold them? He frowned and tried to get angry, but it was not in his soul to speak harsh words to anyone.

The previous year, just as he was finishing his apprenticeship, Lucin's family had been murdered by raiders, and he'd felt lost and afraid ever since. He knew that behind his back people called him Lucin the Timid: and to his shame, he knew they were right.

He was only just out of his own apprenticeship, for his talent at painting had made a master painter take him at a younger age than usual, and he was short of money as well as confidence. People who didn't know him treated him as a lad, because he still looked so young. Felt it, too.

One day he hoped to become a master painter himself. For now, he was a trained and competent painter, selling a few paintings here and there, doing the work he loved –

well, all except for training these children whose parents paid him fees for the privilege.

That night he sat and worried over his meagre supper. He'd have to tell Heller Dyas that the new system for choosing apprentices didn't work, and that he, Lucin, could no longer teach children with no talent, however large the fees. The older craft masters were pretending things were all right, but Lucin couldn't lie about painting. Never! Even if he died for it.

The mere thought of confronting the man who controlled everything in Setherak town made him tremble. Heller had brought peace to the district – well, peace for those who did as he told them, anyway – but he was terrifying when angry. And to make matters worse, Lucin couldn't refund these young apprentices' fees because he had spent nearly all the money on new paints, wonderful expensive pigments, brought from Tenebrak by Leeto the trader.

The next morning Lucin sent the apprentices home and went on leaden feet to see Heller, taking his own best painting. It showed the wildwoods that surrounded Setherak, with foliage rioting heedlessly where it would, the shy flowers of the shaded undergrowth peeping out here and there. Small creatures were creeping and flying through it, and there was a pool at the one side, fed by a stream that cascaded like windblown silk over a small rock face. Lucin had dreamt of this place so often, it seemed real to him.

Maybe, just maybe, Dyas would buy the painting for enough to refund the fees to the parents. It was his only hope. If Dyas refused, Lucin dared not think what might happen.

When his turn came to speak, he stepped forward with his timid shambling walk that made folk laugh. He pretended not to hear them. He knew he walked comically, but he felt as if every step might lead him into danger and he could not do other than tread carefully. He spoke his plea haltingly, losing himself in a tangle of half-sentences.

Heller Dyas looked down at him from the great carved chair. 'You're a good painter, Lucin,' he said, 'but you're a fool. If you beat those children, they'll make adequate painters in time.'

'No, sir. Beating will change nothing. They have no talent at all.'

'Can you pay back the fees, then?'

'No, sir, I can't. I – I spent the money on new pigments and brushes.'

Heller sighed. 'You can't take people's money and refuse to do as you've promised.' For him, this was a gentle rebuke.

Lucin started to unwrap the painting. 'I was hoping—' A corner caught and he stopped speaking to ease the cloth gently off it. The fine carved frame was done by the great Hannaver, the best wood carver Setherak had ever known, but the raiders had killed her all the same. She had been a friend of his family and the frame was the most precious thing he owned. He wished desperately that he could keep it.

When the painting was revealed, Heller said abruptly, 'Bring it over here.' He stared at it for a long time. 'Did you do this?'

'Yes, sir. It's my best piece. I – I thought you might like to buy it and – and then I could pay back the fees. The frame's a Hannaver.'

'I can see that!'

'Hannaver gave it to me herself.' Lucin's eyes filled with tears as he remembered her words to the ardent lad he had been then. 'She said one day I must do a painting worthy of it. And – and I think I have done that with this one, sir.'

'I'll buy it.' Heller named a sum.

Lucin shook his head. 'I'm afraid that's not enough.'

Colour tinged Heller's cheeks. 'I never bargain. Take it or leave it.'

'It's not enough.' He wrapped up the painting and left, feeling Heller's glare scorching his shoulder blades as he tiptoed out. Every minute he expected guards to come after him and take the painting by force. His hands trembled as he clutched it to his side.

When he got home, he knew he couldn't stay here in Setherak any longer. Heller Dyas was angry with him, he couldn't pay back his debts, and so he wouldn't be able to become a master painter.

He filled his travel pack with pigments, brushes and rolled canvases. As an afterthought, he stuffed in a few clothes and some nut meal. Then he took his best blanket and wrapped it around the painting.

Tears were running down his cheeks as he left and when a neighbour spoke to him, he just shook his head blindly and walked on.

2

Three hours' walk out of Setherak town, Lucin left the deeply rutted main road, hoping to avoid pursuit, and took a side track barely wide enough for a small cart. When it forked in two, he dithered for a moment, then took the path which looked as if no one had set foot on it for years.

Eventually his hunger would no longer be denied, so he stopped and listened for pursuit. Nothing. He'd just rest for a short time. He wasn't used to walking so far.

He set the painting down carefully, slipped off the travel pack and stretched his weary shoulders. You could always find food in the wildwoods, so he picked some fruit and nuts, then sat hidden beneath the overhanging branches of a tree to eat. There were no dangerous animals to fear round here, but there were occasional raiders still. And poisonous plants.

He looked around him nervously on the thought. No plant was as dangerous as the redrot bush, for it caused a lethal fever which still broke out sometimes in the newer settlements. Every spring, the settlers sought out and destroyed the plants, and every year fewer of the horrible things grew. But the pretty red petals which were the most poisonous part of all could be blown anywhere by the wind so you could never be quite sure you were safe. Those touched by them died within hours. And anyone touching the sweat of the sufferers died, too, so virulent was the fever. There was no cure.

Fear soon made him move on. Not once did he see a sign that anyone else had passed this way recently, so he began to feel more hopeful. He wasn't sure what he was going to do with himself, but the first thing was to get away. He could think about his future later.

Then he came to a faded sign and stopped in shock. *REDROT FEVER* it said in misshapen letters. *DANGER. KEEP OUT.* Should he risk going on? No, better turn back.

Suddenly there was a crashing noise in the undergrowth to one side. Panic filled him. There were sounds behind him, as well as to the side, voices calling out, 'What's that? Did you hear something?' It must be Heller's men pursuing him. Heller did not like to be refused.

Suddenly a deleff burst out of the undergrowth to his right, towering over him, looking like a giant cousin of the lizards which lived in the eaves of houses, but with longer legs. These great creatures usually drew the traders' huge wagons from village to village, though there hadn't been many traders around since the Discord Wars began.

The voices were getting closer. The deleff bent its head and nudged him so hard it pushed him into the undergrowth at the side of the track. Two more nudges sent him tumbling into a clump of shiverleaf bushes. He looked round for his painting, saw that it had fallen softly enough and dragged it under the bushes with him.

To his astonishment, the deleff turned and trampled off towards his pursuers. What was it doing? He peered out through the leaves, watching in puzzlement.

Back along the track, someone called, 'A deleff!'

'Be careful! It looks angry.'

Some more trampling sounds, then, 'It won't let us pass.'

Silence, then, 'Well, the painter can't have come this way, then, can he?'

'What shall we do?'

'Go and look down that other track.'

Footsteps faded into the distance and Lucin heard the deleff returning. He must have strayed onto its territory. He turned, trembling, to face it and closed his eyes. If it attacked him, he didn't want to see it coming.

But nothing happened. After a few moments, he opened his eyes again and stared at it.

Traders said that deleff were very intelligent, as intelligent as people, though most folk laughed at that idea. The look in this one's eyes seemed to Lucin to be that of a thinking creature. The fear churning within him started to fade a little. Perhaps it wasn't going to kill him. But what did it want? Why had it not gone on its way after it saved him?

The head bent towards him and suddenly he had a desire to lay his hands on it. The grey skin was covered with myriad small scales giving it an iridescent look. However would you paint that?

As soon as his hands touched it, relief washed through him. *No fear*, something said inside his mind. *No danger*.

Pictures began to form in his head. He saw himself carrying the painting, tramping through the wildwoods behind the deleff – digging a grave, carving a headpost, painting a huge tableau on a wall of pure white plaster. Ah, how wonderful that would be!

The pictures faded, the deleff shook Lucin's hands off gently and turned, looking back at him as if to ask him to follow it.

No longer feeling afraid, he retrieved the painting and walked after the great creature.

3

Just as sunset was colouring the sky, they came to a small settlement near a tumbling stream. The deleff stopped, pushed him forward, then trampled away. Another faded wooden plank said DANGER. REDROT FEVER. There was no sign of life, not a whisper of sound apart from the breeze among the trees and a silverbird singing in the distance.

Lucin called out, his voice fluting with nervousness, 'Is – is anyone here?'

No reply.

He crept towards the nearest house. Inside, curled close to one another, were two skeletons. The creeping insects had long since stripped them clean of flesh, and to the artist, the bones had a beauty of their own, gleaming palest pink in the sunset light.

'Your pardon,' he said aloud. 'I'm seeking shelter for the night.'

The house felt warm and welcoming, as if it had been waiting for him. The owners had died holding hands. A man and a woman. They must have loved one another very much. 'Tomorrow I'll bury you together,' he whispered. 'You shall lie peacefully and I'll carve you a little headpost.' He had some small skill as a carver, not as good as Hannaver's, but enough to beautify a few objects.

Then he froze as he realised that the deleff had already shown him digging a grave. 'Ah!' he said softly. 'This was meant to be, then.'

He went to explore the rest of the house. Beyond the big communal room were three bedrooms, but no more skeletons. The bedcovers were thick with dust, and webs of shadow crawlers patterned the ceiling. He would sketch the webs before he cleaned the place up. Some of them were very pretty.

Already he knew that he was going to stay here. Even if raiders found the tiny settlement, they would flee from that sign. And if he died of redrot fever, then so be it. But somehow – somehow, he didn't feel he would.

He slept well, better than he had slept for a good many years.

In the morning he found a well whose water was cool and sweet. He made himself porridge with the nut meal he had brought, sweetening it with the glowberries that grew in abundance near the well. It was a long time since he had felt so peaceful. Not since before his family died.

A little path beckoned to him towards a small burial place, where two wooden stakes marked graves. The first one said: JENNA, INFANT DAUGHTER OF SEM AND KATTYSHA, AGED TWO DAYS. Lucin bowed his head for a moment, and wished the child's soul well. The second one said: MERRIK, SON OF SEM AND KATTYSHA, AGED EIGHT YEARS. The words had been hurriedly painted. He could guess why. The parents must already have contracted redrot fever themselves.

He dug a hole next to these graves and laid the two adult skeletons in it, wrapped in a blanket, arranging them as he had found them, so that one seemed to be holding the other's hand.

Finding a well-seasoned plank, he carved SEM AND KATTYSHA. He was pleased with the straight clean cuts of the letters and the small flower he carved in one corner, a redrot flower like the one which must have killed them.

By then it was late afternoon and he was exhausted, so he went back inside the house to rest. In a drawer he found papers which told him the settlement had been called Yilgarrak and that there had once been thirty people living there.

On the third day, he followed the stream for a little way, crying out in sheer delight to find a pool and waterfall, identical to those in his painting. How often had he dreamt of this place! But the reality was much more beautiful, and the spray's caress was healing, somehow. He cast aside his dusty clothes and bathed in the sun-warmed water, sighing in pleasure.

Nowhere did he find any redrot bushes, though he searched carefully. While returning to the house, he was lucky enough to find an old vegetable patch gone wild. Self-set plants were growing in tangles. Plenty to eat here.

In an overgrown field, ripe grain had self set and was growing in patches. There would be enough here to feed him and provide seeds for the next harvest. His parents had been farmers. He remembered clearly what to do. He only hoped he would be strong enough to do it all before the winter rains came.

There were other houses nearby, together with signs that people had fled in haste, no doubt to escape the fever flowers.

In the largest barn stood an abandoned traders' wagon, its woodwork finely carved and the square canvas hood neatly rolled. He hoped its owners hadn't died here, but he feared they must have. Traders didn't just abandon their wagons. They lived on the road from adulthood, once a deleff came out of the woods and chose to draw their wagon. If no deleff came, they settled in a town or claimed new land to farm.

He thought long and hard, then decided to stay here in Yilgarrak. It seemed the right thing to do. And he had plenty of colours, so he could still do some painting. He didn't think he could live if he couldn't paint and draw.

4

Two years passed. Heller Dyas would have walked past Lucin in the street without recognising the tall, well-muscled young man with the tranquil face. Part of the field at Yilgarrak now grew neat rows of grain. Part of the vegetable patch was tidy and productive. And the early blisters had long since turned into calluses on Lucin's hands.

There were paintings in the house on the new canvases he had made from the sheets he liked to believe Kattysha had woven herself. Good strong fibres, they were, and made excellent canvases.

Then, one evening, a deleff crashed out of the wildwoods with a girl clinging to its back, Lucin ran forward to see what was wrong. The deleff came to a halt and the girl slid off its back in a faint.

He exclaimed in shock at the blue bruise on her temple, the dried blood on her arm, forgetting about the deleff as he carried her into the house and tended her wounds. He blushed as he undressed her body and found her a woman, not a girl, a woman sorely beaten.

She whimpered in pain or maybe fear, but didn't regain full consciousness.

That night he slept on the floor beside her, with a lamp turned low on the chest, in case she woke and was afraid.

At dawn he tiptoed outside to perform his morning ablutions. When he returned, she was sitting and staring round, fear in every line of her body.

'There's no need to be afraid. There's only me here. My name's Lucin.'

'Where am I?'

'A small settlement called Yilgarrak, a long way from anywhere. Can you tell me how you were hurt?'

'Raiders. They,' she gulped back tears, 'came and burnt our farm, killed my father and brothers.' She was sobbing now. 'We fought, but they were stronger.'

'Shh, now.' He patted her hand gently. 'You're quite safe here.'

She shook her head, her expression bleak. 'Nowhere is safe. Especially in the wildwoods settlements. Don't you know what's happening? The raiders have been driven from Tenebrak, every last one of them routed out. But they're stopping at the small places now, looting and killing people.'

He comforted her awkwardly, found that her name was Mishalla and listened to her tale all over again.

When the tears had stopped, he brought her food and coaxed her into eating some.

Within a couple of days, she was helping him around the place, seeming to find solace in hard work.

'Why do you live here alone?' she asked.

'I came here one day, tired of living in Setherak, and felt at home here.'

When he got to know her better, he took her outside to the barn and showed her his paintings.

'Oh!'

Did she not like them? 'Some are better than others—' he began to apologise.

She turned to him. 'They're beautiful. All of them. The most beautiful paintings I've ever seen.'

He blushed.

'You have a great talent, Lucin. Why do you hide it here in the wildwoods?'

'Because I offended Heller Dyas so I daren't return to Setherak.'

'Ah.' Everyone in the land knew of Dyas and the firm hand he had laid upon that town.

A few days later, she said, 'We need to discuss the future, Lucin.'

'I was hoping you might stay here with me.' He spoke humbly and hesitantly, because what had a fellow like him to offer to a pretty young woman like her?

'No. I can't stay here.'

He stared down at his hands. 'No, why should you?'

A small firm hand covered his. 'Not because I don't like you, Lucin – I do – but because I'd go mad from loneliness out here in the middle of nowhere. And from fear that raiders might attack us. I don't think I could face that again.' She kept hold of his hand. 'I don't have a great talent like yours. I need people around me – I want to talk, sing, gossip.'

'Oh.'

'We needn't go to Setherak; we could try Tenebrak. I'm sure you could continue painting there.'

'I'd not make enough to live off. I'm just a – competent painter.'

She stared at him in surprise. 'Lucin, you are a *great* painter. I've never seen such beautiful work.'

When he shook his head in disbelief, she let the matter

drop. He was such an unassuming fellow. He didn't realise how strong and handsome he was, either – handsome enough to turn a young woman's head. But impractical.

He needed someone to manage his life for him, so that he could paint. She had already decided to be that someone. But not here, not hidden away in the wildwoods. It was a dreadful waste to hide a talent like his. It should beautify the world.

The next day, she said to him, 'I shan't change my mind. I want to leave here, Lucin.'

He sighed. 'Where do you wish to go, Mishalla?'

'Where I said, Tenebrak.'

'It's a long way.'

'Yes, but the traders told me that in Tenebrak people are building a temple and a school. Lucin, I'm good with children. I thought – I hoped I could be of use in the school. I've wanted to go there for a while now. Even before the raiders came.'

'Oh.'

'Why don't you come with me? Just try it.'

'Oh, no. I daren't let Heller Dyas know I'm still alive.'

She looked at him fondly. Like a burnt child, he needed coaxing back to the fire. 'Will you take me there, then, Lucin? I should be afraid to travel alone.'

'Of course I will.' He wouldn't dare stay, though, and without her, Yilgarrak would be very lonely.

While they were still debating what to take with them, two deleff walked out of the forest, as deleff sometimes do, saluted them with nods of their heads, then moved across to the big barn. They walked into the padded harness bars of the old traders' wagon and pulled it outside, then began to stamp up and down as if to say, 'Let's go!'

Mishalla laughed aloud. 'This was meant to be, Lucin. Now we can take all your paintings with us and sell them in Tenebrak.'

But she had to plead with him before he would agree to that.

5

Many days of travelling brought them out of the wildwoods and onto a broad track. They stopped on the hilltop to look down at what could only be Tenebrak. It was a big town and they were building something on a hill.

Lucin became very tense and nervous. 'I – I think I'd better leave you here. You can sell the paintings, if you like. You'll need some money.'

The deleff trumpeted loudly.

Mishalla took a firm hold of his arm. 'Please, Lucin, stay with me.'

The deleff speeded up suddenly, and all Lucin and Mishalla could do was hold tight as the wagon rattled down the hill. They didn't slow down until they entered the town itself, with its wide streets lined with huge trees. People out walking together in the evening sunshine waved at the wagon. It was a scene of peace and beauty.

'Does it look like somewhere ruled by a tyrant?' Mishalla asked, still holding Lucin's arm.

'No.'

'Try living here for a while. Just for me. Please, Lucin.'

'Well, perhaps I—'

In the market square stood an inn, a bustling prosperous place. The deleff stopped in front of it without being told.

A small man came out to greet them. 'I'm Evril, keeper of this inn. Welcome to Tenebrak, my friends. Do you have goods to trade?'

Mishalla spoke for the two of them. 'We're not traders. These kind deleff knew we needed to carry our things to Tenebrak, so they came and pulled this abandoned wagon for us. We'd like some food and a room for the night. And where should we leave our wagon, please?'

But the deleff had already pulled it to the side of the square. They backed out of the harness, nodded to Mishalla and Lucin and left, making their way up the hill that led out of the town.

Mishalla nudged Lucin. 'You'll have to stay here now. You'd never find your way back to Yilgarrak on your own.'

And he was glad of that – as well as afraid.

The innkeeper cleared his throat. 'If you and your husband would come inside, my wife will find you a room.'

'He thinks we're married,' Lucin hissed at her as they followed him.

She took a deep breath. *He* would never dare ask, so she must do it. 'Then we'd better get married, so as not to make a liar of him.'

'But I – we—' He faltered to a halt and looked at her, his heart in his eyes.

'Don't you want to marry me?' She smiled and took his hand.

'I'm not good enough for you.'

'*I* think you are. I love you so much, Lucin.'

He couldn't say a word, could only stare at her with

longing written all over his face, so she left it at that.

As they sat over a delicious meal, Evril's wife, Loral, came across to find out about them.

Mishalla gave the information willingly. 'Lucin's an artist and we're looking for somewhere to settle. And we'd like to cry aloud our marriage in the old way.'

Loral beamed at them. 'Well, with a handsome man like that, you'll want to make sure all the girls know he's taken.'

Lucin gaped at her in astonishment. Handsome! He wasn't handsome!

But he was tempted to stay, sorely tempted.

Yet when they went to their room, he told Mishalla, 'You need to think about it more carefully. I'm sure a pretty woman like you could find yourself a better husband than me.'

'I don't want any other husband.'

'I'm not good enough for you.'

'Go to sleep, Lucin. We'll discuss it in the morning.' She blew out the candle, for modesty's sake. His modesty, not hers. He was indeed handsome and she wanted him with her in bed as husband and wife. But since she had done the asking, she felt she should let him take the next step.

6

The following day, the two of them set out to explore the town. Up on top of the ridge, they found some people earnestly discussing where to site the main entrance doors of the new temple they were to build, arguing fiercely about it. The building's position was marked out, but the doors and windows were still to be decided, it seemed.

Lucin listened and looked around, admiring the shape and situation of the building. Eventually, he could hold back no longer. 'No.' He forgot to be afraid in his urgent need to show them their errors of design. Taking the plans from a plump man's hands, he pointed. 'You should place the door here, not over there.'

'Now, look—'

A silver-haired man came up to join them. As the others fell back before him, he smiled encouragingly at the young man. 'Tell us why you say this, my friend.'

Lucin explained about the way sunlight would fall through the door to paint a pathway inside. And there must be windows at each side of the door. 'You've got a good design shape, but some of the details need refining.' Then he realised how presumptuous he had been to interfere and stopped mid-sentence. 'I – I'm sorry. I didn't mean to presume.'

Mishalla came and linked her arm in his. 'My man is an artist. He has an eye for such details,' she said proudly.

As Lucin waited for the older man to speak, he studied his face. What a fine profile the fellow had. His fingers itched to find a piece of charcoal.

'The artist's right,' the silver-haired man told the others. 'Put the door there, where he says. And make more windows.'

'But Deverith—'

'Do as he says. And introduce him to Balas. He was saying the other day that he needs help with the details of the building.'

When they got back to the inn, Lucin couldn't find the strength to resist Mishalla's pleadings any longer. With an inarticulate cry, he gathered her into his arms and fumbled a kiss onto her lips. 'I don't deserve you, Mishalla, but I will stay, I long to stay. And I'll do my very best to make you happy.'

That evening, Loral led them out into the market square and they cried out their marriage in the old way. Deverith came to watch them, smiling and nodding approval. And beside him, arm linked in his, was a woman far gone with child. She looked so radiant that Lucin wanted desperately to paint her.

Mishalla tugged at his arm and teased, 'Where have you gone to?'

Lucin blushed. 'Sorry. I just had an idea for a painting.' His eyes strayed to the woman again.

Mishalla laughed. 'Oh, Lucin, what am I going to do with you?' Then she pulled his head down and gave him a kiss that made the colour come rushing to his face again. Especially when the onlookers all clapped and cheered.

'Now the marriage dance!' ordered Loral.

Lucin took a deep breath and stepped forward to twirl Mishalla round once. Then, one by one, he twirled all the women nearby round, after which he and Mishalla led the line of people in a dance through the town.

Mishalla looked so beautiful and he felt so proud to be her husband that he didn't stumble once.

His wife watched him with great pride, seeing his new confidence. He no longer shuffled awkwardly when he walked, but didn't realise that, any more than he realised how great his talent was.

Her man would paint pictures that filled people's lives with joy and beauty. She knew it.

7

As the years passed, Lucin's fear of Heller Dyas lessened a little, but it still crouched there at the back of his mind and gnawed at him sometimes in the darkness of the night.

Thanks to Mishalla, he prospered as a painter. Indeed, he had so many commissions it was hard to make time for the great tableau he was painting upon the temple's inner wall, the tableau for which he would accept no payment. It was his gift to his Brother the God for bringing him Mishalla, who had made his life so happy and given him three wonderful children.

Karialla, Elder Sister of the temple, had the wall plastered exactly as Lucin specified, and bought him all the pigments a man could ever need.

He had not yet done his portrait of the Illustrious Deverith, because he had decided that it would be presumptuous to ask such a hero to sit for a painting. Deverith and his wife Karialla had led Tenebrak out of violence and driven away the last of the raiders.

Lucin didn't even tell Mishalla of this longing. He tried to draw Deverith from memory several times, but somehow it would never come out right. Deverith had such a special face. Lucin needed time to get that right, not only time, but Deverith himself sitting quietly in front of him, with his wise, luminous old eyes.

8

Five years after his arrival in Tenebrak, Lucin was horrified to hear that Heller Dyas was to come to the opening ceremony of the new temple hall. Its glowing tableau was finished now, showing a scene in the wildwoods and in it, standing to one side, bathed in light, the tiny figures of Deverith and Karialla, who had led the people of Tenebrak out of Discord. He had no trouble getting them right for the tableau, because you didn't need the same detail as you would in a portrait.

As the big day approached, Lucin grew thin with worry. He even contemplated leaving Tenebrak, so that his wife and children would be safe. *No, I shall not flee again*, he decided in the end. *I was a coward once and the deleff saved me. I cannot expect that sort of miracle to happen twice. I must face things myself this time.*

When Heller Dyas walked up to the tableau, moving to and fro, studying the details of the scene, he exclaimed, 'Lucin the Timid! No one else could have painted that.'

'Yes.' Karialla smiled and beckoned Lucin forward. 'But why do you call him timid? His apprentices wouldn't agree with you. They run to do his bidding.'

Heller glared at the artist. 'Where in the name of all the dark demons did you get to when you left Setherak?'

For Mishalla's sake, Lucin held his ground. And as he stood there, it was as if bells rang out great peals of joy inside his head. For the last traces of the fear that had lurked within him for so long vanished completely. He straightened his shoulders. He had never liked being called Lucin the Timid, but now – what a thing for his children to hear! No one should ever call him that again.

'Good day to you, Heller Dyas.' He smiled calmly. 'Do you like my painting?'

Heller's frown faded. 'Of course I do. I like all your

paintings. You're the best painter I've ever met. When are you going to come back to Setherak?'

'Never, I'm afraid. Tenebrak is our home now.'

'You – er – you wouldn't still have that painting, would you? The one you tried to sell to me once. I've never forgotten it, never stopped wanting it.'

'I do still have it, actually.'

'I'll give you your price for it, if it's still for sale.'

'It'll cost you twice what I asked before. And it won't have the Hannaver frame.' Lucin wanted to use that for Deverith's portrait.

Heller cackled with laughter and dug him in the ribs. 'Very well, you rogue. I see you've learnt to know your own worth better.'

He turned to Karialla. 'Do you know, I once refused to buy that painting at his price, and as a result he left Setherak. I even sent men after him to tell him I'd changed my mind, but they couldn't find him.'

He turned back to Lucin. 'So. You shall have your money and I'll even admit I was wrong to force you to take those apprentices. A person needs real talent to paint properly.' He scowled. 'We don't have good painters in Setherak at the moment. I'm hoping to find a teacher to take back with me.'

Lucin nodded. 'Very wise. And there is a young man here who might do. I've trained him myself.'

They chatted for a while, then Heller said, 'You know, I've dreamt about that scene in your painting ever since you left.'

'Come for the painting when you're ready. I live just behind the market square.' Lucin watched as Karialla and the Illustrious Deverith walked on with their guest. Proudly he offered Mishalla his arm and led her home, head held high.

'It's such a beautiful picture,' she mourned. 'Your very best. Do you really want to sell it, love?'

'Yes. But it's not my best. My best is yet to come. From now on, I shall dare to paint anything I wish. And I shall start with the Illustrious Deverith. He has the noblest head I ever saw. I want to do a detailed portrait of him. I'm sure he won't refuse to sit for me.'

She smiled. 'Have you only just realised that?'

He shrugged. 'Yes.'

'About time, dear Lucin.'

She Who Dares Wins

Introduction

Sometimes when you accept a dare, it can be a mistake and lead you into trouble. But just occasionally taking a chance can have a delightful outcome.

I'm not one to accept dares. Nor is my heroine Sally. But when an annoying workmate caught her at a weak moment, she'd accepted before she could stop herself. And she wasn't going to chicken out.

I was feeling in a light-hearted mood when I got the basic idea for this story. I grinned as I wrote it.

It still made me smile as I reread and polished it.

I hope you enjoy it too.

(P.S. In case you're interested, this story went from 1,800 to 3,200 words as I polished it.)

She Who Dares Wins

On their day off, Sally and her friend Madge drove over to Five Mile Beach and strolled along the shore, passing cafés and shops, enjoying the lively crowds and the joy of just doing nothing after an extremely busy week at the hotel where they worked.

Sally had been run ragged at work the previous day and had said at the morning tea break that she wanted to do something different, something challenging.

She'd been called on that in front of everyone. 'Bet you fifty dollars you daren't do it,' Tim Jones ended, sniggering.

She wasn't putting up with any more of that guy's sneers. Just because she'd gained a promotion he'd thought he'd be getting, he'd started making snide remarks about her capacity to do things. Before she could stop herself, she'd accepted the challenge and Madge had offered to be her witness to prove she'd done it.

'I'll believe it when I see it,' Tim said. 'My fifty dollars is quite safe.'

Today Sally looked hard for some way to carry out the dare. But she'd not found anyone suitable at the beach. She was getting tired, had to be back at work soon.

Then she caught her friend looking at her in a way that said even Madge had expected Sally to back out of this dare.

So she raised her chin defiantly and moved on. Just another half hour, she told herself. There had to be someone suitable out today.

Unfortunately, there was a lack of guys her own age at the beach today. There were lots of teenagers, a few older men, some family men, but no guys who looked both single and eligible.

The minutes ticked by. Twenty minutes passed. Enough was enough. At least she'd tried.

She stopped walking and turned to Madge but even as she opened her mouth to say she'd changed her mind, she saw a guy sitting in the café. He was by himself in a corner, staring out across the ocean, lost in thought.

He was, as the dare had specified, reasonably good-looking. Very good-looking, actually. He was tall, blonde and handsome, though rather formally dressed for a beach outing, with tailored slacks and a short-sleeved shirt with neatly knotted tie.

Sally preferred dark-haired men, but attractive guys were pretty rare on the ground any time, so this was no time to quibble about hair colour. She stopped for a second look at this one. Yep, definitely a suitable candidate.

By now her heart was thumping in her chest. Swallowing

hard, she turned to Madge. 'I'll have that one! He's definitely a hunk.'

'Good choice. You go for it, girl. You can do it.'

Firmly refusing to let her feet run in the opposite direction, Sally sauntered past the café again, pretending to admire the view. The hunk didn't even notice her.

Taking a deep breath she went right up to him and gave him the eye. 'Nice day, isn't it?'

He nodded and said in a cool, I'm-not-interested voice, 'Lovely.'

He was already turning away, so she blurted it out before she lost her courage. 'Would you like to have dinner with me tonight?'

His mouth dropped open in shock and he goggled at her, as if he couldn't believe what he'd heard.

From a few paces away, Madge raised one eyebrow in a challenging way, which meant 'not enough'.

Setting her hands on her hips, more to prevent them from shaking than to show off her figure, Sally demanded, 'Well, do you or don't you want to have dinner?'

He gulped audibly. 'Um. Well. No, not just at this moment. But thank you for – um, asking.'

Madge applauded silently.

'See you round, then.' Sally strolled on past, trying to look cool, but feeling herself blushing furiously.

When they were round the corner, she stopped and clutched Madge's arm, letting out a long shuddering sigh. 'I'm *never* accepting a dare again as long as I live! *Never!*'

Madge shrugged. 'You'll win the bet, though.' She giggled. 'I didn't think you'd go through with it, actually.'

'Neither did I. It was the thought of Tim Jones that did it in the end. I'm not having that sleaze bucket winning fifty dollars off me.'

'I don't know what you're making such a fuss about. It wasn't all that hard, was it? After all, women ask men for dates all the time these days.'

'I don't ask men for dates. I've never done it before in my whole life. And if that means I'm old-fashioned and unliberated, I don't care. When he said no I felt like crawling under the nearest table.'

'Pity he said no, actually. He was rather gorgeous.'

'I'd never have kept the date! The bet didn't say anything about that.'

Madge nudged her and chuckled. 'You won, though. You asked a hunk to go out with you. Tim will never dare to call you Miss Tight-Knickers again.'

As they moved on Sally thought of the man and sighed regretfully. Maybe she would have kept the date if he'd said yes. Well, she would have done if he'd looked at all interested. She wouldn't have minded a close encounter with a man as gorgeous as that.

The following day she went back to work. That was the trouble with living and working in a holiday resort. There were beaches all around, beckoning, but she had to pin her hair up, dress in dark office clothes and make sure the tourists had a good time. Oh, well, working as assistant manager in a resort hotel wasn't too bad a way to earn a crust.

The first thing she did was march up to Tim Jones and hold out her hand. 'You owe me fifty dollars.'

'Yeah, Madge has already confirmed that you did it.

So now you know what us guys feel like when we ask chicks out.'

'Nothing to it,' she said airily.

Scowling, he paid up then slouched back to the front desk.

'Don't forget your promise not to call me by *that name* again if I won.'

'Yeah, yeah.'

She'd never have asked someone like Tim to go out with her, that was for sure.

That afternoon was the busiest they'd ever experienced since she got promoted. They filled all the rooms and she had to turn several people away. Why on earth didn't they phone and make bookings first? The town was always packed out for the food and wine festival over the holiday weekend. There wasn't a hotel room to be had for love nor money.

About six o'clock *he* came into The Bensham. The one she'd propositioned. She felt like diving for cover, but she was the only one behind the reception desk so she straightened up and greeted him coolly, praying he wouldn't recognise her with her hair pinned up.

'My name's Jonathon Ryder. I have a room booked.'

As she searched the computer listings she breathed a sigh of relief that he hadn't recognised her. His name wasn't there. 'Are you sure you booked, sir?'

'Very sure.' He fumbled in his briefcase and waved a piece of paper at her.

She took if from him and checked. Oh, no! He did have a confirmed booking, but all their rooms were taken. She studied the initials on the letter. Tim Jones again. Not the first time he'd messed things up, either.

She stole a glance sideways and saw the customer frowning at her, as if he was trying to place where he'd seen her. Please, no! The last thing she needed was for him to recognise her! 'I'm so sorry, sir. I'm afraid there's been a mix-up. Perhaps you'd like to have a coffee while I sort something out?'

'What I'd like is to have a shower and change,' he growled.

She handed him a complimentary coffee voucher and said in her most soothing voice, 'I promise you I'll deal with this as quickly as I can.'

She watched him walk across the foyer. He still looked pretty good, even with that frown on his face. Then she clicked her tongue in exasperation at herself. He was a customer, for heaven's sake. *Out of bounds.*

She went to see the manager. Mr Jenson just about tore his hair out. 'What the hell do we do now? Why does this always happen to me? Haven't I got enough to worry about?'

He always panicked. And his glass-walled office was in full view of the foyer.

She glanced across to the coffee shop and sure enough, Mr Ryder was watching them. When she looked back at her boss, she began to feel worried about his colour. He hadn't looked well for a while now. 'Look, we don't have a guest room to spare, but we do have a couple of empty rooms in the staff quarters. Mr Ryder won't find anything else in town this late, that's for sure. We won't charge him for the room, of course.'

He gave a weary sigh. 'Good idea. See if he'll wear it.'

She walked across to the coffee shop, very conscious of

the cool blue eyes focused on her, and sat down opposite Mr Ryder. 'I've got a solution of sorts, sir. I'm afraid all our guest rooms are booked and claimed, but we do have a staff bedroom we could let you have. It'll be free of charge, naturally, because it's our mistake. It's very comfortable, though it does have a shared bathroom.'

'Very well.' He looked at her and frowned. 'Where do I know you from?'

She'd rather not remind him. 'I don't think we've met before, sir.'

He stared at her, eyes narrowed. 'Then why do you seem so familiar?'

'I couldn't say, sir.'

His watch chimed at him as if reminding him of an appointment.

'Oh, very well, I'll take the damned room.'

By the time her shift was over Sally was exhausted, so she dived straight into bed. In the morning she was on late shift again, so took her time about getting up, then went to the shared staff bathroom for this wing.

He was just coming out of it. He stopped and looked at her with her hair spread over her shoulders. Smiled knowingly. 'I remember now. We met in a café a couple of days ago.'

She couldn't prevent the blush. 'I was off duty at the time.'

'You certainly were.' He chuckled.

She stared at him as coldly as she could, which was not easy when he looked so good. Only you did not mess with hotel guests. Prime rule of the company.

'If you've finished with the bathroom, sir?'

'Yes.' But he didn't move out of the doorway. 'Are you free to have lunch?'

She almost said yes, then shook her head. He was smooth. And rather nice. But so was having a job. 'I'm sorry, sir. I already have an engagement.'

That morning another guest turned up with a confirmed booking and again, there wasn't a room. Mr Jenson tore a strip off Tim Jones, who told him where to stuff his rotten job and quit on the spot.

Mr Jenson clutched his chest and crumpled to the floor.

Was he having a heart attack? Sally leapt into action, using her first-aid knowledge to make him as comfortable as possible. It seemed a long time till the ambulance got there and the paramedics took over.

She watched them cart him off to hospital then went back behind the counter till her shift ended. Afterwards she then went into Mr Jenson's office where she found everything in chaos.

An hour later Madge tapped on the door and pointed out that, 'Now Tim's left there's only me behind the counter. Can you come and help out? We have a queue of guests trying to check out.'

Sally found being in complete charge of the hotel took up every minute of the evening as well as the day. She completely forgot Jonathon Ryder as she tried to do the work of three people.

She stopped a fight in the bar by sheer force of personality, quietened a group of New Zealanders who were celebrating a huge Lotto win and soothed an old lady who had lost her handbag, as well as drawing up emergency rosters for the following day.

And of course she emailed head office to send a replacement for the manager and Tim Jones, as a matter of urgency.

After working for fourteen hours straight, she waited impatiently for the night staff to take over.

It was midnight before she finished handing over.

As she turned to leave, she noticed *him* sitting in the coffee shop watching her. She walked briskly towards the staff lift and to her annoyance, Jonathon Ryder fell in beside her.

'I hope you had a nice day, sir?' she asked in her cool, professional voice. 'We should be able to get you into a guest suite later tomorrow.'

He smiled, a lazy smile that curled her toes right up, and stopped at his bedroom door, raising one eyebrow. 'Fancy a drink?'

She did. She definitely did.

She couldn't. She definitely couldn't.

'Sorry, sir, but you're a guest. Staff don't – um, fraternise with guests.'

'Pity.' He winked at her and went into his room.

She went and took a very cold shower. It didn't help much.

The next morning Sally went on duty at six and hardly had time to breathe till eleven. By then, most of the weekend guests had checked out and there was no one waiting at the counter. She heaved a sigh of relief and turned to Madge, who had come in on her day off to fill in.

'Can you hold the fort while I go and grab something to eat?'

'Sure.' She looked at the computer. 'There aren't many

more due to check out now. Did head office contact you?'

'Sort of. They said they'd find someone to fill in.'

Of course, *he* was sitting in the coffee shop again. Fancy coming on holiday and spending all day indoors! She was beginning to wonder if he was watching her, and if so, why?

'Why don't you join me?' he called.

'Sorry, sir. I'm still on duty. And you're still a guest.' She took a table in the opposite corner, but couldn't resist glancing sideways to see what he was doing. He was still watching her. He even gave her a little fingertip wave. She could feel herself blushing again, dammit.

At two o'clock in the afternoon an email arrived from head office. Sally scanned it rapidly and heaved a sigh of relief. 'They've found someone and are sending him down to help out. They don't say his name, but he'll be here at four. In the meantime, if you can work on for another hour or two, Madge, I'll be your servant for ever.'

By three-fifty all the staff were on edge. Staff seconded from head office could be pure poison, finding fault with everything and reporting back to the bigwigs. No one was in the mood to put up with criticism when they'd all worked so hard.

At one minute to four Jonathon Ryder got up from the coffee shop and sauntered over to the reception counter.

Oh, no, not now! Sally groaned inwardly and gave Madge a poke in the ribs. 'You deal with the hunk. I'll keep an eye open for the big cheese from head office.'

Ryder ignored Madge and leant on the counter. 'I need to speak to you, Miss Hesketh.'

Sally, who had just seen a middle-aged guy with 'manager'

written all over him walk into the foyer, choked off a refusal and stepped forward. 'How can I help you, sir?'

He pulled out a card. 'You can read this.'

When she looked down it said JONATHON RYDER, EXECUTIVE MANAGER, BENSHAM HOTELS.

She gulped. She'd only propositioned the new executive manager to the group of hotels. And Tim had mucked up the man's registration. Ryder had been in the hotel for days, lodged in the staff quarters. It was an old hotel, and he must have seen every fault in the place by now.

'Shall we go into the manager's office?' He was unsmiling.

She gestured to him to come behind the counter. 'This way.'

Once in the office he took charge. 'Please sit down, Miss Hesketh.'

A last flicker of spirit zipped through her. 'I prefer Ms, actually.'

'Sorry. My mistake.' He sat behind the desk and studied her.

She stared at the picture to one side of his head, sure he was about to sack her.

'I'd like to congratulate you, Ms Hesketh.'

Even a desperate swallow didn't produce enough saliva for her to speak. She could only stare at him blankly and wonder what he meant. Then she suddenly realised that he had said something and was waiting for an answer.

'Um, I'm afraid I didn't catch what you said, Mr Ryder.'

'I said how well you've done taking over at such short notice during a very busy time. We're very pleased with your work, Ms Hesketh. We've had several letters from customers since your last promotion telling us how you've gone out of your way to help them.'

'Oh.' It was faint, but at least it proved she was still functioning. Well, more or less.

'If you like, I'll come and back you up here till we see how Mr Jenson is doing. But if he does come back to work, I think he'll be happier managing one of our smaller hotels, so we need to look for another solution long-term.'

'Yes.' It was faint, but she was still hanging in there.

'And in the meantime, I'd like you to take over as acting manager.'

She nodded, hoping she looked businesslike, but not feeling very optimistic about that.

He pulled his tie off. And his jacket. Undid the top button of his shirt.

She blinked at him in shock.

He put his feet up on the desk and shoved all the bits of paper aside, not seeming to care how they got mixed up.

What was going on here? she wondered.

'I hereby declare us both off duty,' he said solemnly. Then he winked at her. 'And we both know that I'm not a guest. Now what were you saying the other day when you came up to me in the café?'

When she didn't reply, because she couldn't think what to say to that, he winked again. 'Or is it my turn to pick you up, Ms Hesketh?'

She let out her breath in a whoosh, then a smile crept across her face. 'D'you fancy a date with me, fellow?' she drawled.

'I'd love one, honey pie.' His eyes were twinkling.

'Good. Meet me in the foyer at seven. Dress casually and bring your bathers.'

'Um – can I ask where we are going?'

'It's a surprise.'

She might have asked him out the first time because of a bet, but this time she was doing it because she wanted to. Very much.

And where they were going was to have a champagne picnic on a secluded beach she knew a few miles up the coast.

After that, it was up to him.

Good Terms

Introduction

This is another fantasy story and a bit of a spoof. It's dedicated to all public servants everywhere. I endured several years of bureaucracy and what I learnt (usually the hard way) about how to proceed in a new situation is what inspired this story.

I wrote it in the early '90s, but it could just as well apply to the world of big organisations today.

Red tape and spin doctoring were alien to my nature. I was dreaming of writing, and as I was writing both fantasy and historical novels then, I dreamt of other worlds, too.

Coincidentally, there have been articles in the newspaper recently about genuine alien sightings. Whatever you think about that, let your imagination fly a little and join me in a look at how a future government bureaucracy might struggle to cope with the first meeting with an alien.

To the best of my recollection, this story was never published because my historical novels were doing well and I had to concentrate on them. Submitting stories to magazines is very time-consuming, you see.

What I wrote seems to apply to the world of commerce now even more than it did then – or is that just my imagination?

Good Terms

'They said *what*?' Dell Barrath, chief administrator of Lunar Colony, turned white with shock.

The deputy administrator looked at her sympathetically. 'They said you're to go and negotiate with the aliens, ma'am, see what sort of terms they're offering for a treaty, and then report back. You're not to agree to anything, just report back.'

'Just like that! Take a little trip into space, chat to the nice kind aliens and negotiate terms for a treaty.' Dell thumped her desk. 'Why did this have to happen to me? I'm forty-three, less than two years to go to retirement. I don't *need* any hassles with aliens!'

She managed to calm down enough to ask quietly, 'What happened while I was asleep, Lee? Last I heard, the UN was debating how to deal with the aliens. That should have kept them busy for weeks.'

'Well, the aliens started orbiting the moon and broadcasting a second message, which we think translates as, "Let's talk terms".' He looked at her anxiously. 'That wasn't an emergency. You said only to wake you in an emergency, ma'am. You were out on your feet when you left the com-room.'

'All right. I'm not reprimanding you. Go on.'

'I was watching the holocasts from the UN. The delegates started running round in circles when they heard the second message. They couldn't decide whether it was – well – threatening. Or whether these creatures came in peace.'

'It's me who's going to be running round in circles,' Dell said sourly. 'Do you realise that there aren't any regulations covering negotiations with aliens. Not – even – draft – guidelines!'

He was suitably awed. 'Yes, ma'am. I mean, no, ma'am. What'll you *do*, then?'

'I'll have to "act on my own initiative".'

He shivered. This was the stuff of which bureaucrats' nightmares were made.

She pulled herself together. 'Go on, Lee. What happened next?'

'Well, ma'am, the main political factions in the UN started demanding places on the negotiating team. I kept my eye on the holochannels – that Pan-African bunch are very touchy lately, aren't they? – and then someone from the Security Council came in and announced that the aliens had chosen the ideal orbit for attacking the major cities on Earth. There was another uproar, then someone else thought of Lunar Colony. I've never seen any motion passed as quickly, ma'am. It was approved before I could even send for you.'

Dell was near to tears. 'Why, why, *why* didn't I take my leave, as I'd arranged? I'd have been safe on a beach in Surfers' Paradise by now. Best holiday complex on Earth. Top security resort. Ultraviolet barriers. Medi-screening of guests. Introduction services. What more could anyone want? I should have just taken a break and never mind that new filing system.'

Lee breathed a silent prayer of thanks to whichever deity was watching over him. What if it'd been he who had to act on his own initiative? He felt sick at the mere thought of having to do that.

She realised she had gone off at a tangent, and took a deep breath. 'What happened then, Lee?'

'Well, ma'am, I woke you because a formal order was sent here as a joint communiqué from our three agency heads. Triple A status. To be acted on immediately. It printed itself out automatically in hard copy for the permanent records.' He lowered his voice, unable to conceal how much that had impressed him. 'Your name will be right there in history, ma'am.'

'Oh, sure. And if I put one toenail wrong, they'll wipe the floor with me – with all posterity looking on. You've studied Diplomatic History. You know what happens to scapegoats.' She began to gnaw her fingernails. 'I bet those holo-news teams have been making a feast of this.'

'Well, yes, ma'am, they have rather. It's not just the aliens, you see, it's the Pure Earthers. They're staging No Contact demonstrations in all the major cities and demanding that Lunar Colony be closed down immediately. Traffic's come to a standstill in most capitals. They've got a really well-planned demo series going there. And no violence.

They'll probably win an efficiency award from the Public Conscience Trust for these demos.'

'Those Pure Earthers sure are nuts,' said a cheerful voice behind them. Sergei Anatolov, head of Lunar Colony Security, who had been maintaining his usual blank silence up to now, stretched out his oversized mitt to pat the administrator on the shoulder. 'Now, Dell, honey, it does make sense for you to go out there and do some talking with those idiots.'

'Don't call them idiots. The correct term is aliens.'

'Whatever. It still makes sense whatever I call them.'

'Oh, does it?'

'Sure does. You'll be all right. Why, those aliens have been broadcasting "We come in peace" ever since they hit the solar system. Couldn't have a plainer statement of intent than that.'

'That doesn't mean we have to believe them, Sergei! And if they come in peace, why haven't they shown us what they look like?'

'Who knows?' He shrugged and gave her one of his fatuous grins. 'Hey, what is all this? You'll be joining the PEs yourself next and demonstrating against the Unholy Invaders in Lunar Square.'

It always amazed her that such a large man could produce such a girlish titter. No one else even smiled at his feeble joke, but Sergei was used to that and continued to punctuate the conversation with titters for several minutes longer.

'Never mind the Pure Earthers,' Dell said impatiently. 'What am I going to do now?'

Lee shook his head. 'I couldn't say, ma'am. It's – er –

rather delicate.' He wasn't going to buy into this one.

Sergei had no such inhibitions. 'You'll have to do what they said, of course. Start negotiating the terms for a treaty. Aw, come on, Dell! The UN knows what it's doing. That's what it's there for. And we're all behind you here in Lunar Colony.'

She stared at him for a minute, head on one side, then she felt a nasty little smile curve her lips. He wouldn't notice the subtleties, though. 'You certainly will be, Sergei my friend. *Right* behind me, in fact, because I'm taking you with me, you and Yamashe both.'

It took a minute or two for this to sink in, then alarm crept across his big square face. 'Now, Dell, there's no need to be hasty about this, honey! That Triple A communiqué didn't say anything about taking anyone along with you.'

'I haven't been a bureaucrat for twenty years without learning a few prime rules, Sergei. *Never stick your neck out alone* is the main one. I learnt that within a week of starting in the Space Bureau. So I'm taking the head of Lunar Security and the head of the Lunar Science Foundation along with me to help negotiate the treaty terms.' She grinned at the panic on his face. 'You and Yamashe make three of us. What could be more appropriate?'

Lee permitted himself a quick grin.

'Another good rule is: *Always cover your butt with paper*,' Dell continued, turning back to her deputy. 'Therefore, we'd better see that the paperwork is done properly. That's your job, Lee – but don't send anything till just before the shuttle leaves, hmm? A memo to all three agency heads should do it, I think. If no one objects before

I leave – and they won't be able to if you time it carefully – I'll be well papered.'

Lee inclined his head, admiration in his eyes, then set to work on a suitable memo. Ten standard pages or so, he decided. Enough to look good, but too much for anyone to read carefully in a short time. The phrases tripped fluently off his tongue into the voice-corder. He had, after all, graduated top of his year in Administrative Language Skills. The final result added very little to the basic information on who was going to meet the aliens, but did it at considerable length and in the most polished of styles.

Five minutes after the memo had been sent, Dell and her two unwilling companions went to board the shuttle.

Lee heard her ask for the third time as they got ready, 'What have I *ever* done to deserve this, Yamashe? Just tell me that!'

Her voice cut off abruptly as the com-engineer began to check their personal broadcasting equipment.

When she started speaking again, Lee heard her smooth official voice saying, '. . . for the good of Earth and humankind.'

He smiled. Dell Barrath was a skilled performer. A real professional. She could make any situation she found herself in look good. He had learnt a lot from her.

He watched on the main com-screen as the shuttle took off, wondering if it would return safely. He hoped so. He didn't want this hot chestnut dropping back into his basket.

* * *

Her surging adrenalin did not improve Dell's temper. *Our transmission will give those Pure Earthers triple hysterics,* she thought, staring at the viewscreen as the shuttle approached the alien spacecraft. *In fact, I wouldn't mind having hysterics myself.*

Aloud she said calmly, with due regard for her massive audience, 'Yamashe, was that size estimate of the spacecraft confirmed?'

'Yes. It's about half a kilometre in diameter, ma'am.'

'Thank you.' Her expression stony, she brooded on the mountain of paperwork this encounter was going to generate. New forms to design. New procedures to be worked out. New guidelines to be written. She'd never get the leave due to her now! She'd be lucky even to retire on schedule.

'Gee, that's a big one!' said Sergei uncomfortably as they reduced speed and drifted towards the alien craft.

For once she agreed with him. The spacecraft was gigantic by Earth standards. Obviously the product of a far more advanced technology. How, she asked herself bitterly, could a mere Class 3 administrator be expected to negotiate on behalf of the whole of Earth with creatures whose technology enabled them to zip around the galaxy in a spacecraft that size?

She tried not to show how angry she was at finding herself in this situation. It should have been an agency head, at the very least, up here running these preliminary negotiations, or better still, a UN diplomat. Without even a draft protocol to guide her behaviour, she felt more vulnerable than ever before in her whole well-ordered life.

A hole opened up in the side of the saucer and the shuttle

began floating towards it. The pilot swore under her breath and banged the panel in front of her. 'They've taken over our controls! What do we do now, ma'am?'

Sergei gasped loudly and opened his mouth to spew out more inanities. Aware that everything they said was being broadcast back on Earth and would later be all too thoroughly dissected by posterity, Dell got in first. 'We must assume that this is standard docking procedure. Do nothing unless they commit a hostile act.'

While the slow drift continued, the pilot muttered over her control board and Dell exchanged worried glances with Yamashe. The tension even penetrated Sergei's thick skull and he responded by starting to suck his thumb.

After what seemed like an eternity, the shuttle came to rest inside the alien spacecraft next to a narrow opening surrounded by sinister-looking protruberances. 'I hope that's only an airlock, ma'am,' the pilot whispered.

'So do I.' Dell did her best to look calm and collected. 'Better maintain things on red alert.'

'I don't think any of our defence equipment is functioning, ma'am.'

'Then behave as if it is!' Dell bit her lip as she heard how sharp her voice sounded. She must remember to stand and speak in a more relaxed manner.

Sergei removed the thumb and took the line that had stood him in good stead in a dozen other crises. 'Er – I think it'd be better if I stayed here on the shuttle. You'll need someone to guard your rear, ma'am. Provide you with an escape route, if necessary.'

He was standing as far back from the exit port as he could, a magnificent picture of muscular blonde manhood in a trim grey dress uniform. His very appearance seemed to inspire confidence in the lunar colonists he was employed to protect, but Dell, like all those who knew him better, was always amazed that people could be so gullible as to trust someone as stupid as Sergei. Well, she thought, eyes narrowing, *she* was not going to let him get off the hook that easily!

'I sure hope we can breathe their air,' he added chattily, before she could stop him. 'Be a real shame if we can't. Got my grandson's first birthday next month. Wouldn't want to miss that.'

Posterity would make a meal of that stirring speech! Dell wondered for the millionth time how such a moron had managed to land a top security job. 'Stay ten paces behind me throughout these negotiations, Commander Anatolov!' she ordered before he could speak again.

'Oh – er – are you sure, Dell? Isn't that a little – close? For your safety, I mean.'

She contented herself with glaring at him. *If he puts that thumb in his mouth again*, she thought savagely, *I'll slap it out myself*. 'Yamashe, ten paces behind Sergei.'

'Yes, ma'am.'

A voice echoed around them, rather too loudly for Dell's taste. '*THE AIRLOCK WILL NOW CONNECT TO YOUR VESSEL. PLEASE HAVE NO FEAR. WE BREATHE VERY SIMILAR AIR. WE ASK YOU TO LEAVE ALL WEAPONS BEHIND. WE, TOO, SHALL BE UNARMED.*'

Dell pulled her stungun out of its holster and attached it to the nearest magnet panel. She waited for a minute, then, when Sergei did nothing, pointed to his handlaser.

'Whoops! Silly me!' He pulled it out of the holster and slapped it on the panel, tittering softly to himself.

Yamashe removed five knives and a needlegun, shaking his head regretfully as he placed them beside the handlaser.

Dell gaped. Quiet, studious Yamashe, armed like an assassin!

He bowed slightly from the waist. 'My colleagues were nervous, or I'd not have brought the needlegun, ma'am.'

'Nice little blades, those,' commented Sergei, momentarily diverted. 'Sure like to try them out in the practice range when we get back.'

Yamashe bowed his acquiescence. 'Perhaps next week.'

I don't believe this is happening, thought Dell. *We'll be planning a picnic next.*

There followed a series of clangs and hisses which had Sergei wincing visibly and which tested even Yamashe's self-control. Dell was beyond fear. By now, she would not have been surprised if purple mice had started crawling out of the bulkheads and singing the 'Hallelujah Chorus'.

When the airlock opened, she took a deep breath, straightened her shoulders and led the way out of the shuttle. A heroine she had never wished to be! For the past eighteen years she had steered a careful path through mountains of red tape, protocols and regulations, without once blotting her copybook. She was praying desperately that she would not smudge the ink now, to use an ancient metaphor.

The tunnel led upwards. Another airlock. They seemed to be waiting inside it for a very long time. Was this a trap? Sergei looked at his watch and opened his mouth to comment, but Dell shook her head and he closed it again, pouting. She ignored that. He had already given posterity enough to chuckle about.

At last the airlock door opened. Dell stepped out into the alien spacecraft first, feeling self-conscious and exposed. Her two companions prudently remained as far behind her as was possible, but in spite of her instructions, Sergei managed to be the last one out.

She scanned the chamber ahead, stopped dead and gasped in shock. Sergei's voice floated forward. 'What – on earth – is *that*?'

In front of them stood a smiling humanoid, its arms spread wide in what Dell hoped was a gesture of welcome. A smile was plastered across its face. She hoped it was a smile.

She shivered and remained where she was. The creature was humanoid only if you didn't mind bright green hair and a double row of sharp white teeth, all of them clearly exposed by that smile. She found that she did mind.

Nor was she at all taken by the creature's striped crimson and yellow pyjama suit. Apart from its vibrant colours and eye-catching neon braid, it was too baggy. Heaven alone knew what it was concealing.

The thing took a step towards her, still beaming all over its rather vulpine face.

Oh, those teeth! thought Dell. *I now know exactly what Red Riding Hood felt like when facing the wolf!* 'Er – I'm Dell Barrath, administrator of Lunar Colony.' *Surely*, she thought feverishly, *no one could quibble at those words of greeting.*

The thing came closer and closer. Only by the firmest exercise of willpower did she manage not to flinch away as it loomed over her, two metres tall at least, and stuck out one large greenish-pink hand to grasp hers.

'My *dear* Ms Barrath! Welcome to our space store!'

Space *store*? What did he – or was he a 'she' or an 'it'? – mean by that?

'A thousand times welcome! I'm so *thrilled* to meet you!' It continued to pump her hand vigorously. 'My name is Yichi'Hann'Llarass.' Its speech was extremely sibilant and its smile was, it seemed, a permanent fixture, which permitted maximum tooth display.

'On behalf of the people of Earth and the United Planets,' Dell began, for the UN in its wisdom had decreed that the planets were to be united, even before they had all been settled, 'may I welcome you to this star system. Our government has asked me to extend its greetings to your government.'

She felt that she had done that rather well, all things taken into account, and had kept her voice firm and resonant.

Yichi'Hann'Llarass pulled a face and sniggered. 'Oh, governments!' It flipped a limp hand. 'Who cares about *them*?'

Dell heard two loud gasps behind her and hoped that she had concealed her own horror at this heresy, but she had a strong suspicion that her jaw had literally fallen several centimetres. She tried desperately to maintain the dignity of the occasion, in spite of those pyjamas, in spite of those teeth. 'Er – Mr—' She broke off as a thought struck her. 'It *is* Mr, isn't it?'

It waggled its hips and leered at her. 'Yes, Dell honey.' Another waggle, then it struck a pose. '*Mr is me. Just try some and see*. I just love your raps – or do you consider them to be poems?'

She gulped, repressed a shudder and persevered in the best diplomatic tradition. 'Mr – er – Yichi'Hann'Llarass, surely you are here as the representative of your government?'

'Not me, baby!'

'But you're the first aliens – er – extra-terrestrials to visit us! Mr Yi—'

'Oh, *please*! No one uses that mouthful after the first introductions are over. Just call me Yichi. All my friends do. And I'm sure we're going to be good friends, you and I.' Another leer and wriggle.

She swallowed and tried to take her eyes off those teeth. 'Yichi, then.' Best not to annoy him in any way until she understood what it was he really wanted.

He smoothed a stray green lock from his brow and eyed her roguishly. 'That's *much* better. And may I call you Dell? Thank you, Dell. We've so much in common, my dear, that I feel we're close friends already. I mean, we're an almost identical species, if we ignore your lack of teeth – how *do* you manage to chew your food, by the way? – and our research and marketing team thinks we'll be able to work up some good deals together.'

'Oh?' It sounded like, it couldn't be . . .

'Yes. We've *never* found a species so close to us physically! Never! We're all *so* excited! Think of the products we can share. You've no idea how hard it is when there are chemical incompatibilities, and as for the non-oxygen breathers, well, you can keep them, baby!' He clicked his teeth twice to emphasise the point.

Dell could not help wincing. 'Er – yes,' she said faintly,

not quite sure where all this gentle eloquence was leading.

'And talking of deals . . .' He clasped her nerveless hand in his for a moment.

The hairs on his hand were as green as those on his head, she noted in revolted fascination.

Then he waggled one finger in a beckoning gesture. A large rainbow-coloured container full of packages floated over to hang in the air beside them, chiming softly.

Yichi pushed it gently towards her. 'I want you to have these free samples for your very own self, Dell. No charge. No obligation. Except that you give our other offers fair consideration, of course.'

She could only goggle at him. 'But – but – what about your government?' She was always to regret how feeble she sounded and certainly posterity found it exquisitely humorous. 'But – but – what about . . . ?' became quite a catchphrase on the holochannels.

'Oh, the Galactic Confederation's already got *far* too much paperwork to sort out without us adding any more. There are simply *hundreds* of planets applying for federation since Snee'Snith'Ferrith invented the space hopper drive, bless his little rear molars! He won a company prize for that, you bet! Those hoppers get you along far faster than the speed of light and at a fraction of the cost of other drives. The company president himself was there to congratulate him and present the prize. Old Snee's made for life.'

She continued to stare at him, her eyes feeling glassy, but he seemed to enjoy the sound of his own voice and continued unabated, while she was still struggling desperately to come to terms with what he was saying.

'No, you can forget about governments, Dell baby!

You'll not see anyone from GalCon here in the outback for centuries. Your best bet is just to put your trust in the company. *Service across the universe: universal service*, that's the motto our PR branch dreamt up for you Earthers. Pretty neat, eh?'

'Company?' she queried faintly, trying to find out who was in authority. 'You're representing a company?'

'Yeah. Universal Traders, Always First on the Frontiers.' He drew himself up and warbled tunefully,

The only firm that you can trust.
We are honest. We are just.'

'Universal Traders?' She was beginning to feel like Alice in Wonderland, falling down the rabbit hole.

'Who else? It's free enterprise that really gets things moving in this little old galaxy, baby, not governments.'

Her bewilderment at last began to register and he looked down at her, frowning. 'You must understand how it is with government bureaucracies, honey.'

Her 'No!' was a mere scrape of the vocal chords.

'But our R and M team says you've got the most advanced bureaucracies we've ever encountered. More forms to fill in per head of the population than even the Seerinans.'

Dell gulped audibly at that.

'Now,' Yichi went on persuasively, edging closer and exposing all his teeth once again, 'let's you and me talk turkey, huh? Our ship, *Spacemart 969827F/3Z/XX8*, has the most up-to-date and inexpensive range of trade goods that you're ever likely to see in this neck of the woods.'

She couldn't believe what she was hearing. It was a nightmare, it had to be.

'How'd you like a personal franchise for the Earth

trade in some new communication equipment, Dell baby? Just a licence to coin money, that one is. All we ask in return is a little help in settling in.'

He waited a little, then added, 'And we'll offer you *such* good terms . . . You have come to talk terms, haven't you?'

Going Out in Style

Introduction

I wrote this story before the turn of the century, when a women's magazine wanted a short story of about 1,500 words. I tried to write a romantic story for them, but no ideas came to me because I kept seeing feisty old Mrs Kelly instead.

So I wrote the story as I 'saw' it and sent it off without much expectation of the magazine accepting it. To my surprise they loved it and bought it.

Good old Mrs Kelly! She not only earned me a nice little chunk of money back in the day, but she's made me chuckle every now and then for years as I've remembered her. I'd forgotten the details of some of my stories when I started putting this collection together but I never forgot this heroine.

I thoroughly enjoyed polishing this story and adding more colour and details that wouldn't fit into a 1,500 word short.

In general, when I write about old ladies (and old gentlemen too) I refuse to show them as meek, grateful semi-puddled creatures, a stereotype you still see in adverts and drama in 2018! There is one particular advert at the moment where a nurse is uber-kind to a grateful old man, treating him like a helpless child. I shout at it every time it dares to come on my TV!

I'm old now, to my surprise in my late seventies, and I grow less meek by the year, believe me. I once stood up for equal opportunity for women. Nowadays ageism is alive and well, but I make sure it gets a bit battered when I'm around. For instance, I've been told to my face that I'm costing young people money to keep me alive. Hey, I'm working full-time and paying tax! How does that cost anyone money? I certainly gave that young man what for!

I've also been told that I should stop writing and leave 'slots' for the younger writers because I've had my day! I was very sharp in my response to that, too. I'll stop writing when I drop off my perch and not until, thank you very much.

I grow especially angry – and blunt – in shops, where they quite often treat elderly women kindly, in a patronise-the-child way. Computer shops are especially bad this way, in my experience. I put one incident involving that sort of ageism plus sexism into my book *Bay Tree Cottage*. They don't treat my husband like that and he's even older than me (six months!).

My generation have been feisty all the way through, from the lively '60s onwards, and I'm going to stay the same. So go get 'em, Mrs Kelly, and all oldies like you.

Going Out in Style

Vera stormed out of a bedroom in the hospice. 'If I have to go in there one more time, I'll strangle her!'

The other nursing assistant pulled a face. 'One of her bad days, is it?'

'One of her bad *weeks*! Threw her soup down the wall yesterday, tipped water over the bedcovers the day before – *on purpose*. I saw her do it.'

Just then the manager came round. 'Someone's coming to do voluntary service, a young woman on her final chance. It'll be prison if she offends again. She's not violent, so you can let her help with the residents.'

Vera smiled. 'I suggest you assign her to look after Mrs Kelly, then. Sounds like they'll suit one another.'

'Oh, I don't think—'

'Go on. It'll give us a bit of a break, at least.'

The girl leant against the doorpost, sighing. She had short spiky hair, heavy make-up around expressionless eyes, and mismatched, garish clothes that clearly came from a charity shop.

'This is Raelene, Mrs Kelly. She's here for some work experience. She'll be helping you for the next few days.'

'I don't want her.'

'You know how short-staffed we are. She'll be able to fetch and carry for you and—'

'*I do not want her!*'

'Well, I didn't want to come here, either,' Raelene snarled. 'They're lying to you. I'm not on work experience. Think I'd want to work in a dump like this? I'm on community service. It's that or prison, so I'm staying here and you can like it or lump it.'

Vera hid a smile as Mrs Kelly gobbled in incoherent rage. 'Let me show you what's needed, Raelene,' she cooed.

Grimly the girl helped Mrs Kelly to the toilet, washed her hands and face, brought her meals. When the old woman tried to throw her plate at the wall, Raelene snatched it out of her hands.

When she tried to do it again, Raelene threatened to spill it down the front of Mrs Kelly's nightie. 'You're not going to get me sacked, you silly old fool! They'll blame me and I'm not going to prison if I can help it, not for you or anyone.'

Mrs Kelly studied her, grinned and began to pick at the bland food. 'Well, you've got spirit, girl, I'll say that for you. Them others just grit their teeth an' clear up the mess. Can't get them angry no matter what I do.'

The girl gaped at her. 'Do you mean you've been doing all they told me about on purpose? That you've got all your marbles?'

'Course I have! Got to do something to pass the time, haven't I?' She scowled. 'If I had my way, I'd just press a button and exit quick smart. It's no fun waiting to die, I can tell you.'

Raelene looked at her with the first real interest. 'They say you've got cancer.'

'Yeah.' She patted her sagging breast. 'It's sitting there chewing away at me. But I don't pay it much attention. An' I don't take them painkillers in the daytime, just have the injections at night. Turn your brain into mush, them tablets do, and I haven't got many days left.'

'Aren't you frightened of dying?'

Mrs Kelly shrugged. 'I'm nearly ninety. Had a good life, looked after myself till I was eighty-nine. So I've not done badly.' She glared at the remaining food. 'It's horrible. Take it away. I can't face it.'

'What do you like eating?'

'Pizza. They used to deliver them to my flat. Good, they were. I always had extra cheese. But them nurses won't let me send out for one. They say it's not good for me. As if that matters now.'

'I love pizzas.'

The sunken old eyes gleamed suddenly and Mrs Kelly put her head on one side like a bird about to peck at a seed. 'Wouldn't like to bring me one, would you? I'd bribe you generously. You could hide the box outside that sliding door and sneak it in when they're not looking. Even cold pizza would be a treat after the slop they serve here.'

'I don't want to get into trouble.' Raelene frowned down at the scrawny old figure, stared at the lumpy, greyish mashed potato left on the plate and felt a sudden surge of sympathy. She shrugged. 'Oh, why not? I wouldn't feed that stuff to a dog. I'll fetch you a pizza tomorrow.'

'All the trimmings, mind. Except anchovies.'

The rest of the day passed quite well.

'How did you tame her?' Vera asked Raelene as she got ready to leave.

'I didn't do anything. I think she's a nice old thing, actually. She makes me laugh.'

'Wonders will never cease.'

Raelene sneaked the pizza into the hospice grounds and it was still quite hot when she arrived. Mrs Kelly's face lit up as she pulled off a strand of the melted cheese that was running over the edges.

'You're a good kid, whatever anyone says.' She ate three pieces and gave the rest to her fellow criminal.

Afterwards she chortled when the girl produced some air freshener spray. 'You're not stupid.'

Raelene slumped in her chair. 'No, I'm not. I'm a troublemaker an' a thief, though. I've got a record as long as your arm.'

Mrs Kelly pulled a face. 'Well, *I* think you're a good kid. And you don't preach at me like that chaplain. Silly young fool he is. What does *he* know about life? Wait till you've raised six children single-handed when your husband runs off, I said to him, *then* I'll let you come and preach at me.'

'Did you really raise six children single-handed?'

'Course I didn't! Think I'm too stupid to know where babies come from? I only had two. But the chaplain doesn't know that and it shut him up.'

'How many grandchildren do you have?'

Mrs Kelly's face grew sad. 'Four. But they don't visit. And both my daughters are dead now, poor loves. My Katie would have visited me if she'd been alive, I know she would.'

She scrabbled at her pillows, let Raelene puff them up then sank back with a sigh. 'I have one big regret: when I got married, it was a shabby affair. I always wished I'd waited and done it properly, with a white dress and veil. I still look at them bride magazines. Silly, isn't it? A wrinkled old prune like me imagining myself wearing one.'

Raelene patted her shoulder. 'It's not silly. I look at photos of dogs. I always wanted a pet dog but I was a ward of the state and they don't let you keep pets. Shall I get you another pizza tomorrow?'

'Yes. Let's have pepperoni this time. Got a nice bite to it, that has. Here, let me give you the money. Keep the change.'

'No need to tip me. I don't mind doing you a favour.'

'No, take it. I'm not going to need it.'

It was like a miracle, the nursing assistants said. Mrs Kelly had never been so quiet. She wasn't eating much, but that was to be expected in her condition.

And Raelene was behaving herself, a bit sulky with the nurses but seemed to have taken a real liking to Mrs Kelly. Well, birds of a feather, they were.

'I'll give her an excellent report,' Vera said. 'She's earned it.'

When the community service ended, Raelene continued to visit Mrs Kelly. It pleased her probation officer no end. Raelene didn't tell her she went visiting because she enjoyed Mrs Kelly's company.

The old bird was a real hoot. She still had a bucket list. One thing on it was to try smoking marijuana before she died. So Raelene took her in a spliff. It put a very happy smile on her face.

She said she'd had a really good night's sleep after that and asked for more, but Raelene wasn't risking it.

Mrs Kelly was fond of a nip of gin, too, so Raelene brought some in. She wouldn't leave it there, though, just in case.

The nursing staff never twigged what was going on, because Mrs K developed a sudden liking for strong peppermints and Raelene brought the gin in her water bottle which she took away afterwards.

One afternoon, however, the girl found Mrs K slumped back against her pillows, face chalk-white.

'It's starting to win on me,' the old lady said in a faint voice. 'Been gnawing at me something cruel today.'

'That's tough. Want some gin?'

'Not tonight. But it's nice to see you, girl, real nice.' She patted her companion's hand. 'I've grown fond of you. If I were a bit younger, I'd take you under my wing and show you a few tricks.'

'Ha! What does a respectable old grandma know about tricks?'

'Grandma! When do I ever see them grandchildren of mine? And I know more than you'd believe about tricks, girl. How d'you think I coped with my husband and kids? They had to stick to my rules, or I gave 'em what for. I've been thinking. What *you* should do is start your own business. You're too feisty to work for someone else.'

'I wouldn't know what to do.'

'How about you start a business visiting old people in

hospitals or hospices when their families are too busy to go. Not a lot of the oldies here get visitors.'

Raelene blinked and grew thoughtful. 'I'll . . . consider it.'

As the visit drew to an end, Mrs Kelly sighed and scowled at the room. 'I don't want to die in here. I want to go out in style. Look, I've got an idea.'

'Oh?'

'I've been saving my pills. Time to use them, I reckon. You don't have a friend with a car, do you?'

'Might have.'

'And you don't know how to break into shops with burglar alarms, do you?'

'Might. The easier sorts of alarms, anyway.'

'I've got a couple of thousand dollars hidden away an' it's all yours if you'll help me do one last thing. Come closer. I don't want anyone overhearing us.'

Raelene laughed all the way home, then she had a good old cry, too. She was going to miss Mrs Kelly.

The papers and TV news programmes were full of it.

Ninety-year-old woman escapes from hospice and breaks into bridalwear shop. Found dead wearing white wedding dress and veil, holding bouquet of real flowers, with a smile on her face.

Raelene missed Mrs Kelly even more than she'd expected to. But it was very satisfying to have helped her go out in style. The old woman had cried happy tears over that bouquet, which had been Raelene's personal contribution to 'the wedding'.

The girl had learnt a lot from the old lady and when she eventually married, she intended to call her first child Kelly in memory of a friendship that had meant a lot to her when she was feeling at her lowest ebb ever.

Her business was doing really well and she was actually visiting old folk for busy relatives. Some of them reminded her of Mrs K. They soon perked up when she encouraged them to rebel against stupid restrictions.

And the photo she'd taken of Mrs K, all dressed up, had pride of place in Raelene's flat. It always would. Beautiful, the old lady looked. And so happy. She'd gone out in style, just as she wanted.

Just Seven Words

Introduction

I wrote the first part of this story nearly twenty years ago and couldn't work out how to end it. So I set it aside to wait for inspiration.

When I'm writing one thing and get ideas about another story, I write a few pages to capture the idea, then store the file in my 'fragments' folder. I'm not always sure whether they're the beginning of a novel or a short story.

The main thing is that I've saved them, because you can't possibly remember every word you've written. To tell you the truth, I can't remember all the details of my early novels, even though I spent several months of my life on each one. I just remember the main storylines.

Isn't it amazing how things can suddenly slot into place, though? Putting this collection of stories together must have awakened something in me and suddenly, I could 'see' what would happen to Ellie. Images slipped into my mind and the words poured out. I had a lovely afternoon writing another 3,500 words to give you a longish short story with a lovable tongue-tied hero.

I don't usually write so much in one day, partly because there are other jobs involved in being a novelist besides the actual writing. I manage around 1,000 words a day when I'm beginning a new story, till I've settled in, then around 1,500 to 2,000 words. And I never write after teatime. That's the time reserved for spending with my lovely husband.

Just Seven Words

1
1860

Two groups moved towards Alleton churchyard and the five people on foot paused at the gateway to let the hearse with its black horses and plumes pass them.

Ellie Pearson patted the shoulder of her daughter as she waited. At two, Nan didn't really understand what was happening, didn't understand what it meant that her father had died. At four, Johnny was more aware of what death was, because he'd seen neighbours die, but he didn't understand what Petey's death meant for them beyond his father 'going away'.

She brushed vainly at her dusty ankle-length skirts. You ought to be better dressed than this for your husband's funeral, whether you grieved for him or not, but she'd sold everything she could during the past weeks to put food on the table for her children, including her Sunday-best clothes.

The young men pushing the handcart had been sent by the farmer for whom her husband had only recently come to work, since neither she nor Petey had any close relatives in the district. Well, she had no close relatives anywhere now, come to that. One young man took out his handkerchief and wiped his forehead, because it was a warm day.

Ellie wiped her eyes, then wiped them again. She must be brave, must find a way, somehow to survive.

The larger group moved away along the path. She didn't recognise the man walking behind the hearse, but she did one or two of the others. Farmers. Rich folk by her standards, comfortable enough to give one of their own a fancy funeral, not send the dead woman to a pauper's grave, like Petey.

Well, it was all he deserved after how he'd treated his family, but angry as she was at him still, it had seemed right to come here with him. One last time.

Isaac Matthews walked stolidly behind his wife's coffin. The village church was so close to his home that he'd insisted on walking instead of taking the carriage with his wife's family. One cousin was walking with him, to preserve appearances, though the two of them had never been close.

There were neighbours walking behind him, too. Other farmers. Kind of them.

Isaac's thoughts were miles away. What was he going to do now? How was he to care for his three children, one still a babe in arms?

Eugenia's family would step in, he knew, and make their usual efficient arrangements. But he didn't want them managing his life any longer. Or the lives of his children. He intended to dismiss that starchy governess immediately. She didn't beat the children, he wouldn't have stood for that, but they had been so subdued since his wife had hired her.

As they paused to allow the hearse to stop at the lychgate of the churchyard and unload the coffin, his attention was caught for a moment by the sad little group standing to one side. They'd stopped to let their betters through. Betters! Ha! His wife's family were a bunch of greedy bigots, whom he'd grown to detest. They cared only for money and status.

He studied the wraith-thin young woman in worn clothing who had two children pressed against her. Her thin hand rested briefly on the little girl's head and the child nestled against it, as if she'd done that many times before.

He'd seen the rough coffin jolting along on a handcart pushed by two sturdy young men. Who had this woman lost? A husband? If so, her life would be hard indeed.

But his life wasn't easy, either. Was anyone's?

The young woman bent to whisper to the little boy, dropping a kiss on his forehead as she spoke.

He couldn't ever remember his own children going to their mother for comfort, or Eugenia offering it. And yet her family had asked him to marry her for the sake of the children he could give her. They'd said she longed for them.

He'd never have thought of offering for her, but as a younger son, he was tempted as much by the land she'd bring with her as by Eugenia herself. It had seemed as though she was fond of him but once they were married, he had quickly discovered that she cared about no one but herself.

And yet she'd desperately wanted children. He'd never understood that.

He forgot about the other group as he plodded on into the church behind the coffin. He mouthed the hymns, but afterwards couldn't have said what had been sung.

He had refused to deliver a eulogy himself, because he couldn't tell lies about Eugenia, not in church. He told them he wasn't good with words, which everyone knew. When his father-in-law had offered to give the eulogy, he'd shrugged, which they'd taken for agreement.

As he endured a flowery eulogy, full of lies about his dead wife's supposed virtues, he wished he hadn't agreed.

Eventually that part of the service ended and he could follow the coffin out to the churchyard.

Nearly done, now. Thank goodness.

There would be battles to come, he knew. He hoped he'd find the words to tell them what he intended to do, how he wanted his children to live, and convince them he meant it.

They wouldn't change his mind. He wanted happy children, a peaceful home and land which brought forth its wealth in stock and seed.

Once the carriages had passed, the two young men set off again and Ellie followed the handcart to the area where they buried paupers.

The curate arrived and gabbled through a shortened form of the burial service. She listened stoically. He didn't say anything about Petey, thank goodness, just went through a few prayers and then looked at her rather guiltily and added that it was sad to see a man die so young.

She bowed her head to him, but couldn't think of anything to say. Petey had died because he got drunk again and fell in the river on the way home, lying there all night and coming home with a fever. She'd tried to nurse him better, because he was the wage earner and even the house they lived in depended on his labour, but oh, it had made her so angry.

The men lowered the coffin into the grave and started to fill in that section of the big trench.

The curate looked at her as if expecting something. Well, if he thought she could pay him, he was wrong. She had only a few coins left.

She had only a few days left, too, had to be out of the cottage by the end of the week. That's when she'd have to go to the workhouse and confess that she was a homeless pauper. They'd take her children from her in that horrible place, she knew. But at least Nan and Johnny would be fed and kept alive.

She needed feeding too. She was weak for lack of nourishment, too weak to tramp the roads and beg, even.

What she couldn't work out was how she'd get out of the poorhouse once she was stronger. She had to get out quickly because they'd send the children away to an orphanage as soon as they could arrange it, and might not even tell her where it was.

Just a few days, she prayed. *Give me a few days with food to pull myself together.*

She felt so dizzy and weak she could only walk slowly and it took her a long time to get back to the cottage.

Mr Sharpe, the farmer, was waiting for her there, showing the cottage to a young couple. No! He couldn't turn her out, not today of all days. He'd promised to let her have two days more.

He turned round. 'Ah, Mrs Pearson. I'm just showing James and Harriet round. They'll be moving in as soon as you move out. Um, they were wondering whether you'd like to sell them your furniture?'

She felt sick at the thought, then realised that if she did, it'd give her some money, maybe enough to leave Alleton without going into the poorhouse.

'How much are you offering?'

'I thought a guinea,' the young man said.

Anger filled her. 'Five guineas.'

'Two. And that's my final word.'

The anger flared into rage. 'I'd rather burn the furniture than be cheated. You know it's worth much more.'

'It is, you know,' Mr Sharpe said. 'Five guineas is a good bargain.'

The young man scowled. 'They'll only take the money off her when she goes into the poorhouse.'

And then it really sank in: she'd have enough to get away. The lie slipped easily from her tongue. 'I'm not going into the poorhouse. If I can raise the money for the train fare, I'm going to stay with my cousin. I wrote to her when Petey died and she wrote back to say I can work in their shop.'

Mr Sharpe gave her a disbelieving look, but said nothing, thank goodness. 'Right then. If you give me the money, James, I'll see Mrs Pearson gets it before she leaves.'

'Don't let her take anything away with her,' the young woman put in.

'I'm only selling the furniture and household goods. I'm keeping my Bible and personal possessions,' Ellie said firmly.

Both of them scowled at her, then Mr Sharpe said, 'That's fair enough.'

The man handed over the money to Mr Sharpe and they walked away without a word to Ellie.

When they'd gone, the farmer looked at her. 'We both know there is no cousin and you haven't received any letters.'

She lifted her chin and stared him in the eye. 'No, but I know someone I can ask for help only I never thought I'd find the money to get to her. Thank you for making them pay a fair price.'

'It was my wife's idea for them to buy your things.' He frowned. 'I didn't think that young man would treat you so meanly. I'll have to keep an eye on him. I'm not having cheats working for me.'

When he didn't say anything else, she ventured to ask, 'I wondered – could you do me a favour?'

'Oh? What exactly?'

'If I pack my things, could you please store them in the barn till I can come back and collect them? Not the furniture. I won't cheat those two. But there are a few other bits and pieces that are worthless to anyone else but mean a lot to me.'

'I'll have to check through the things first.'

She nodded, forcing herself to stay calm. It was only one more humiliation among many. What did it matter?

'My wife sent some food. I put it on the shelf. She says she'll send you down some more tomorrow.'

A couple of tears escaped Ellie's control but she dug her fingernails into the palms of her hands and managed to stop others following them. 'That's generous of her. You've both been so kind, letting me stay on here after Petey died, and I'm truly grateful.'

'Yes, well. We felt sorry for you and the children. He turned out to be a drunkard. If he hadn't died, we'd have had to send you all packing. I need the cottage for my labourer.'

He grew very brisk. 'Well. I must get on. I'll bring more food tomorrow and some bread and cheese to take with you for the journey. I'm sorry, but I have to make a living and these are difficult times.'

She knew that. Everyone knew that. But he was kinder than most.

She didn't let the tears fall till she'd got the children to bed and was on her own. And even then she didn't allow herself to sob for long, because she didn't want to walk about with red puffy eyes tomorrow.

There was no one to go to for help. That was another lie. But she'd leave the district and go to a town, where there might be a chance to find some way of earning a living now that she'd have a little money to tide her over.

There must be something she could do.

2

Isaac endured the funeral gathering, though the sight of people stuffing their faces with food sickened him. He remembered suddenly the young woman at the churchyard. If ever hunger had been written on a face, it had been there on hers and her children's, too. What was she going to do now? Go into the poorhouse probably.

After the visitors left, Eugenia's father and the family lawyer stayed behind and the rest of the family left them alone.

'There is the question of the will.'

Isaac looked at him in puzzlement. 'What will? I didn't know that Eugenia had made one. Can a wife leave her husband's property?'

'No, it's nothing to do with Eugenia; it's the will of my uncle I'm talking about. He left this house and land to her on condition she married within three months.'

Isaac stared at him. 'That's why she married me so suddenly? To get this property.'

'Yes. We thought it unnecessary to tell you.'

He knew why. In case he fled like the other man she had once been betrothed to.

Mr Carter nodded. 'There were other conditions we didn't tell you about.'

Isaac felt horror trickle through him. Had he endured the years with Eugenia only to lose this land he'd grown to love?

'The uncle who left this property put a caveat on it. He was a firm believer in marriage. Eugenia had to marry within three months of inheriting or else it would pass to another cousin. And the same condition will now apply to you.'

'Dear heaven, was he a madman?'

Mr Carter shrugged. 'Eccentric.'

'Could you not have contested the will?'

'I didn't wish to do that. I wanted my daughter to marry.'

To get rid of her probably. 'Well, I intend to contest it.'

'You won't win, Isaac. My uncle had a good lawyer who tied things up tightly. You must do as he stipulated or lose the land. I want my grandson to inherit one day, so I beg that you'll agree to the condition.'

'This is – ludicrous.'

Another shrug greeted this.

'Have you already chosen a woman for me?' Isaac asked.

'No. But I'm sure my wife will be happy to introduce you to suitable women. Not young ones, older ones with a bit more sense. Ones who'll be grateful for a husband. And we'll make sure she has a better temper than poor Eugenia.'

Isaac looked at the lawyer, who had said nothing and seemed rather uncomfortable.

The lawyer shrugged, as if guessing what he wanted to know.

'I'll do it on one condition.'

They waited.

It took him a couple of minutes to put it into words. 'I must choose my own wife.' He didn't intend to be caught by another shrew.

He said it again. 'I must choose my own wife.' Surely they hadn't found anyone suitable? Eugenia's death had been very sudden.

'Everyone knows you get tongue-tied in the presence of women. Perhaps you'll let us help you, make a few introductions?'

'I'm sorry if this offends you, but I don't want another wife like her.'

Mr Carter nodded wearily. 'She always was very headstrong. Difficult in some ways.'

Difficult in all ways, Isaac thought, but didn't rub that in. That was why they'd trapped him, a stranger who didn't know her reputation, into marrying her.

'I want it put in writing now that I can choose my own wife,' he said firmly.

There was a pause, then Mr Carter said, 'On condition that she's respectable.'

'I wouldn't choose someone not respectable to mother my children.'

'No. We appreciate that. But we'll still put it in the condition.'

They waited till the lawyer drew the condition up and made a copy, then they both signed them, with him acting as witness.

By then Isaac could take no more. He stood up. 'If that's all, I'll go and see my children.'

'Thank you for being so reasonable about this,' Mr Carter said.

Was he being reasonable? Isaac didn't *feel* reasonable. He felt angry. But he also felt entitled to this property, which he'd worked so hard to make productive, so if he had to marry some female to keep it, he'd do that.

3

The next day Isaac was so busy he felt like his little daughter's spinning top. He started the day by dismissing the governess. The woman had no kindness in her.

That was a dreadful ordeal and even though he'd practised what to say beforehand, he found himself stuttering as he had when he was a lad.

In the end she left the house and was driven to the railway station.

After that the servants were very nervous of putting a foot wrong, he could tell, and they kept asking him things. As if he knew the details of keeping house!

By the end of the day, he realised that he'd need a housekeeper. But he didn't want another woman in the house. He just wanted things to be peaceful and to see more of his children. At least the housemaid was a friendly young lass and she was keeping an eye on them for the time being.

Two days later he got up early and went for a walk round his land, breathing in the cool air and planning what he'd do with each field now they were truly his.

Then he stopped and scowled. No, they wouldn't be legally his until he'd found himself a wife. Would it be difficult to do that? He didn't know, but he'd guess not. After all, some woman was bound to be found who would marry him for the comfortable life. But she'd better be a hard worker. Farmers needed wives who weren't afraid of work.

Suddenly he heard screams from the other side of the hedge and ran round to see who was in trouble.

Further along the lane a young woman was trying to fight off a man, while two small children were clutching one another and crying with terror.

'Get away from her!' he roared.

As he ran towards them, the man made one last attempt to take her bundle from her. She held on tightly even though he dragged her along the ground and as Isaac drew nearer he ran off.

There were some advantages to being tall and strong, Isaac thought grimly as he helped her stand up. 'Are you all right now?'

'I will be – in a minute – I have to be. I—' Then she fainted.

He caught her and tried to shush the terrified children. 'Your mammy will be all right in a few minutes.' He'd recognised them, of course he had. The other group burying someone the day he buried Eugenia.

He couldn't stand here holding her up, so he moved back into the meadow and sat down, telling the children to sit next to him.

When she stirred he moved away a little, but still sat next to her, in case.

She stared at him blankly, then gasped and looked round. 'Did he get my bundle?'

'No. I turned up in time.'

'Thank you, Mr Matthews.'

'That's a heavy load you're carrying.'

'We had to get out of the cottage, and I needed to bring some clothes for the children.'

For some reason he had no trouble speaking to her. 'Where are you going? To relatives? Could they not have sent a cart to fetch you?'

'I have no relatives. I'm just . . . going.'

'To the poorhouse?'

'No. I'm going to look for a job in the town. I sold my furniture and have enough money to manage for a while, if I'm careful.'

'What sort of job?'

'Anything honest, where I can keep my children.'

He remembered suddenly how tenderly she'd held her little daughter. 'Would you work as a nursery maid?'

She looked at him suspiciously. 'At your farm?'

'Yes.'

'You didn't have a nursery maid while your wife was alive; you had a governess.'

'I dismissed her yesterday. She was unkind to my

children. I need someone to look after them. You could look after your children at the same time.'

She was still looking suspicious.

'It's honest work. I'm not trying to trick you. I have other maids who'll sleep in the attics with you.'

She sagged in relief and suddenly began to weep. 'Thank you, Mr Matthews. I'll work my fingers to the bone for you if you'll let me keep my children.'

'Good. Let me take your bundle and we'll go home.'

She closed her eyes for a moment and stood up. It seemed to him as if the sun came out from behind the clouds at that moment and haloed her in light.

Strange fancy! He wasn't usually fanciful.

And strange how easy she was to talk to.

Nobody approved of him hiring this young woman. His maid threatened to leave, his father-in-law remonstrated with him about bringing 'paupers' into the house, and even his mother-in-law came to give him a lecture on how bad it would look to bring a woman into his house.

That made him thoughtful and he went to Tom the ploughman's old mother for advice. She was as shrewd as anyone he knew and he'd spoken to her before when he met her out walking in the fields.

She sat thinking, then said hesitantly, 'I could come and help out, Mr Matthews, if you have another bedroom for me. If she was sleeping next to me, no one would think anything wrong was going on.'

'You could?'

'I know I'm old and can't work as hard these days, so I'd not need paying, just my food and keep.'

'Would you want to leave your son's house?'

'I like to be useful, and they're expecting another child, so I'm taking up space.'

'Yes. Come and live with us.'

She laid one wrinkled old hand on his and said quietly, 'I think this will be a good thing.'

She was another woman who was easy to talk to. 'What makes you think that?'

'I can sometimes sense such things, just a little. My family have a gift for it.'

'Shall I send someone to fetch you and your things?'

'No. It'll be much better if I ask my daughter-in-law whether she minds, and let her think I'm following her advice. Then my son can bring me.'

He strode back feeling that his world was settling down again. He'd enjoy having Mary Janson in the house. She was good company and he often stopped to speak to her. The children would like her, too.

He chuckled aloud when he thought how furious Eugenia would have been.

It amazed him at how well Ellie and Mary Janson got on, how little discord there was in the house these days.

He tried to find a governess and had difficulty, because the lady the agency in the next town brought in to be interviewed was so full of starch she looked down her nose on him.

Time was passing. He realised one morning that he had only two more months left to find a wife, so when his mother-in-law suggested he come and meet a few young women, he agreed.

There was no shortage of available women, it seemed. He was also invited out to tea at the neighbouring farms and always there was a single woman present – at one house three of them at once! They gave him false, sickly smiles while the relatives talked of their virtues.

He tried to like them, because he was desperate to keep his land, but there was always something wrong. He didn't like meek women, or scrawny little women who barely came up to his shoulder. One laughed like a braying jackass and he certainly didn't want a stupid wife who would bore him to tears.

One day Mary Janson asked if she could speak to him privately.

'You need a wife,' she said bluntly.

'I know.'

'You've met at least ten young women in the past few weeks. Tell me what was wrong with them.'

He shrugged and at her prompting went through the reasons.

'I know one who would suit you.'

He sighed. Here they went again. 'Who?'

'Eh, you men can't see beyond your own noses sometimes. What's wrong with Ellie? Your children love her already. She's a clever lass and she's getting quite pretty now she's being properly fed.'

'Ellie?'

'Yes.'

He considered her suggestion and waited for protests to well up, only they didn't. 'Ellie?' he asked again, still feeling surprised.

'Talk to her after tea instead of disappearing into the sitting room. She's good company. Watch her with the children.'

He had watched her with the children many times already, just keeping an eye on things. She was wonderful with them. But as a wife? Would she fit in?

Mary stood up. 'I won't push you any more, but remember, you'll lose your land if you don't find someone.'

He sat there for a long time, then went into the kitchen. Mary was sitting by the fire knitting. All four children were sitting in a circle on the rug while Ellie read to them.

She looked up when he came in and flushed. 'I'm sorry. You don't usually sit in here. I'll take the children up to the nursery to finish the story.'

'No, don't leave. I, um, wanted to see how they were going on.' They had never looked so rosy and happy.

'They're good children.'

'Go on reading.'

As she continued to tell the story, he got his own book out and pretended to be looking at that. But he couldn't help stealing glances at her. Mary was right. Ellie was very pretty these days.

After a while, Ellie looked at the clock. 'Time for bed, children. Give your father a kiss, you two.'

When his children came to do that, little Nan followed them, so he kissed her too.

When they'd left the room, he looked across at Mary. 'Speak to her for me,' he begged. 'I'm not good with words. It'll come out wrong.'

'I can see if she's interested, but you'll have to do your own proposing.'

He nodded.

4

The following day, Mary followed him outside after breakfast. 'I spoke to Ellie. She would be interested.'

He didn't know what to say to that. He'd half convinced himself that Ellie would refuse. 'She's not still grieving?'

'Are you grieving for Eugenia?'

'No!' The answer was too vehement.

'And Ellie isn't grieving for Peter Pearson. She had a very unhappy marriage.' Mary paused. 'Any other questions?'

'No.' He stood thinking, waiting for his heart to sink at the idea, but it didn't. He'd seen Ellie laughing and playing with the children, chatting to his other servants, who all seemed to get on with her now they knew her. 'Please . . . ask her for me, Mary?'

'No, Isaac. Some things a man should do for himself.'

'I'm not good with words.'

'You only need to say four words: Will you marry me? Repeat them after me.'

He did that twice.

She smiled. 'Better do it tonight before you grow too fearful.'

After the evening meal, he looked across at Ellie. 'Could you please come into the sitting room? I need to ask you something.'

Mary nodded approval. 'I'll look after the children.'

He led the way, stopping at the door to let her enter the room first. 'Please sit down. I believe M-Mary t-told you about my – my – um – situation.' He could feel his face going red and his tongue seemed to have grown too big for his mouth.

'Yes. She did.'

He watched Ellie move her hands in her lap and saw that they were trembling. Then she clasped them together so tightly her knuckles turned white.

She was as nervous as he. Of course she was. That gave him the courage to continue. And he suddenly found the words, not just the four he'd rehearsed but seven of them, and they came out easily.

'Then would you marry me, please, Ellie?'

'You're sure?'

Seven more words slipped out easily. 'Yes. I'm sure. It wouldn't upset you?'

She looked at him in surprise. 'No, of course not. As long as you're *sure*. I've watched you since I came to live here and you're a kind man. You don't speak a lot but you say what you mean. And you work hard. I admire that.'

Another seven words joined the others in the air between them. 'I'm glad, Ellie. I admire you too.' He waited for panic to set in, as it had when Eugenia proposed to him, but it didn't.

'I'm glad about it, too, Isaac.'

She had such a lovely open face, he didn't doubt she was telling the truth. He put an arm round her and gave her a brief shy hug. She smiled up at him from within the circle of his arm, and his heart gave a happy little skip.

Just seven words. What a difference they'd made.

ANNA JACOBS is the author of over eighty novels and is addicted to storytelling. She grew up in Lancashire, emigrated to Australia in the 1970s and writes stories set in both countries. She loves to return to England regularly to visit her family and soak up the history. She has two grown-up daughters and a grandson, and lives with her husband in a spacious home near the Swan Valley, the earliest wine-growing area in Western Australia. Her house is crammed with thousands of books.

annajacobs.com

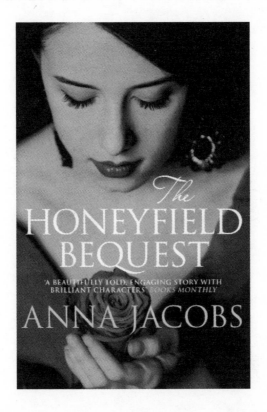

The
HONEYFIELD
BEQUEST

'A BEAUTIFULLY TOLD, ENGAGING STORY WITH
BRILLIANT CHARACTERS' *BOOKS MONTHLY*

ANNA JACOBS

1901, Wiltshire. Young Kathleen Keller is being forced
into marriage by her cruel father and runs away in a bid
for a safer life. But when tragedy strikes, Kathleen is left
vulnerable and one man threatens her fragile peace.

Meanwhile, Nathan Perry works for his father's
accountancy firm but yearns for something more satisfying.
He is brought in to help with the purchase of Honeyfield
House, intended as a safe house for women in trouble, and
there encounters Kathleen. Their lives are set to intertwine
and neither will be the same again.

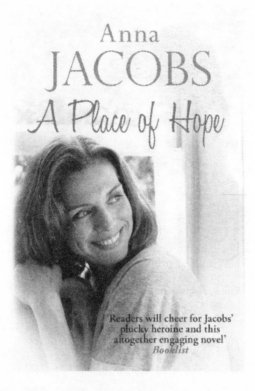

Anna
JACOBS
A Place of Hope

'Readers will cheer for Jacobs'
plucky heroine and this
altogether engaging novel'
Booklist

When Emily Mattison is the victim of a near-fatal accident shortly after receiving an unexpected inheritance, her ruthless nephew George seizes the opportunity to take control of his aunt's assets.

It's only when Emily reaches The Drover's Hope, a former pub on the edge of the Lancashire moors, bequeathed to her by her late cousin Penelope, that she begins to feel safe. She also discovers that love can be found in the most unexpected places. But it's not so easy to escape the clutches of someone as determined as George . . .

HEIR TO
Greyladies

'Anna Jacobs is adored by a whole army of women readers
for her heart-warming stories of love and life'
Lancashire Evening Post

ANNA JACOBS

Hampshire, 1900. With the sudden death of her father, Harriet Benson is forced into service at Dalton House, where she becomes friends with the owners' crippled son Joseph.

But Harriet is unprepared for a life-altering the event: her unexpected inheritance of Greyladies, a supposedly haunted house in the country. While Harriet and Joseph grow ever closer, the plots and actions of both their families threaten to destroy their happiness. Will their love, and the legacy of Greyladies, be able to survive?

Cherry Tree Lane

THE SPELLBINDING NEW NOVEL FROM THE MUCH-LOVED
AUTHOR OF *FAREWELL TO LANCASHIRE*

ANNA JACOBS

Wiltshire, 1910. With her stepfather threatening her with a forced marriage, Mattie Willitt flees home in search of a better life. She is soon lost and at the mercy of the elements – until her life is saved by Jacob, a widower who takes her in and nurses her back to health. Finding consolation in each other's troubled pasts, the pair soon grow close.

But when pressure is put upon them to marry, and Mattie's stepfather discovers her whereabouts, they must face their fears and stand up to those who threaten their future happiness.